Kill the Stuart

Ronald Bassett

Table of Contents

Part I - The Scent

Chapter 1

The tall, rawboned Highlander drew his ragged plaid over his shoulders and dropped to his soiled knees in the grass. A few minutes earlier he has started a hare in the dusk, and had given chase, hoping to drive it into the narrow mull from which escape would be difficult and where he might fell it with his cudgel. A hare would have been fine for the pot, and he'd not had meat in his mouth for a week, since the Laird had given him a sheep's head and liver — but now it was forgotten.

It was late July, but unseasonably chilly, and he shivered, wanting the warmth of his peat fire, even if its smoke did make his eyes red-sore. Soon it would be dark. The shore was no place for a body at night, and a fried oat-cake was better than an empty belly.

Below him was the sound, with the calm sea purple in the failing light and, a mile offshore, the shadowy hummock of the Isle of Eriskay. A few stars were beginning to show to the eastward, tiny jewels set in grey velvet. And off Eriskay, motionless, was a ship.

He had not seen it arrive, and it had not been in the sound that afternoon, he'd swear. It wasn't a big ship — not as big, that is, as the English frigate that had anchored off Loch Boisdale last year, but a great deal bigger than any of the boats native to the Isles. It was difficult to imagine what business it could have here. There was little enough in South Uist, *Mo Dhia*, for the MacDonalds who scratched the thin soil, manured by seaweed, for a meagre living, fished, or ran a few shaggy cattle in the hills — and nothing to attract visitors, traders or smugglers. The Highlander ran his tongue over his lips. But here was a ship, to be sure, firmly anchored off Eriskay, and with a longboat lowered.

There could be no good in it, and the Laird must be warned. MacDonald of Boisdale, who had travelled to Edinburgh, London and Paris, who spoke Gaelic, English, French, and whose grey stone house stood three miles away, on the far side of the Loch, would know what to do. The Highlander rose cautiously to his feet, drew a deep breath, then plunged into the wiry grass which slashed at his bared legs. Above him a gull screamed. The Laird would know — but there could be no good in it.

Chapter 2

Sir John de Courcy, merchant banker and Justice of the Peace, balanced clumsily on his sound leg as he gazed through the great bow window of Halstead Hall at the rooks circling the far elms, his head thrust forward over a paunch that strained at his waistcoat buttons and his hands clasped firmly beneath his coat-tail. The noise of the rooks' scrawking came faintly on the warm air.

'He sailed from Bel Ile in the sloop *Du Teillay* three weeks ago, wi' guns, money, and a handful of hangers-on — and in company wi' the French frigate *Elizabeth*. Yesterday we heard that the *Elizabeth* was made to stand by our own Lion, and the two of 'em shot each other to rags while the *Du Teillay* escaped northward. There's naught been seen or heard of her since, but ye can be certain she's reached the west coast o' Scotland.' He turned, groping for his snuffbox. 'And that's why ye're here, Tom. Ye're going to Scotland to find him.'

Major Thomas Margery, of His Majesty's 2nd Regiment of Foot Guards, placed down his glass of brandy very carefully, then stared at de Courcy. 'Scotland? You want me to go to *Scotland*?'

There had always been something mysterious about de Courcy. Seventy years old, portly, and with a leg lost in Spain during the old war of Marlborough's, yet the old man still had a sword wrist like steel and an eye that could pistol a spot from a playing card at thirty paces. There was no secret about his fortune, based on slaving, tobacco, sugar and furs. The de Courcy house flag was flown by eleven ships out of Deptford, and he had agents in Bristol, Liverpool, the Gambia, the Cape Coast, Jamaica, Charleston and Norfolk — and likely a few other places if the truth be known. It was de Courcy who had presented Thomas with a commission in one of the British Army's most expensive regiments — once de Courcy's own — the 2nd Foot Guards, and that must have cost a few thousand guineas in addition to a great deal of influence.

But de Courcy was obviously more than just a wealthy, mildly eccentric old man. He was a Justice of the Peace, but gave a minimum of time to the Bench and, for a seventy-year-old country squire, spent a great deal of time in London — not at Lloyd's, or White's, or 'Change Alley, but stumping among the courtyards of Westminster, and disappearing in his closed chaise as suddenly as he arrived. Night-walking folk of Halstead could tell of cloaked riders in the moonlight — and Harwich, the gateway to the Continent, was an easy ride away.

'Scotland', de Courcy nodded, as if it were no further than Chelmsford market. 'Ye'll travel in the brig *Hopewell*, waiting at Harwich for ye, to Leith — which'll be faster than by road. In Edinburgh my man will provide ye with money and the latest information — and anything else ye need. Be clear on one matter, Tom. Speed's the important thing, and ye needn't spare money to buy a day — or even an hour. The affair must be settled wi', and this damn' spark stamped out before it sets Scotland afire — and provokes a torrent o' blood before it's quenched.'

Thomas sighed. Only a few hours earlier he had been roused from his bed after a night duty at St. James's and ordered to flog his horse into Essex. It had happened twice before — on the first occasion only to find himself joining Sir John and some whooping local gentry in a mud-spattered fox hunt, and on the second to merely make a fourth in a prolonged game of cards. Each time he had shrugged away his annoyance and put a good face on it, but this time it was a little different. De Courcy had been a firm friend of his own father, Adam Margery — dead now for fifteen years — although Thomas had never completely understood the relationship between a wealthy ship-owner and a Cambridgeshire farmer, and he had never needed the generous allowance that de Courcy made him, although — i'faith — it made life in the Guards tolerable. In return, since his pink-cheeked ensign days, he'd always humoured the old man. But this —?

Aye, it was plain that de Courcy's years were getting the better of his senses. Scotland, did he say? And what was all this nonsense about the Pretender? There had been nothing about it in the London news-sheets.

Thomas chuckled. 'It'll be a diversion, Sir John — always allowing I'm back in London by tomorrow evening. I've a fitting at Millerd's on Thursday —'

Sir John de Courcy eyed the carpet at Thomas's shining feet thoughtfully for several long seconds, his lower lip out-thrust. Then he nodded. 'Aye — it's to be expected.' He stumped across to the fire-place to reach up for a long clay pipe. 'Sit ye down, Tom lad, and fill ye' glass.

Ye won't be in London this Thursday, or many a Thursday to come.' He glanced at the clock. 'It's four o'clock, and by midnight ye'll be aboard the *Hopewell*, which can out-run anything that floats on the East Coast.' He waved Thomas to a chair. 'Aye, ye're thinking that the old fool's gone soft-brained at last but, when ye've heard what I have to say, likely ye'll think different — or I've been mistaken in ye for a long time.'

'I'm sorry, Sir John —'

'I'm not blaming ye, but listen. Ye've not too much time. Some o' this ye'll know already, but there's a lot ye don't.' He tapped the clay pipe against a fingernail. 'For fifty years or more the Jacobites have been dreaming o' putting a Stuart back into St. James's. They've tried four times, and they're about to try for a fifth.' He paused, his eyes narrowed. 'The Stuarts were a disastrous breed, Tom lad — and England can't afford 'em, especially now that the country's on the brink of prosperity. I'll not live to see it, but there's India, the Americas, Canada — all ripe plums for the picking, and naught but France and Spain to dispute us. In a few years ye can discount Spain — and that leaves France, the old enemy.

'And France knows it. She would like to see a Stuart king in England, but she also knows it's too late, even if the Jacobite rag-taggle don't. Still, a Jacobite uprising — albeit abortive — would be to her advantage. We'd be wasting troops, ships, money, and killing our own kind, while France is picking the plums.'

'Sir John, Whitehall's well aware of all this —'

'Aye, and more. All the time the French are nursing a Stuart they're holding a pistol they can put at our head. Aye, it'll grow less dangerous as the years pass, but we haven't got too many years to spare.

'The last time a Stuart landed was in 'Fifteen. Partly because the French declined to commit any regular troops and partly because the whole affair was bungled by the Jacobites, it died of apathy after Sheriffmuir. With better planning and support it might have given England a deal of trouble. As it was, the Crown was too damn' lenient. The Scots should have been given a lesson that would have kept them quiet for a hundred years, but they weren't. And now we have the same business again.'

Thomas shrugged. 'What can a handful of Scottish peasants do against the British Army, Sir John?' He dropped a glance to his own impeccable scarlet coat, blue-faced, his tailored breeches and silk hose. What, for instance, could a horde of untrained, ragged Scots do against the solid, disciplined ranks of his own guardsmen, loading and firing by platoons like a beautiful, lethal machine? Sir John hadn't seen a battlefield in forty years —

De Courcy had permitted a light smile to twist his lips. 'Badajos, under Galway, in 1705, Tom. That's where I lost this.' He lifted his timber leg, and Thomas flushed. 'Aye, Tom — forty years, but it weren't so different.' He shook his head. 'If the British Army were all Guards regiments, and *if* there were ten thousand of 'em in Scotland wi' a decent artillery train, ye'd be right.' He limped across to a bureau, withdrew a drawer, then thumbed through a sheaf of papers.

'There's less than four thousand troops in Scotland, none of 'em better than second rate and none that have smelled real powder smoke.' He read from a paper. 'The infantry battalions are Guise's, Murray's, Lascelles's and Lee's, the cavalry Gardiner's and Hamilton's — both Irish. There's a few other detachments — invalids and recruits — and not a single gunner, mattross or bombardier north of the Tweed.'

Thomas sat up, frowning at de Courcy. ''Sblood!' He hesitated, not wishing to enquire how the other was in possession of such facts, of which he, a serving officer at St. James's, was unaware. Four thousand redcoats, with no artillery, to garrison the whole of Scotland? 'Still — all they have to deal with is a few ignorant clansmen —'

'Now we'll deal with that,' de Courcy nodded. 'We're not concerned with the Lowlanders. I'll hazard they'll sit on the fence and cheer Prince Charles on Monday and King George on Friday. It's the Highlands, north and north-west o' the Tay, that'll spawn trouble — as they've done before.' He drew a deep breath, impatient with the task of explaining a situation that was obviously lucid to himself but not to his listener. 'Some clans will support the Pretender, some won't. It depends on the clan chieftains — entirely. Mark my words, Tom —' he pointed a finger, '— when a chieftain calls out his clan, *every* clansman obeys. There's no choice, no feet-dragging. And that's the crying pity of it all.'

De Courcy poured himself a brandy, sipped it, rolled it around his tongue. 'As I say, some of the chieftains — 'specially those that remember the 'Fifteen, won't support an adventure *that's certain to fail eventually*. Whatever history calls 'em, they're the wise ones, and there's plenty o' Scots mothers that'll bless their names. But there's others — too festerin' many, an' too damn' stupid — who'll lead their clans out, to be butchered.'

He raised his hand to forestall Thomas's protest. 'Ah — they'll win a few initial skirmishes, kill a few hundred redcoats, capture a few towns. These'll persuade one or two wavering chieftains to throw in their lot, and likely a few fool Jacobites from England. It might take months before an adequate punitive force can be gathered and marched from the South — but those months will do more for us than a half dozen battalions, Tom. Among the clans there are jealousies, old feuds, resentments — and they're not soldiers. They've got to be kept together, fed, clothed and armed, despite the needs of their families and farms, d'ye see —?'

Thomas nodded, amused. 'You're saying, Sir John, that the Pretender will never keep them disciplined — that they'll be melting away at harvest time —?'

'No. A few might, among the unattached and the Lowlanders. The clansmen will stand as long as their chieftains do. A deserting Highlander could never again return to his clan. But, after six or seven months in the field, with no commissariat, no supply bases or magazines, no replacements of killed and wounded, and a dozen other inadequacies that plague a rustic army led by novices, they'll not be the same men that marched from the glens. Aye, they'll still fight, when the British Army has finally cornered them — and they'll be massacred like blind cattle.'

'Then I don't see —'

'Don't ye? The whole damn' thing is unnecessary! And those scheming devils in Versailles can predict its failure just as well as I can. I told ye before, when a Scots chieftain calls out his clan, every clansman must obey — but hundreds of 'em don't want to, Tom. What does a simple Highland crofter care about the balance o' European power and the machinations of ambitious statesmen, eh? Nothing — but he has to fight, or have his hovel burned about his ears. He, and likely thousands like him, are going to die — one way or another — for nothing, while the French laugh.' De Courcy paused, his head to one side. 'But, Tom lad, if ye and I can help it, it's not going to happen.'

I'll hold my peace, Thomas decided. Either I'm lunatic or the old man is. The Scottish Highlands are four hundred miles away, as remote as

China. This is Halstead in Essex. There's a Secretary of State in London who must know all that de Courcy does — if it's true.

De Courcy had not quite finished. 'And that's why ye're sailing for Leith, Tom — tonight.'

I'll still hold my damn' peace, Thomas resolved. He owed the old man at least a pretence to courtesy, if only in return for fifteen years' allowance. The Margery acres in Cambridgeshire were not yet his, nor would be until the death of his mother, Mary Margery. At thirty-eight and unmarried, Thomas had been independent of his mother's purse by virtue of de Courcy's generosity, for which there seemed little motive other than a vague paternal interest. It was odd, but de Courcy could afford to be odd.

Sir John seemed mildly disappointed at Thomas's lack of response. He talked on. 'If matters go unchecked, the Pretender will be faced by the regiments I've mentioned, under Sir John Cope, Major-General.' He paused. 'I've known Johnnie Cope since Spain, forty years ago — and he was at Dettingen. He's a better soldier than many give him credit for, but he's never fought Highlanders and his troops have never fought anyone. Johnnie Cope will get a drubbing, and that's when the real trouble will begin.'

'But —' his finger was pointing again, '— you, Tom, must reach the Pretender before Cope does.'

''Od's blood!' Thomas could restrain his impatience no longer. 'Sir John — even if it were possible — to what point? The Pretender, *if* he's landed, and *if* I could find him, isn't going to abandon his campaign because of anything I can say or do. He can't be completely a fool, and he must have balanced the odds. His interpretation is obviously different to yours. He'll also have a staff, of some kind, which apparently supports his view, and an army officer from St. James's isn't going to change it. Besides —' he shrugged, '— I'm not free to spend weeks tramping over Scottish mountains in search of something that may not even exist —'

As Thomas was speaking, de Courcy had stumped his bulk back to the window. Now he turned. 'First, it exists, Tom. It'll take too damn' long to explain how I know, but I'll just say that my intelligence is as reliable as the Gospel. Second, ye're free. Ye've already been released by ye' Colonel under direction from the Secretary of State. Tomorrow I'd be able to show ye it in writing, over Tweeddale's signature, but ye'll not be here. Third, ye're not going to Scotland to parley wi' the Pretender. Ye're going to kill him.'

For several seconds Thomas could hardly credit his ears. Then he reared to his feet, staring. 'Kill? Did you say *kill* the Pretender?'

De Courcy returned his stare impassively. 'Kill, Tom lad. And I don't mean at the head of a company o' Guards. Ye'll be alone. Ye can shoot him, stab him, throttle him — I don't care. Ye're a soldier, and ye aren't paid to just strut around in a scarlet coat. Ye should know something about killing.' His voice had hardened very slightly.

Thomas quelled his own rising exasperation. It was true, then. The old man was lunatic. 'It would be assassination,' he said quietly, 'and officers —'

'Ye can call it what ye festerin' like,' de Courcy snorted. 'And before ye begin bleating that ye're an officer and a gentleman, remember that I made ye so.' He leaned forward. 'And this is *why* I made ye so, d'ye understand?'

Thomas shook his head, nonplussed.

'It was plain to a lot of people,' de Courcy explained, 'that the 'Fifteen wasn't going to be the last of the Stuarts' murderous escapades, and some of us began to make preparations. Ye, Thomas, were one o' mine. There's others, but ye're the closest to hand and the only one I can get to Scotland in time. All the while that Charles Edward amused himself in Rome, I've not been concerned with him — but from the moment he determined to come to Scotland he's been under sentence of death. Aye, I sent a man to Paris and another to Gravelines. They both failed. Now it's your turn, Tom. Remove the Pretender and ye remove the linchpin o' the whole bloody business. The clans will disperse and there'll be peace in the Highlands. The French'll be deprived o' their Stuart pocket-pistol and the Jacobites can abandon their hopeless conspiracies — which'll be safer for all of 'em.'

Thomas sat down again. For a lunatic, de Courcy was presenting a very plausible story. If he were speaking the truth, then a number of things were beginning to make sense — uncomfortable sense —

'Now ye're fitting the pieces together, eh?' de Courcy smiled. 'The fencing master I sent to ye? And the pistol training I gave ye myself? French lessons? And how many times have I had ye ordered from ye' bed — to see how fast ye could ride from London to Halstead?'

Thomas swallowed. So that was it. 'Sir John,' he said, 'I'm grateful for the generosity you have extended to me since my father's death. I shall repay that generosity, in full, in due course — but not in the manner you are suggesting. I am an officer of His Majesty's Guards, and assassination is not numbered among my duties —' Damme, he thought, I sound like a pompous archdeacon. 'If there's naught else, I'll take the Chelmsford road within the hour.'

De Courcy was eyeing Thomas thoughtfully. 'I didn't think ye'd accept it easily, and — ye can believe me — I'd never intended assassination for ye, but now I've no choice. There's two men failed, and still in France. There's others, in Rome, Stockholm an' Hanover, and one on the high seas between London and Lisbon. As I say, Tom, ye weren't intended for this cloak an' dagger business. Ye were being kept for better things — yeself, young Wolfe on Hawley's staff, Richard Howe, Lieutenant in the *Firedrake*, Bob Clive wi' the East India in Madras, an' others — ye were all part of a grander scheme, until this festerin' Stuart puppy decided to drench Scotland in blood. Then I had to use one of ye, dammit —'

'And what "grand scheme",' Thomas enquired sceptically, 'did you have in mind for me?'

'In ten years ye'd have been commanding a British army to take Florida from Spain.' He paused. 'And then Mexico.'

Thomas's jaw dropped. 'And Wolfe?'

'He'll drive the French out of Canada.'

'Lieutenant Howe?'

'He'll smash France at sea.'

'And this Madras fellow — Clive? He, I presume, is intended to annexe India for the Crown?'

De Courcy nodded. 'In a word, precisely.'

Thomas pulled a mock-wry face. 'And now, Godammit, the Union Jack will never fly over Florida and Mexico.'

De Courcy ignored the jibe, turned, and limped to the door. Opening it, he spoke to the room beyond. 'Brigadier? If ye would —?'

Thomas sprang to his feet as through the door strode the tall figure of Brigadier-General Lord John Avershaw, commanding officer of His Majesty's Foot Guards, first soldier of St. James's and doyen of the

16

King's personal retinue. Nodding at Thomas as the latter bowed, he drew off the long cloak that hid the scarlet and gold of his uniform.

'Major Margery. You've heard Sir John?'

'I have, m'Lord.' Thank God, Thomas thought, here was sanity. He could not guess the reason for Avershaw's presence, but there was nobody less likely to tolerate wild flights of fancy than this dour old soldier, before whom officers trembled and guardsmen became speechless with awe.

Avershaw went on. 'Like Sir John, I regret the necessity for applying an officer of my command to the dirty business of assassination. I particularly regret that it has to be you, Margery. On His Majesty's return from Hanover you were to be offered a colonelcy. Not —' he smiled coldly, '— in the Guards, but a good line regiment — and a step towards bigger things. A pity. Even if you return from Scotland you may well be a marked man, hunted by the Jacobites and despised by your friends. You will have to resign your commission. Indeed, I may have to cashier you.' He shrugged. 'But there's always the Continent or the Colonies and, under another name, you can make a tolerable life for yourself. Needless to say, you will not be left in poverty.'

Thomas choked. 'You mean, m'Lord — ?' He had the taste of ashes in his mouth. 'You mean that everything Sir John said —?'

'If he said what I suspect, then you can accept every word. I understand that a ship is waiting at Harwich to sail for Leith tonight. Once in Scotland you will avoid any association with the military, who will be ignorant of your task. Our own intelligence is vague, but in Edinburgh you'll be provided with better, and it will almost certainly direct you westward — Inverness, Argyle, or the Isles. The method of your task is your own affair, and if you are apprehended we shall disown you.'

'M'Lord — surely this is something that any penniless vagrant — any Newgate blackguard — could do better? For a few guineas —'

Avershaw shook his head. 'We've tried, twice — and both times failed. This time must be certain; our time is running out. You must remove the Pretender, Margery. Those are your orders — from a higher authority than I — and Godspeed.' He picked up his cloak. 'Sir John — if you'll forgive me — I must be at St. James's before dawn.' He nodded again at Thomas, and was gone.

Deflated, Thomas slumped again into his chair. Within the space of a few seconds his loyalties and ideals had been brutally shaken. It was incredible that a man of Lord Avershaw's image could be an accomplice to the assassination of a royal prince — Stuart or not. Equally incredible was Sir John de Courcy's earlier disclosure that Thomas had been one of a selected few destined to dispute with France and Spain the possession of a world-flung empire. But Avershaw had mentioned 'a higher authority'. Who could that be? Mr. Pelham? The Duke of Newcastle? Mr. Pitt? Or — could it be His Majesty? The reasons for the King's absence in Hanover at this particular time might be innocent; they might not. The merest whisper that the King of England had stooped to murder would be viciously damaging. A mere army major, on the other hand, was expendable. With luck he would not survive his assignment. If he did — and despite Avershaw's assurances — it was unlikely that he would be permitted to live out his days with the fire-brand knowledge that he held. He would be silenced — and on such intrigues were royal houses built upon.

'It's not a pretty picture, is it?' de Courcy murmured. 'But ye've no choice, Tom lad. If it's any consolation —'

'No choice?' Thomas retorted. 'What if I refuse?'

De Courcy considered. 'Aye, there's *that* choice, but I'd not recommend it. Ye see, Tom, ye've been committed. There's only one road for ye tonight, and that's the Harwich one. If ye returned to London I couldn't guess what would happen. Ye might not even reach ye' quarters. Certainly ye'd not be given the chance to air ye' knowledge tomorrow, whether ye intended to or not.' He grimaced. 'I'm telling ye this because I fancy I owe it to ye in return for the dirty cards I've dealt ye. And ye' father and I were friends —'

'Friends?' Thomas spat. 'Aye — and a fine, friendly gesture you've made — ''sblood —!'

De Courcy's voice had hardened again. 'Tom — I've explained, I've apologised. The issues at stake are far more important than one army major's honour. If ye fail, perhaps a thousand men — Scots and English — will die, and a dozen peers will go to the scaffold. This time there'll be no leniency. Scotland will bleed for a hundred years, and the balance o' world power could tip in favour o' France. Any of these things is of more account than Thomas Margery or John de Courcy. Ye're a soldier,

Tom, and ye have ye' orders. They may choke in ye' throat, but ye'll obey 'em.'

Thomas sat in cheerless silence for several minutes. Then he roused himself. 'I've never killed a man in cold blood,' he gritted, and chuckled humourlessly. 'Damme — I've just never killed a man.'

De Courcy sighed with relief and stumped forward. 'The Pretender'll have some kind of bodyguard, so it's unlikely ye'll be able to engage him wi' a sword. I'd say shooting's the most reliable. I took the liberty o' having ye' pistols brought from ye' quarters. They're the pair I gave to ye' father twenty-five years ago — from Coutts o' Houndsditch — and ye'll not buy better today. If ye prefer, I'll give ye a rifle-barrelled musket. It's more accurate than the "Bess" and throws further, but I'm thinking that a musket will draw attention to ye when ye're travelling.' He paused. 'There's a dozen other ways o' killing a man wi'out regular weapons —'

'Pistols will do,' Thomas said sullenly.

'I'll have them packed with ye' baggage,' de Courcy nodded. 'And clothes. Ye can't travel through rebel country in the King's uniform.' He went to the bureau again and returned with a small package wrapped in oiled silk. 'There's no need to open this until ye dock in Leith. It contains the identity and address o' my man in Edinburgh, and gold — although there's plenty more if ye want it. There's also an authorisin' letter which my man will destroy as soon as he's read it. The packet's weighted, so it'll sink if thrown overboard.'

Thomas gazed at him cynically. 'You were confident the assassin was going to be me, eh?'

'It was yeself, or nobody, Tom lad. And ye can console yeself wi' the knowledge that ye're going to do something that all o' Johnnie Cope's horse an' foot can't. Unfortunately it's a story ye'll never be able to tell ye' grandchildren.'

'If —' Thomas observed, '— I ever live to have grandchildren.'

Chapter 3

The sign over the door had said simply 'D. MacDonald. Tailor'. Inside, sunlight through the narrow, mullioned window gleamed on a waxed floor and the shelved bolts of broadcloth, rateen, taminy and serge that climbed to the low ceiling. There was a tall mirror, two high-backed chairs, and a table on whose polished top were strewn the instruments of a tailor's trade — shears, a measuring tape, chalk, a box of pins — and a plaque repeating the legend:'D. MacDonald. Tailor to Gentlemen. Fine English Cloths.' Beyond the window, the cobbled street that twisted towards the Cathedral and the old tolbooth echoed with the screech and rumble of iron-clad wheels.

Donald MacDonald was a short, square man, middle-aged, wearing his own greying hair neatly tied on his neck. He raised his eyes from the letter he was reading and studied Thomas sombrely.

'Ye know what's written, Major?'

'I can guess,' Thomas said.

MacDonald folded the letter deliberately. 'Aye,' he nodded, then drew a deep breath. 'It's a bad thing. A bad thing. Nothing good ever came out of murder. Ye might halt the rising, Major, but ye'll provoke a hatred for the English that'll live for centuries. No countryman o' yours will walk safe in Scotland again —'

Thomas shrugged. 'I've had ample time between Harwich and Leith to consider the consequences, Master MacDonald, and I don't like them either — but I've persuaded myself that two men's lives against a thousand, and all the other implications, is a reasonable barter.'

'Two men's lives?'

'The Pretender's and mine. You'll not pretend that my own chances of survival are anything more than slender.'

'I'll not, and I've been in English pay too long to give ye a lecture on morals, Major. I'm a Scot, from Uist, and half the year I travel the Highlands. I'll be away westward within the week, collecting debts — and spying on my own clansmen. That makes me a traitor, if ye like. But I also share the opinion o' Sir John de Courcy — that Charles Edward means only disaster for Scotland. Mind ye —' he stared at Thomas, '— if he'd come wi' twenty thousand French regulars behind him, I'd likely be whistling a different jig. As it is, the sooner the business is finished wi', the better — and if it has to be murder, well, so be it.'

The little *Hopewell* had run swiftly northward under clear skies, and the fresh, salt wind had softened the despair with which Thomas had embarked. A great deal must happen, he had told himself, before he achieved an opportunity to kill Charles Edward. In the first place there was no proof that the Pretender had even landed and, i'faith, Edinburgh showed no awareness of an impending rising. Everything in the city was normal —

'Charles Edward landed on the Isle of Eriskay on the 23rd of last month,' MacDonald said, and Thomas's heart sank. 'He got short shrift from MacDonald of Boisdale, but on the mainland, two days later, he was joined by the MacDonalds o' Keppoch, Glencoe and Scotus, and Lochiel's Camerons. That was at Glenfinnan, not ten miles from Fort William, and it's the last information I have of him.' He sucked his teeth.

Festerin' blood, Thomas gritted — that was his first hope shattered. The Pretender was in Scotland and had raised at least some support. That meant that the rising was fact, and there was bound to be some blood spilt. How much depended upon how soon he — Thomas — could reach the Pretender. As de Courcy had said, he was committed.

'The news is a week old,' MacDonald went on, 'and the military in Stirling will have it tomorrow — but it'll take Cope two weeks to have his column marching, and likely another three or four before he can get within reach o' Charles Edward. So ye've time enough — given the luck.'

'And the Pretender's movements?'

MacDonald sniffed. 'I'm no military man, Major, but if I were the Pretender I'd want two things quickly. First, more men. I'll hazard he's got less than two thousand at present. Second, a success or two that'll bring in the clans that are wavering. Nothing kills a rebellion quicker than inactivity. So —' he nodded, '— I'll say he'll push inland, eastward, say towards Perth, calling out the chiefs as he goes. Then, to impress the clans — and Whitehall — he'll march on Edinburgh.'

'If you're right, then there's no sense in my leaving. I can wait here — and that being so, I'll wager there's more than one hungry kern in

Edinburgh that'd put a bullet into the Pretender in exchange for a hundred guineas and a fast horse.'

MacDonald considered. 'Aye —' Then he frowned. 'No. Charles Edward won't reach Edinburgh for a month — and in a month another two thousand clansmen can put their necks into nooses. And I could be wrong about his movements. He might decide to march northward, to Inverness. It's a good clan country — the Frasers, the MacBeans, and the Chisholm. On the other hand he could stake everything on one throw — and march straight for the border, hoping to raise the English Jacobites.' He shook his head. 'No, it's the Highlands for ye, Major. Stirling first, then northward and still northward. Sooner or later ye'll find the Pretender and his clansmen. Ask any goat-boy, and ye'll get better intelligence than from Major-General Cope himself.'

The Highlands? To Thomas — as to most Englishmen — the name provoked a vision of wild mountains and trackless moors, the tribal territories of savage, uncouth clansmen continually warring between themselves and periodically swooping on Lowland farmsteads to murder, plunder, and drive off cattle. They were illiterate, quick to anger, spoke a bastard Irish, and most of them had red hair. Some of them, properly drilled and firmly led, had made good soldiers under the Crown although, in battle, there was always the hazard that they would abandon all discipline and hurl themselves like wolves on a bewildered enemy expecting only slow-plodding time-servers.

If the primitive Highlanders wanted to pit themselves against the British Army, Thomas decided, then they deserved the consequences. He did not share de Courcy's and MacDonald's solicitude towards them; it was the wider issues that mattered. Nor was he convinced that the Scots would embarrass Sir John Cope's redcoats, whatever de Courcy said. A few rounds of canister would settle the affair in minutes — but then, Cope had no artillery —

So the Highlands it had to be. Stirling first. There'd be Englishmen there, and in the forts — William, Augustus and George — further northward, where at least he might find reasonable quarters and civilised company. The method of assassination, de Courcy had said, was Thomas's own business. If he could persuade one of the garrison commanders to loan him a dozen men and a veteran sergeant, then an ambush would be the easiest way. The untrained Highlanders, in their own glens, would likely be careless about picquets and patrols —

'Ye're to have no intercourse with the military,' MacDonald reminded him. 'The Scots have their spies as well as the English, and ye'll be marked. And there's no sense in pretending to be a Scot. Ye've got Englishman written all over ye. But that's of no account. There'll be more than a few English Jacobites trickling into the Highlands to join the Pretender, and there's English traders that the clans tolerate. Aye, when I think on it, trading's probably ye' best pretext. Let's say cattle-buying. If ye're stopped and searched, it'll explain the gold ye're carrying and the pistols for protecting it.'

He paused, plucking at his lip. 'But if ye are stopped, ye'll likely be robbed o' gold, pistols and everything. So, in the first place, ye've got to appear harmless and not worth investigating.'

'I can dress shabbily, leave my hair untied, ride a broken-down horse —'

'No — it's a trick that's been overplayed, and the Highlanders aren't fools. Besides, ye'll need good horseflesh where ye're going. It's not a Sunday canter on ye' Newmarket Heath.' He pondered. 'There's two hazards. First the military, who'll be suspicious of any Englishman travelling into the Highlands — remembering they'll be looking for Jacobite renegades. Then there's the Highlanders, who are suspicious of anyone who's not a clansman — or at least an Englishman they recognise. Ye see, Major, once the news of the rising has spread, nobody's going to believe ye're going into rebel country just to buy cattle. Lowland stock's plentiful and fatter — and safer to come by.'

Thomas chuckled. 'Why not disguise me as a Methodist preacher? Or, i'faith, equip me with a wife and four puking infants?'

MacDonald looked up quickly, his eyes narrowing. Then he walked to the window and stared, unseeing, at the distortion of the street beyond. 'Aye,' he murmured. 'Aye — it could be. It could be.' His calculating eyes turned to Thomas.

'A preacher?' Thomas retorted.

MacDonald snorted impatiently. 'Damme, no. I've told ye, ye'll never pass for a Scot, and certainly not a Scottish preacher. If ye were exposed, things might go badly for ye. But —' he fingered his chin, '— no man goes about villainous business accompanied by his wife and child.'

'I'll agree with ye.' Thomas raised his eyebrows. 'But I've no wife or child, Master MacDonald — and, s'blood, if I had, I'd not take them with me to an assassination in the Highlands.'

MacDonald was not listening. He walked several steps, turned, and retraced them, then halted, staring at Thomas. 'Ye'd need two horses for riding — one wi' a side-saddle — and a pack-horse. North of Stirling ye'll not find shelter every night, but the weather's mild, and there's worse beds than heather.' He seemed to be talking to himself. 'Ye'll make good time — twelve, perhaps fifteen miles a day.' He hesitated. 'No — say ten, with the bairn. In two weeks that'll be a hundred and fifty miles — and that's more than enough —'

'More than enough what?' Thomas enquired. 'Fester it, man — what are you muttering about?'

'If ye *had* a wife and child with ye, nobody would suspect anything — military or clansmen. Ye may suppose the clansmen are a savage breed, Major, but they have a peculiar respect for womenfolk — their own or another's.'

'I'll accept your word for it.'

'So —' MacDonald gazed at the ceiling. 'I have a son, Major — Ranald MacDonald. Three years ago he married a Glengarry girl and took farmland in his wife's clan country — Glen Moriston, north o' Loch Lochy. Ranald's in Glen Moriston now. I see him once in a year, sometimes in two. He's a good lad, but strong for the Stuarts, and certain to come running when he hears the Pretender's drums a-beat-ing. He doesn't know, o' course, that I take English money.

'His wife and bairn are here — under this roof. The child had been sickly, and we thought it better to have it close to an Edinburgh doctor than on a remote farmstead in Glengarry country. Now, the child's well enough, and ready to return to Glen Moriston. D'ye see?'

Thomas could see very well. 'You're saying that I travel with your son's wife and infant?' The suggestion was so incongruous that he found it almost impossible to visualise. The infant — well, he knew nothing about infants. He supposed they had to exist, but he was scarcely aware that they did. Women were different. For twenty-five years he had strenuously avoided the mildest association with any members of the opposite sex save his mother and an ageing housekeeper. Women were a plague, perverse, demanding, contributing nothing to the world of men

— and Thomas was a professional soldier with no tolerance for irrelevancies. That his philosophy was unwarranted he would have disputed, and pointed to the many promising young officers whose military careers had been ruined by an unfortunate marriage. Tall, well-figured, passably good-featured — and with prospects that had claimed the attention of more than a few spouse-seeking females — he had persistently declined invitations to masquerades and match-making soirées, until now he was no longer asked. He knew every yard of the campaigns of Marlborough, Eugene, Berwick and Villeroi, but not an inch below the lace bertha of a woman's bodice. Although lacking a natural dexterity, assiduous practice had made him an excellent horseman, swordsman and marksman, but he had never danced to music, or sat through an opera. His brother officers, whilst respecting his qualities, considered him a dull fellow — and Thomas did not care. And it was inconceivable that he should spend several weeks in close company with another man's wife, pretending her to be his.

'I'll go alone,' he said.

'Then ye'll get as far as Stirling,' MacDonald nodded. 'And one o' two things'll happen. Cope's provost will throw ye into the tolbooth and ye'll still be there when the army marches. Or if ye're lucky —' he sniffed, '— or more likely unlucky — ye'll avoid the military and get a day's ride beyond Doune. Perhaps even two days, into Murray country, and then ye'll have a dirk at ye' throat. They'll leave ye wi' not so much as a breek-cloth, Major — if they leave ye alive.'

'Master MacDonald,' Thomas suggested, 'I'm not enraptured by my task as it is — and it doesn't include escorting your son's family. And I would have thought — with this business brewing — that this is a poor time to send a woman and infant into the Highlands. Likewise, if any of your starveling clansmen decide to play footpad, they'll find the adventure expensive, I promise you. As for the military, well, perhaps you'll allow that my experience is somewhat better than your own. If I'm apprehended, an interview with Cope will set the matter right, and I believe I can convince him of the importance of secrecy. I have some thoughts of my own on the manner of handling this affair —'

MacDonald was unfolding de Courcy's letter again. 'Ye don't know all that Sir John wrote, Major. I suspect he's determined there'll be no whisper of the British military being involved. In ye' absence from

London, the *Courant*, the *Tatler* and the *Spectator* have all carried notices of ye' desertion with regimental money, wi' speculation on ye' Jacobite loyalties. The master of the *Hopewell*, in which ye travelled, also carried despatches for the Edinburgh and Stirling garrisons, among which was an order that, if identified, ye were to be shot on sight.'

Incredulous, Thomas stared. 'You mean that Sir John de Courcy did this —?'

'Aye. When it comes to matters o' state, de Courcy's a ruthless scoundrel. I could tell ye a story or two that'd leave ye shivering. The Frenchman that was responsible for taking off Sir John's leg at Badajos left his country a vicious legacy, Major. Ye might be intrigued to know that the French had intended to support the Pretender wi' 3,000 regulars in the Highlands and a main force of 12,000 under Marshal Saxe, landed within march o' London. The history books'll find other reasons, but I can tell ye that the French were foiled from Halstead Hall in Essex. So ye see, Major, individuals don't figure much in his calculations, and if the Crown's likely to be compromised, then the 2nd Foot Guards will have to be deprived of ye' services.'

Thomas sat in silence. If MacDonald spoke the truth, then he — Thomas — was a renegade in the eyes of his own people and a potential assassin in the eyes of the Scots. 'And in case ye suffer a change o' heart,' MacDonald added slowly, 'and decide to lie low in Edinburgh until the situation resolves itself otherwise, I've orders to have ye arrested — and disposed of quickly. I'd be sorry, o' course, but —' he shrugged, '— as I said, individuals don't figure much.'

Fester it — he couldn't return to England, and he couldn't stay where he was. 'This daughter-in-law o' yours,' he said cautiously. 'Ye've no qualms about sending her travelling with a stranger?'

MacDonald smiled for the first time. 'I've no qualms about yeself, Major. De Courcy penned a mark against ye' name that puts ye beyond any doubt in that respect. As for Isobel, she comes from good Glengarry stock, and she's got a year-old infant. The two things don't contribute towards wanton behaviour. She also has no taste for Englishmen — although, i'faith, she's not met many — and she's most of fifteen years younger. No, Major, I've no qualms, although —' he hesitated, '— it's likely her husband might, if he knew. He's a quick-tempered rogue — but ye can cross that bridge when ye come to it —'

''Od's blood, it's a captivating scheme, and no mistake. And if I survive the military, footpads, the Highland army, the Pretender, and your son, what then?'

MacDonald considered. 'I am sure Sir John de Courcy will have something arranged. But aren't ye thinking a little far ahead —?'

Thomas grunted. 'Aye, you're right. There's no profit in thinking about anything beyond the day after tomorrow. Alright —' he nodded, '— the woman can ride with me — and the infant, dammit. If she speaks English, tell her I've no patience for female prattle, nor do I entertain a fancy for dandling an infant on my knee. In short, unless circumstances compel otherwise, I should prefer that our relationship be detached and silent.'

'I don't think,' MacDonald said wryly, 'that she'll find ye' requirements vexing.'

'She'll leave my company immediately I tell her so and, if I must choose between my duty and her safety, she must be prepared that I abandon her. I am not a knight errant, Master MacDonald. I'm an assassin. I didn't ask to be. I have to murder a royal Stuart, or die — or both. The fourth possibility — that I fail and live — has been removed. I may perhaps, then, be pardoned if I consider the welfare of an unknown Scottish housewife of small importance.'

'It's a reasonable sentiment,' MacDonald agreed.

Thomas gazed at him, mildly puzzled. 'I confess I find it strange that a man should volunteer his own kin for this venture, even allowing for your motives. And the woman's loyalties, I take it, are with the Pretender?'

'It's likely they will be, Major, but she'll not need to know the real reason behind ye' journey. She'll be content that ye're a cattle buyer, and the ruse o' travelling as man and wife still applies. Glengarry women are accustomed to doing as they're bid wi'out questioning. As for her safety in the matter, well, it'll be better now than in four or five weeks time. And in a week, as I said, I'll be away westward myself.' He paused. 'And that's another thing. It's unlikely that we'll meet, Major — but if we do, ye'll be careful to show no recognition.'

So that was that. Only a week or so earlier, in scarlet and gold lace, he had ridden his gleaming mare at the head of a company of high-stepping guardsmen. The drums had ruffled and the hautboys trilled, the sun had shone on a gay St. James's and all had been right with the world. Then a hastily-penned note from Sir John de Courcy had marred his complacency, and he had ridden into Essex ill-humouredly, but resigned to the old man's whims. And now this. In a few hours he'd be travelling northward out of Edinburgh accompanied by a strange woman and an infant. She'd probably have no English, eat with her fingers and spit out bones — and she'd probably never used soap. As for the infant — he shuddered. He'd seen year-old children in the gutters of London's slums, in scraps of mired rags, their puny legs sore-covered and their noses streaming. The prospect of playing guardian to such a woman and brat was scarcely to be preferred to that of putting a bullet into the twenty-five-years-old Charles Edward.

What was today? Wednesday? This morning his sergeants would be drilling the company in loading, priming and firing by flams of the drum, and he would have strolled the ranks as they knelt, calculating that the skirts of the scarlet, piped coats were neither more nor less than two inches from the ground, that gaiters were unspotted and hair neatly clubbed above the leather stocks. Fester it, two hundred of his phlegmatic guardsmen in the right place would have shattered the Pretender's rabble with three musketry volleys, and with cold steel driven the barbarians neck and crop into one of their own stinking lochs.

'Dawn tomorrow,' MacDonald was saying. 'Ye can be on the Falkirk road before the City's awake. I'll have three good horses for ye — Yorkshires. They're a mite heavy for saddle, but ye'll need their bone before ye're finished. Pistols, shot. A purse o' fifty guineas, and another twenty sewn in the waist of ye' breeches. If ye're wise, Major, ye'll not make too much show of ye' money, and beware of anyone displaying more than a casual interest in ye.'

'I'm not a damn' fool —'

'Not in London, Major. Not at St. James's. But once beyond Stirling — even Falkirk — ye'll be in a foreign country, three hundred years behind England — and I'm a Scot that says it. Ye'll not credit the Highlanders' ethics. They think higher of a rogue who steals a dozen cattle than of the honest man who owned them. Ye might think ye've seen poverty — until ye see how some o' the humblies live, and remember — most of 'em have never had a guinea in their hands during their whole lives.'

Falkirk, Stirling, Thomas mused, and then northward until he reached the Inverness forts — or the Pretender's army. There were a few military roads, but otherwise only pack-horse tracks and more often nothing at all. Well, if he had to fall foul of moss-troopers or Jacobites, he'd sooner do so in open country than in some dark alleyway. The riff-raff who preyed on travellers were unlikely to be more valiant in Scotland than they were in England, and would not lightly attack a well-mounted man with a sword and a brace of pistols.

He nodded. 'Dawn, then.' The sooner the better.

Chapter 4

The dawn was chill, with drizzling rain and a dank mist that had drifted in from the river. Wetness glistened on the cobbles, streaked the silent, ash-coloured buildings of the Canongate, and soaked quickly into clothing and leathers. Among the narrower wynds and closes there was a pervading smell of night midden.

He had broken his fast in his room under the roof, on a mess of boiled and salted oatmeal that he pushed aside after the first mouthful, bacon, and bread hot from the oven. In the street the horses were already waiting — the two big bay Yorkshires and a smaller animal for baggage. There would be little of his own, he knew. Most of it must be the woman's, fester it. He loaded and primed his pistols with meticulous care, buckled on his sword and laced his cloak high to the neck. Damn the rain. It added yet a further discomfort to an already burdensome journey.

MacDonald had said little and, when Thomas emerged into the street, the woman was already in her saddle, tiny against the bulk of the big Yorkshire and hooded against the rain so that he could see nothing of her face. The plaid-swathed bundle that she held must be the brat. Thomas checked his mount's girths and then the woman's, giving her a nod and a grunt which she did not acknowledge but merely shrugged herself deeper into her cloak. That, Thomas decided, was a good beginning — but he'd wager it wouldn't last long. The woman who could hold her peace for more than a half hour hadn't been born yet.

But he was mistaken. They rode free of the Canongate to the mist-shrouded line of the Flodden Wall, Thomas leading the pack-horse and the woman following. The streets were deserted save for occasional dirt-men shovelling gutter refuse or hauling their laden and reeking creels to the foreshore. Behind them the Castle and the huddled, peak-gabled houses were congealing, disappearing in the haze. The scattered cottages on Corstorphine loomed and were past, then Kirkliston's crossroads and the mound of Niddry Castle like broken, grey teeth against the sky. The mist was dispersing and, with it, the rain. The woman had not spoken.

A signpost pointed a weathered finger in the direction from which they had ridden. Edinburgh 8 miles. Thomas reined. Eight miles, b'God — and it wasn' even noon. MacDonald had said ten miles a day with the brat.

The brat? Goddam — didn't the thing need feeding and watering? He turned in his saddle. 'My apologies, Madam —' he began grudgingly, then stared.

With the rain stopped, she had thrown back her hood, and her hair lay over her shoulders — neither gold nor brown, but like polished copper glinting in the sun. He had never seen such hair. Her face was small, well-boned — not classically beautiful, but with a strange, wild pride emphasised by cinnamon eyes that met his coldly and lips pressed firmly together. There was a whisper of freckles over her nose. She sat straight-backed on her side-saddle, as regally as a young queen, and the swathed child in her arms was rousing.

'My apologies, Madam,' he repeated. Did she understand him? 'I've been neglectful —'

'If you're expecting that I shall dispute it, Master Margery, you will be disappointed.' Her voice lilted, making him think of music, but with an underlying hardness that betrayed her vexation. 'I am not a dragoon.'

'Indeed no, Madam.' Thomas flushed. Damme, this was no ignorant, Celt-speaking peasant woman. Why, fester it, hadn't MacDonald said something about her? He cleared his throat awkwardly. 'I'm sorry — I hadn't thought — not being accustomed, you'll understand —'

'That's mightily plain, sir — and we'll not mend matters by sitting at the Kirkliston crossroads. There's an inn, a half mile further, below the Castle — and if you'll not begrudge a halt. I'd welcome a respite from three hours of looking at the back of your head.'

The comment stung. Thomas had abandoned his wig in Edinburgh, and his own hair was too short-cut to be queued and tied on his neck. He grunted.

The inn would hardly have justified the title in England. A warping, shingled roof covered a barn-like interior, an earthen floor covered with matted straw, and a hearth that spilled as much smoke into the room as into the chimney. Thomas had dropped from his horse and then reached up for the woman. 'If you'll take the child,' she suggested, 'I'll not plague you further.' He clutched the child gingerly until, dismounted, she

31

retrieved it with an air of mild impatience, but she was equally cold towards the unkempt Lowlander who brought ale, milk and buttered girdle-cakes. The child, freed of its voluminous plaid, clung closely to the woman's skirts and surveyed Thomas with grave eyes. It was darkhaired and sturdy, and continued to watch Thomas over the lip of a cup.

'You've a fine child, Madam,' he ventured.

She placed down her own cup. 'If you're to succeed in the deception you've undertaken, Master Margery, it would seem more convincing if you addressed me as "Isobel", or "wife". It will be irksome, to be sure — but safer.'

Thomas swallowed. 'Aye — of course.' He hesitated, then, 'and I'm Thomas.'

She nodded. '"Husband" will be better,' and watched the flush climb into his face. For a moment her expression showed perplexity, and then suddenly softened. She drew a deep breath. 'I do believe, husband, that you're not as ill-mannered as I thought — but just timid.' Her lips parted, and she laughed softly, then glanced over her shoulder to ensure that the inn-keeper was out of earshot. 'And you almost old enough —'

Thomas seethed. 'To be your father?' Fester it — a damn' slip of a girl —

She tossed her head. 'I wasn't going to say that, but you can keep it in mind — and something else. I'd not have an Englishman for a husband, or father. I'd sooner be wed to a Laplander or a heathen Turk —'

'I didn't ask —'

'And nor I, but I must do as I'm bid. The sooner we reach Glengarry country —' She halted, and both turned at the sound of a discreet cough. A man stood at the door, as tall as Thomas and leaner, in a long serge cloak and a claymore at his waist. His dark, thin-jowled face was lowered as he slapped his hat against his knee to shake the wetness from it. Then he looked up and grinned.

'Good day to ye, sir —' he glanced at Isobel, '— and lady. It's a raw morning for the season. I saw ye' horses. Ye're for Falkirk?'

'Aye.' Thomas pushed his nose into his ale. The man was probably an innocent traveller, but he might not be. 'Falkirk and beyond, in easy stages. We have the child —'

The newcomer nodded, eyeing the infant. 'A stout little lad —' he put his head to one side, '— or is it a lassie?'

Thomas gulped at his ale again. 'Sblood, he didn't know. Why, i'faith, hadn't MacDonald —?

'A boy, sir.' It was Isobel. 'A year old.'

'Ah —' the other grinned again. '— a Glengarry voice. Glen Moriston? But ye, sir, if ye'll forgive me —' he turned to Thomas, '— ye're English?'

'Aye. My wife is visiting her people while I buy cattle.' Dammit, the kern was inquisitive —

'Cattle?' The man pondered. 'Faith, it's a long way to travel to buy cattle. Still —' He sensed Thomas's growing ill-humour and turned his head to shout for the inn-keeper. 'Scottish inns, I fear, compare unfavourably with your own, sir.' He tossed down his hat. 'My name is Campbell, sir. Patrick Campbell, at your service.' His eyes flickered mischievously towards Isobel, who had suddenly stiffened, then smiled back at Thomas. 'It's a name that your goodwife's people do not regard with favour. A small matter of clan hostility —'

Thomas shrugged. 'I'm not concerned with your damn' feuds, Master Campbell, so long as they don't interfere with me.' He might as well make matters plain now. He shook back his cloak to reveal the hilt of his sword and his two pistols. 'Campbell, Glengarry, or anyone else, will get short shrift, I'll promise you. And my name's Margery. Thomas Margery.'

'Ye're wise to be prepared, Master Margery — 'though ye'll not fear Highlanders this far south. It's bad country for footpads an' highwaymen. Sawney Beane were a native o' East Lothian.'

'Sawney Beane?'

'Aye. It was a long while ago, in old King Jamie's time. Sawney Beane and his family lodged in a cave off the shore road — a lonely stretch if ever there was one. Every traveller the Beanes robbed, they murdered, then cut up the corpses and threw the remains into the sea. They were a big family, with Beane's eight sons and eighteen grandsons — apart from daughters, all living incestuous. Food became short, so they turned cannibal — eating the flesh from their victims. Finally, after several years, they attacked a man and his wife, travelling ahorse —' he grimaced, '— likely the same as yeself and ye' lady. They dragged down the woman and killed her, but before they could finish off the husband they sighted a larger band of travellers approaching — thirty or forty — and fled. Well, the husband lived to tell his story in Glasgow. The Beanes were hunted down with soldiers and hounds, and carried off to Edinburgh. They were hanged the next day, without trial, in Leith Walk — a total of twenty-seven men and twenty-one women.'

'Did you say their name was Beane?' Isobel enquired. 'More likely it was Campbell.'

Campbell threw back his dark head and laughed. 'Ah, Mistress Margery, will ye never forget that old sin? It was more than fifty years ago — and what can a few MacDonalds mean to ye, eh? Ye're a Glengarry — and not even that. Ye're a Margery, and ye' son is a Margery. Are ye going to teach him to hate the Campbells because of a clan skirmish in Dutch William's day?'

'Clan skirmish? You call the murder of forty unarmed men a skirmish? And there's more. Morven and Ardgour —'

Campbell threw up his hands. 'When ye're surrounded by animals ye must fight like an animal, or be savaged. And the Camerons and Stewarts have savaged the Campbell glens too often.'

'Enough!' Thomas barked. 'B'God, I've no patience with this damn' squabbling. You're worse than children with these clan trivialities —'

Campbell shrugged. 'When the glens are dark, and ye hear the howl o' "Gregalach!" as ye lie in bed, ye'd not think it trivial, Master Margery.' He paused. 'But ye're right. I mentioned the Beanes because, if ye're believing that the company of ye' wife and child offers ye some immunity against marauders, ye're mistaken.' Thomas glanced up at him quickly, but the Scot was continuing. 'If ye've no objection, I'll ride with ye on the road. Two swords are better than one.'

Thomas frowned, and Campbell chuckled. 'And if ye're infected with ye' wife's mistrust, Master Margery, I'll ride in front of ye' so's ye can shoot me in the back whenever ye wish.'

'And that would be fitting,' Isobel murmured. 'I'd sooner ride in a plague cart.'

Campbell raised his eyebrows. 'Ye might suppose that Highlanders wear plaid petticoats, Master Margery — but their womenfolk don't wear the breeches. Do English wives choose their husbands' travelling companions?' He winked.

'Dammit, they don't — and my wife doesn't choose mine. Aye, you can ride with us, Master Campbell, and if my wife has been uncivil, I apologise.' He drew his pistols from beneath his cloak, laid them on a chair, and began checking the primings of each in turn. Campbell watched him amusedly. 'They're fine weapons, Master Margery.'

'And he'll need them.' Isobel was sitting rigidly with the child at her knee.

Campbell sighed. 'A woman, a dog, and a walnut tree — the more ye beat 'em the better they be. I'll not answer for the dog and the walnut tree, Master Margery —'

'Women-beating is a common Campbell occupation —'

''Od's blood!' Thomas pronounced. 'If the plaguy pair of you don't stop spitting I'll do some beating of my own! I don't care a damn about your juvenile feud, and I've got a road to ride. If you're coming, you'll keep your prattling tongues between your teeth.' He snatched up his hat.

They were a mile further on the road, with Isobel riding in sullen silence and the grey huddle of Linlithgow ahead, before Campbell spoke again. 'Ye've the bearing of a soldier, Master Margery. Have ye ever served in the Army?'

Thomas shook his head. 'I'm a farmer.' Fester it, the man was full of questions.

'Of course. Ye said ye were buying cattle. Mind ye, I'd have thought ye'd have done better in Galloway, but ye'll know ye' business better than I.' He began to hum thoughtfully.

'And yourself, Master Campbell?'

'My business? Ah — a little o' this, and a little o' that. Sometimes legal, sometimes not.' He grinned. 'Mind ye, I'm no felon, ye understand.'

And that, Thomas considered, explained nothing at all.

All evidence of the earlier rain had disappeared, and he could feel the warmth of the sun on his shoulders. The horses were in good fettle and, following a halt in Linlithgow, there seemed no reason why they should not push on to Falkirk — a mere eight miles further — where they could lodge for the night. And he'd be happier without the company of this Patrick Campbell, who was too inquisitive by half. It might mean nothing, but Thomas recalled MacDonald's warning.

Campbell shot a glance at Isobel, then at Thomas. 'Strange ye should wed a lass from Glen Moriston, Master Margery. Save for the garrison redcoats, there's not many Englishmen seen that far north. D'ye travel there often?'

'No.' Damn the man. 'I met my wife in Edinburgh. She has kin there.'

'Ah,' Campbell nodded, 'so that was it.' He was humming again. 'And did ye give ye' son an English or Scottish name?'

The brat's name? Goddam — he didn't know that either. This was the penalty of his over-hasty departure from Edinburgh. Damn everything. Campbell was looking at him expectantly, and Thomas shrugged. 'English or Scottish? I don't think we considered the question, Master Campbell —' He drew rein to allow Isobel to overtake him. 'What would you say, wife? Did we name the boy English or Scottish?'

Her eyes, wide with spiteful innocence, met his. 'As you said, husband, I don't think we considered the question.' She was exulting, and did not care that he knew so.

'D'you see?' He returned to Campbell, indifferently. 'What does a name mean?'

Campbell persisted. 'A George or a Duncan? A Henry or a Donald?'

Isobel was deliberately studying the sky. Thomas snorted. 'Master Campbell, I am beginning to find your interrogation annoying. You seem to have an unusual interest in the affairs of a travelling cattle-buyer —'

Campbell was immediately contrite. 'Master Margery — my apology! I didn't mean to offend ye. It was just a friendly curiosity, and conversation lightens a weary road, don't ye agree? What profit could I gain by knowing a bairn's name —?' He laughed.

'If it's a Campbell asking,' Isobel interjected, 'there'll be a treacherous reason behind it. But if it pleases you to know — it's James.'

'James! Ah — Scottish. And not only Scottish but Jacobite, eh? D'ye toast the King across the water, Master Margery?'

'And why not?' Isobel flared on the instant, her golden eyes hot with anger. 'If the Campbells sell themselves as running dogs to a fat German and his English lackeys, there are others who don't — and there'll be a bloody reckoning in Argyll. There's been a Judas in the Highlands too long —'

'Faith — and there's peculiar sentiments for the wife of an Englishman.' Campbell's lips were smiling, but his eyes were not. 'What d'ye say, Master Margery?'

'I'll say that I'm sick to the teeth with your questions, and your company, Master Campbell, and I'd be well rid of both.'

Campbell nodded ruefully, his lower lip out-thrust. 'Aye, I'll not blame ye.' He raised his hat with a flourish. 'We may meet again, Master Margery — and if so, I promise there'll be no more questions.' He paused. 'North o' Stirling, ye'll do well to keep ye' primings dry.' He kicked his horse to a trot, waved his hat in the air, and was gone.

Thomas turned angrily to Isobel. 'Are you stupid, woman? He was right — you're a damn' peculiar wife for an Englishman. He could have been a spy —'

'I'm *not* the wife of an Englishman — and never would be. As for him — all Campbells are spies. They're lying assassins. But I didn't invite his company. You did. And if you think that because the Campbells are mercenaries of the English, you're safe from them, then you'll be painfully mistaken. A Campbell would dirk his own mother for a pair of kine!'

In London, Thomas mused — with that remarkable hair piled high, and in a long gown of, say, emerald green — she'd have the gallants swearing her a goddess and vying to toast her in her own bath water — the damn' fools. Mind you, it was refreshing to see a woman whose hair had not been mangled by curling tongs into creve-coeurs and confidants, favourites and passagères, and whose complexion did not depend upon pomatum and Spanish red. 'I don't understand you Scots,' he said. 'If you stopped these plaguy disputes, forgot this Stuart farce, and devoted yourselves to some honest industry, you might make the country a respectable place to live in — instead of what it is.'

The anger she had shown towards Campbell was nothing to the storm of indignation that broke over his head. 'Farce? *Farce*? You have the arrogance — the effrontery — to call the loyalty of the Scots to their royal house a *farce*? You English? You murder one king and banish another in exchange for first a Dutchman and then a German — and you talk of a farce?' She tossed her head contemptuously. 'You can sit as many foreign jack-puddings as you wish on your Westminster throne, Master Margery, but when our Prince returns there'll be an end to it, and your drunken redcoats won't bring English oppression into the Highlands. If they try, they'll fill the glens with their dead.'

He raised his eyebrows, mildly amused. 'Those are stirring words, Madam, and for a woman — damn' bloodthirsty. Ladies talk of gentler things in London although, I'll own, there's more than a few enjoy the cock-pits and fist-fights. But it's not women who have to do the fighting, Madam — in the ring or on the battlefield — or likely you'd be less inclined to incite a blood-letting. I'll not question the gallantry of your menfolk, but be sure of one thing, they'll not challenge the British Army and survive. There's no need for it. Your Stuarts'll not do any more for Scotland than King George, and possibly a deal less.' At her knee the child began to whimper, and he glared at it impatiently. 'And there, Madam —' he pointed, '— is where you should confine your loyalties. It'll be wiser, and safer.' He turned his horse.

Women. They knew nothing about fighting — real fighting, in which men died or, torn and maimed, wished desperately that they had. And Scotland, whatever anybody said, was part of Britain. De Courcy was right. Every man killed in both sides of a civil war, every town spoiled, the costs, the bitterness — these were all self-inflicted hurts. There was no reparation for the victor, no territories conquered, only loss — and the French would laugh in their sleeves to see such havoc at so little expense to themselves. He was beginning to develop a hate for the French that he'd not had before. There was no nonsense about a battle. Two armies faced each other, fought out the day, and there were no excuses. It was all very clear cut and, given reasonable odds, the English had usually hammered the French, on land and sea. Now the Pope-ridden, frog-eating French, mauled at Dettingen, were employing more devious ways of discomfiting their enemy. Let the Scots do the fighting and dying — the ignorant Scots, dazzled by Versailles promises and prodded into a murderous conflict of which there could be only one ultimate consequence. Aye, he was beginning to hate the French.

They left Linlithgow behind them, a scattering of houses around the tall church and the grey huddle of the old Palace half-curtained by green trees. There were sheep and cows, knee-deep in damp grass, and somewhere off the road a millwheel clattered. They pulled to one side to allow the passage of a creaking farm tumbril, and in a field of barley several workers straightened their aching backs to eye them silently, but there were none others abroad. The road to Falkirk, rutted and uneven, stretched westward before them.

Falkirk, however, seethed with excitement, apparent as soon as they clattered over the clogged Roman ditch into the town. Twice in two hundred yards they saw platoons of marching redcoats, and at the conduit in the market-place a file of women, waiting for water, halted their chatter and stared at Thomas on his big English horse, their faces half apprehensive, half derisive. Beyond them a sergeant of Lascelles' Foot stood with his spontoon over his shoulder and, at his side, a boy drummer wiping the sweat from his face with his cuff. Thomas reined. 'What news, Sergeant?'

The man looked up with a scowl but, gauging his questioner to be someone of quality, choked back the oath ready on his lips. 'The Jacobite bastard's landed, in Arisaig, they say, an' set to raise the clans and claim his father king.' He hawked and spat. 'An' there's some say there's three thousand French troops an' artillery landed north o' Inverness. Johnnie Cope's ordered all regiments to muster at Stirling — though it's not likely we'll clear Falkirk before tomorrow —' he turned to give the boy a stinging buffet, '— an' not by tomorrow midnight if ye don't keep that festerin' tattoo beating!' The boy flayed his drum desperately.

Over the clatter of the drum Thomas heard Isobel laugh, but he had neither time nor disposition for dispute now. Cope was mustering his forces to march on the Pretender, and he — Thomas — had to reach the Pretender first, destroy him, and provide opportunity for the clans to disperse before Cope arrived. Well, he knew how slowly an army moved, and he had time still, but none to waste. Below him, the sergeant was gazing at him thoughtfully, and he kicked his horse into motion.

He could move more quickly and easily without the woman, but he could not dispense with her company yet — not until he was at least beyond Stirling. In Stirling the military would be questioning the motives of any armed man travelling northward, and he had to avoid detention and interrogation at all costs. If MacDonald had spoken the truth, arrest would result in his being placed against the nearest wall and shot.

There were three inns, none of them large, in the marketplace. The first two could offer no accommodation — all being already taken by officers of Lascelles's and Murray's, awaiting orders to march. The innkeepers were apologetic, morosely thumbing through sheaves of commissary notes that, with the uncertainties that the latest news had promoted, might or might not ever be redeemable. At the third, Thomas met with similar frustration. There was nothing, with already the serving wenches sleeping in the kitchen and the boy in the stable — and these damn' port-swilling English redcoats thinking themselves lords o' creation —

Thomas's own opinion of the slouching officers he had seen about Falkirk was already approaching contempt. He'd give a deal to have a company of them on Hounslow Heath for a week. They all held His Majesty's commissions, and when he returned to Whitehall — He turned away sullenly, but at his elbow a voice hailed him.

'Ah — Master Margery —!' It was the lean Campbell, cup in hand. 'We're to have ye' company?' He laughed. 'My apologies — I said no more questions —'

'I'll answer you that one,' Thomas growled. 'It's no. The place is gorged wi' military.'

Campbell laughed again. 'No room at the inn? Ye've an inspiring precedent, Master Margery — but it's likely ye're not inspired.'

'There'll be other places.'

'Perhaps.' Campbell was thoughtful. 'An' perhaps not. It's late in the day, and I know the locality. There's not much else in Falkirk fit for decent folk.' He paused. 'But it's easily mended. I've a bed here — no more than the cock-loft under the roof where the wenches usually sleep, but better'n anything ye're likely be offered elsewhere, and better'n a hedgerow. Ye and ye' goodwife can have it, wi' pleasure.'

'That's damn' civil —' Thomas was surprised. 'But what of yourself?'

'Och, it's no inconvenience. I can bed under the stairs — which is better'n I usually achieve — and ye' lady an' bairn need privacy more. To tell ye the truth, I only took the room to prevent another of ye' shave-tail redcoats from robbing the innkeeper wi' a scrap o' paper.'

'I'm indebted.'

Campbell waved a hand, grinning. 'It's naught. Take it as recompense for the annoyance I caused ye earlier — and ye' wife. And that being so —' he shrugged, '— ye'd best not tell her how ye came by the room. It's certain she'll swear it's all a plot to murder her i' the night. And I'll keep out o' view.'

'Damme, I'm grateful —' But Isobel and the child were still in the street, and it was dusk and beginning to chill. He could make amends with Campbell later. He had misjudged the man.

As Campbell had confessed, the room under the eaves was hardly palatial, but it was dry and tolerably clean, and Isobel made no complaint. She drew off her cloak, shaking free a deluge of untrammelled hair and, as he ordered food to be brought up, she undressed the child, already with eyes half-closed in weariness. They ate by candlelight, in silence until he pushed aside his plate.

'Well, your "Prince" has returned, Madam, and the redcoats are marching. D'you still think they'll fill the glens with their dead?'

From beyond the tiny window came the sound of tramping, iron-shod feet, and Isobel smiled. 'You hear them? As you say, Master Margery, the redcoats are marching. The poor, puny little men from your English slums and prisons, disciplined by the lash, fed on skilly and rotten mutton, hating their officers — and being hated — for sixpence a day. And you think they can subdue the Gordons and Frasers, the MacDonalds, Mackays, Maclarens — prouder than eagles, fiercer than wolves, knowing every rock, every blade of grass among their glens? What will your puny little men do, Master Margery, when they hear the battle cries and see the lines of claymores across the heather?'

Thomas was amused. 'Those puny little men, as you call them, Madam, are soldiers. Not, perhaps, the flower of the British Army, but trained to obey, march, fight — and those claymores of yours'll not be flourished so bravely when they've suffered the musketry of an infantry battalion. Those puny little men out there are the same as those that have fought and defeated the armies of France and Spain. They'll not be awed by a rabble of clansmen.'

'You'll not understand.' She lowered the slumbering child to the bed. '*This* is what my clansmen will be fighting for. Their sons, their heritage, their future, and King James. What will your redcoats be fighting for? And you —?' She glanced at him. 'You'll be abandoning your cattle-buying.' She frowned, then faced him challengingly. 'You never intended to buy cattle. The Campbell was right in one thing, Master Margery. The Highlands are no place for a cattle-buyer. There's better beef in Galloway and the Cheviots than ever came out of the North. And what dealings would an Edinburgh tailor have with an English cattle-buyer?' She looked at his sword and pistols, laid carefully on the floor, then back at him, calculating. 'You, Master Margery, are going into the Highlands to find the Prince. If the news of his landing reached Falkirk today, it could have reached Edinburgh yesterday. You knew —' she nodded, '— and Donald MacDonald knew. Why didn't you tell me?'

Thomas laughed. 'You're mistaken, Madam —'

'It's plain — your weapons, your big horses, and your need to get past the military without suspicion. That's why I'm with you, isn't it? Who would join the Prince's campaign with a wife and child? You're an English Jacobite —' her eyes were wide, deferential, '— and you didn't tell me. I'm sorry for my ill temper, but if I'd known —' she shook her head miserably, '— I would never have betrayed you. I would have died rather.'

'Madam, I told you — you're mistaken. I'm buying cattle, and I'm not concerned —'

'There's nothing for you to buy in Glen Moriston or Glen Mor. A thousand men of Clanranald, Keppoch and Glengarry — including my husband — will be digging up the broadswords and axes that have been hidden for thirty years, and they'll not be in the mood for selling cattle. They'll need all they have for the campaign.' She was smiling. 'But I know. You want to continue the pretence because the less I know, the less I can reveal. I don't blame you, after my prattling — but it will not happen again.'

'Dammit —!' Thomas snorted, but she put a finger to her lips. 'Not so loud. This is Falkirk. There could be royalist agents —' She gasped. 'The Campbell!' She reached forward to lay a hand on his sleeve. 'I know you didn't believe me, but the Campbells can't be trusted. He could have been an informer in English pay — and even now there could be soldiers watching for you. Why did he question — and why did he leave us to go ahead so hurriedly?'

Why indeed, Thomas mused — and why had Campbell so cheerfully relinquished his lodging to someone casually met on the road? He *might* be an informer and he might have suspected Thomas. To be arrested as a suspected Jacobite would be a monstrous irony.

There was one thing he must do immediately — ensure that Campbell was still in the common-room below. If an informer, he would be wasting no time in running for the nearest guardroom — although, i'faith, the inn was already swarming with English officers. As Thomas turned, Isobel's fingers tightened on his arm.

'I didn't tell you,' he said. 'Campbell's here — below stairs. Leastways, he was. If he's still here, likely he's safe enough — for tonight, anyway. If not —' he shrugged. 'Besides, you'll be wanting to bed, and I —'

'No!' She placed herself between him and the door. 'That could be just the sign he's waiting for. They're crafty jackals, these Campbells. Don't you see — he could still be doubtful. If he laid false information, the English would have him flogged. So he has to be quite sure. He'll want to see if we —' she nodded at the sleeping child, '— are really your wife and child —'

Thomas's mouth was a little dry. He was, for the first time in his life, in a woman's bed-chamber, even if it were only a garret in a wretched Scottish inn. It was something else he had not contemplated when he had agreed to this ridiculous arrangement. When he thought about it, the whole thing was stupidly unreal, unbelievable. Was he *really* on his way to assassinate the Pretender? And was he *really* in danger of arrest and death? He couldn't compel himself to accept any of it, but somehow it was going on, and on — like a dream —

'Madam,' he said stiffly, 'I have no desire to cause you embarrassment —'

'Embarrassment?' She lifted her small chin, her eyes resolute. 'What is a little embarrassment against what you are doing for Scotland and our King? Do you suppose that, one day, I could explain to my son that a brave English gentleman — a follower of Prince Charles — died because I feared a little embarrassment?' She shook her head. 'For Scotland I would go as naked as your Godiva —'

''Od's blood — that'll not be necessary, Madam,' Thomas said hastily, 'but I'll agree you could be right about Campbell and, if you're determined, I'll roll myself in my cloak against the wall.'

'You'll not!' she retorted. She gazed at him oddly, then sighed. 'When it comes to knavery, you're a child, and you'll never reach the Prince with your own efforts. What would happen, do you suppose, if the Campbell forced the door — to find me in bed, and you rolled in your cloak —?'

'Damn the Campbell!' Thomas promised. 'He'd find a foot of cold steel in his belly.'

'That would rid you of the Campbell,' Isobel agreed, 'and put a halter around your neck. No —' she was talking quite firmly, '— we shall share the bed.'

'Share the *bed*?' Thomas choked. 'Godammit, Madam — you're married, with your child in this very room!' But she was already unlacing her bodice. 'Madam — you're under no obligation —' She turned her back, slipping the bodice over her white shoulders, and he watched the red-gold hair tumble to her waist. She plucked at the fastenings of her skirt. 'If you're a gentleman, Master Margery, you'll put out the light.'

He jumped as if stung. A moment later both stood in darkness, the candle-light snuffed between his nervous fingers. Within feet of him she was pushing her petticoat over her knees, and he heard the creak of the bed. He made another appeal.

'Madam, think of your marriage —'

'I am not going to. And are you intending to stand there for ever? If you're coy about dropping your breeches, I can't see you — and if I could, it wouldn't matter. In a few years, when King James has made you an English marquis, you'll laugh when you tell your children — who'll all be viscounts. But first you have to reach the Prince —'

He shed his coat and breeches, then stood, barefoot, in his shirt. He'd as soon face a battery of eight-pounders as this. He groped for the bed.

Chapter 5

He lay for several minutes, enveloped in warmth, his mind bemused by half-sleep. As from a great distance he could hear the steady tramp of marching feet, the threatening growl of a sergeant, the familiar slap-slap of a hundred cartouche boxes on the infantrymen's coat-skirts. It must be a full company. With his eyes closed he could visualise the immaculate column swinging past the gatehouse into the Park. In a few more moments he'd hear the discreet tap of his orderly at the door. There was the fitting of his new regimentals at Millerd's — scarlet coat lined blue, waistcoat embroidered with gold and a hat laced the same —

But why a full company so early? And wasn't that the jingle of horse —? The only cavalry at St. James's were the Horse Guards' escort, and the King was in Hanover, wasn't he?

He opened his eyes slowly, apprehensively. A shaft of sunlight flared on the stained floor-boards, and his coat, breeches, hose and neck-cloth lay in a tumbled heap. Inch by inch, he raised his head.

She still slept, her face cradled in one arm, the other loosely embracing the child, who, eyeing the ceiling silently, sucked at a thumb. Her hair flowed like molten gold over the pillow, hot-glowing in the soft light, and he followed the luxuriant deluge over her white shoulder to the full cupola of her breast, rising and falling gently. His eyes stayed, guiltily stealing.

So this was a woman. Another man's woman. What had Shakespeare said? *Her breasts, like ivory globes circled with blue, a pair of maiden worlds unconquered. Save of their lord no bearing yoke they knew …*

He swallowed. Godammit, she was beautiful. Aye — he'd never thought it of any woman before, but she was beautiful. The others, with their paints, powders and patches, their fantasies of false curls, their ribbons and brocades, had interested him no more than a stale Holland cheese. In comparison, Isobel MacDonald had the freshness of an April morning, the artlessness of a wild primrose, and if he'd ever unconsciously considered the ingredients of a tolerable woman, they would have added up to someone like her. But she belonged to another.

He glanced back at her face, and in that second her eyes opened and met his. She frowned, then her cheeks flushed, and she fumbled for the blanket to pull it to her neck. Thomas, confused, and with the sick feeling of a thief caught with his hand in a cash box, wrenched himself to a sitting position.

'I'm sorry —' He was contriving to reach his breeches without uncovering his own legs. 'Od's blood, what was he apologising for?

'Master Margery,' Isobel said, 'in the Highlands, men's legs are as naked as Nature designed them, and I'll hazard that yours are neither better nor worse — save perhaps a little whiter. But, not sharing your schoolboy curiosity, I'll turn my eyes to the wall whilst you recover your breeks and get you to the pump.'

When Thomas reached the common-room, Campbell was gone, and only the two Yorkshires and the pack-horse remained in the stable. That suggested, Thomas calculated, that the man had not laid information with the military in Falkirk — but he could be delaying his move until Stirling — eleven miles further — where there was an organised provost. Thomas, his head under the pump, tried to recall what he could of the maps he had studied during the *Hopewell's* dash northward. There was the more direct military road from Falkirk to Stirling, through Bannockburn, which the troops — and probably Campbell — would take. There was an alternative — a less frequented route that followed the south bank of the Forth river, curving in a half circle to approach Stirling from the eastward. There would be few, if any, military bodies on this road, and he wanted to avoid the military. He might even be able to avoid Stirling. The garrison town offered him little except a tolerable lodging, and now that Isobel MacDonald was an accomplice in his desire for caution — even for the wrong reason.

In the street the last of the marching redcoats were passing — a platoon of infantrymen in ill-fitting scarlet, white crossbelts and gaiters, and with muskets shouldered, followed by a troop of dragoons on stump-tailed cobs. Thomas watched their untidy progress with all the disdain of a Guards officer for regiments of the line. They were a scrubby crew and no mistake. Still — fester it — they must know how to load and fire, how to advance with the bayonet, and they must surely be more than a match for any horde of undisciplined clansmen.

The innkeeper was regarding the soldiers' departure with unconcealed satisfaction. 'There's eggs an' beef for ye' breakfast, fresh milk or ale — for them what pays. The blood-suckin' English had porridge an' stale bread.' He shrugged. 'Beggin' ye' pardon, o' course. There's English an' English. The worst kind wears redcoats an' gold lace. Yeself, now —' he looked at Thomas slyly, '— wouldn't be riding by way o' Arisaig, eh?' He grinned.

That was it, Thomas decided. Once beyond Stirling — beyond reach of the Army — he could abandon this cattle-buying pretence and become, ostensibly, a Jacobite. In a few days, i'faith, there would be hundreds of English Jacobites filtering across the border, and the guise could be his most reliable passport to the vicinity of the Pretender. He even had the alliance of Isobel MacDonald, convinced of his Jacobite sympathies. He frowned. It was a contemptible deception, doubly so because of the woman's naïve trust in his motives and her loyalty to an unseen Charles Edward. But there were no gentlemanly rules in assassination. If a royal Stuart had to die — followed almost certainly by himself — then the bruised feelings of Isobel MacDonald were of small importance.

And there was another thing. The murder of a royal prince was a matter for history. How would the name of Thomas Margery be written? As patriot or arch-traitor? Probably the latter, even by his own countrymen — and that would sour the Margery tradition. His father had fought under Marlborough, his great-grandfather under Cromwell, and there had been a Margery at Flodden and at Acre. He, Thomas, might even have been the most renowned of them all. What had de Courcy said? The conquest of Florida and Mexico? Whose name now, then, would be written alongside those of Cortez and Pizarro — and Wolfe, Howe and — who was it — Clive? Not that it really mattered. He would be dead. A dead assassin.

His army promotion had not been rapid. It seldom was in His Majesty's Foot Guards except by political manipulation or the favour of a royal mistress, and Thomas had never sought either — but he had been marked for a colonelcy. That meant he might well be a major-general in ten years, sufficiently senior to command the forces to take Florida. Still, there was no time for speculation, or to loiter over eggs and beef. The Pretender was loose in the Highlands and a British army was preparing to march. He ordered the horses to be saddled.

The road was scarcely better than a bridle track and, clear of Falkirk, plunged downward through the russet bracken almost to the edge of the river, on the far side of which were occasional red pantiled roofs. To their left and high above them, however, they could just see the distant marching platoons, a fragmented scarlet thread that throbbed and twisted against the skyline until, as the two roads fell apart, they disappeared. 'That,' Thomas pointed northward, 'must be Clackmannan. If we could only cross hereabouts, we'd shorten our road by five or six miles — and avoid Stirling.' He had taken the infant, Jamie, cautiously on his saddle before him, and the child's small hand clutched at his neckcloth. The track beneath them, although still puddled from the previous day's rain, was firm, and the air was warming. 'If there was a ferryman —' he calculated.

She nodded, but her cinnamon eyes, disturbed, followed the route of the vanished redcoats. 'Do you really think they can break the clans?' She turned to him. 'If you did think so, you wouldn't be here.' She paused. 'I'm sorry. Perhaps you would.'

Thomas laughed. 'You've not lost heart since last night? The Gordons and Frasers, you told me — prouder than eagles and fiercer than wolves, eh? And the puny little men from the English slums?' He shook his head ruefully. 'No general concedes a battle before the first shot's been fired.'

'But you weren't joking when you said that those were disciplined soldiers, Master Margery. And they are. When I talked about the clansmen I thought I was speaking to an Englishman —' she smiled impishly, '— I mean — I thought you were an *English* Englishman.' Her face resumed its earlier gravity. 'And I was trying to silence my own doubts, but I didn't. You said it was not women who have to do the fighting, but there are things worse than fighting, Master Margery — believe me — like watching your husbands and brothers, and the other men, taking up their claymores and marching over the hill, full of oaths and laughing like boys. Why do they always pretend that a battle's no different to an apple-stealing?' She drew a deep breath. 'Then the waiting and loneliness, with only boys and a few old men to drive the cattle and watch the fields, and listening through the wind for the distant pibroch, praying for them — and dreading them. Have you seen the faces of women as they count their returning men? One — two — three — with their eyes in agony, searching for faces. And the corpse across a man's shoulder? Who will it be? Donald or Cluny? Jamie or Ewen?' She gazed at the child on his saddle-bow. 'Then one of you is suddenly a widow, or a mother without a son, and there's weeping. What comfort is it that the men swear his life will be paid for? That a Campbell will die tomorrow? Does that bring back your man?'

She was thoughtful. 'That is why Scotland must have its king — not a Secretary of State who never leaves London and a few King's Servants that the clans detest —'

For the wife of an illiterate Highlander, Thomas mused, she had an interesting, if twisted, grasp of politics. Likely she'd listened to the men talking over their ale — or perhaps MacDonald of Edinburgh as he masked his true colours behind Jacobite avowals. It was the clan system, i'faith, that bedevilled Scotland and split her into fragments, and a Stuart, restored and supported by that system, would be more likely to perpetuate its feudal structure than destroy it. No, the Stuarts wouldn't bring a ha'porth of gain to the Highlands. Emotion was a fine thing, but it didn't build ships and mills, hew coal or smelt iron, or the dozens of things that might put good broadcloth on the clansmen's backs and solid food in their bellies. Not that the English common people had cause to be satisfied, but there was a flagrant gulf between the fortunes of the two countries. Bitter pill though it might be for the Scots, it would require the phlegmatic and callous English, if necessary with bayonets, to tear down the throttling tentacles of clan society — not an unfledged boy, half Scottish, half Polish, with an armoury of only stirring platitudes and a charming manner.

'But you're English,' she persisted, anxious for reassurance. 'You're not swayed by a regard for Scotland or loyalty to a clan. You must have reasons for believing in a Scots victory. If the Prince is defeated, and you are not killed, then you'll hang for treason. Are there thousands of Englishmen ready to rebel against King George? And will the redcoats declare for King James?'

'It's not as simple as that,' Thomas grunted, and he meant it. 'These are early days, and for the moment you'd be best out of matters — in Glen Moriston.' When the rebels were smashed — and he agreed with de Courcy that it was inevitable — there'd be murder, pillage and rapine in the Highlands, the inescapable atonement of a defeated people, and no woman — particularly the wife of a rebel — would be secure from outrage. Still, that was something with which Thomas could not concern himself. He might kill the Pretender, but he couldn't hold in check thousands of blood-hungry redcoats. It was all the more reason for ridding himself of the company of Isobel MacDonald as soon as he was able. Damnation on French Louis — the 'Well-beloved' — and his murderous-minded ministers. And damnation on the Stuarts, persisting in a lost cause that could only bring death and misery to thousands of innocent people and shatter the unity of a nation. 'The dispute'll be settled, one way or another, long before the Prince can reach Inverness.' He hoped it would. 'You'll be safe enough there.'

'And Ranald will be fighting.' She had not mentioned her husband before, and he experienced a sudden stab of resentment. Fester it, what sort of man was this Ranald, to go roaring off on a brainless adventure whilst his wife and child wandered the Highlands with someone else? 'Likely he'll not go,' he suggested. 'He'll wait for your return.'

She shook her head. 'He'll go. There'll be no stopping him when the pipes are screaming, the cross burning, and Keppoch swearing for the Prince. He's a good man in his manner, but he'll not allow womenfolk or children to stand in his way when his mind's determined. Give him a broadsword, good shoes to his feet and a cock-feather in his bonnet, and he'll be shouting with the others for English blood.' She lifted her chin. 'And that's how it should be, Master Margery.'

'Aye.' He shrugged. He was not anxious to pursue the subject. The road narrowing, he reined to allow her to pass ahead. Above her riding cloak her hair lay on her slim shoulders, tossing rhythmically with the motion of her horse, and she sat like a young queen. Dammit — she was wasted on a churlish, unlettered rustic who had no ambitions beyond a few scrubby cattle, a peat fire, and a periodical opportunity to brawl with neighbours and authorities. He tugged at the halter of the unoffending pack-horse, angry at the thought and with himself for harbouring it. What business was it of his? He was becoming possessive. Towards Isobel MacDonald? 'Sblood — this was the result of being alone with a woman's company. Would he have given her a second glance in London?

He wrenched his thoughts away from her. Fester it, there were more vital things — Stirling, for a beginning, and Campbell. Well, the road under their feet ran for Stirling, with not much in between, but if the river could be crossed northward, then both Stirling and Campbell could whistle a jig, and he — Thomas — would be deep into Perthshire before the foot-weary redcoats had drawn their night's rations. Then north-west, towards Fort Augustus — a route which must allow him to intercept the Pretender's probable line of march and also an opportunity to despatch Isobel MacDonald on the road to Glen Moriston. Alone, he could move faster, more confidently. It was impossible to predict the circumstances under which he would encounter the Pretender, but there must be no delay in killing him. Every hour brought more men to the rebel colours, and made General Cope's attack more imminent. He had two pistols. One bullet in the head would suffice, with a second if he missed or misfired. Then, God help him. The big Yorkshire he rode wasn't bred for speed, but it would be trotting stolidly long after the ill-fed Highland ponies had fallen in exhaustion. Everything depended upon how well the Pretender's person was guarded. And if Thomas survived, what then? Should he ride for the Border? Or Edinburgh? It was impossible to decide. The whole damn' business was so lacking in reality. The sun shone on bracken-covered hills and scattered silver coins over the grey surface of the Forth below them as it reached slowly towards Leith and the open sea. Birds sang, wild flowers danced and nodded in the breeze, and the world was at peace. It was incredible that, only a few miles away, thousands of men were preparing for bloody battle, and that he, Thomas, was riding to a rendezvous with murder.

He did not see the ferry until they were almost upon it, and then cursed. The flat-bottomed scow, large enough to accommodate a waggon, was moored with one square end against a rough, log jetty. A man and a boy, bare-foot, sat idly on the dirty planks, and on the bank, only yards away, stood four dismounted dragoons and a cornet.

It was too late to turn, too late to do anything. The redcoats had already twisted their heads, eyeing with interest the approaching bays and the trailing pack-horse. The cornet was scarcely more than a boy, lacking the authority, Thomas noted, to have ordered his horses to be linked and his dragoons to stand with muskets shouldered. The men lounged indifferently by the water's edge, one with his coat unbuttoned and toeing pebbles into the river. In the Guards, Thomas had time to muse, they would have earned twenty days on bread and water — but then, it couldn't happen in the Guards.

The cornet held up his hand. 'Your business?'

'Is my business, sirrah.' Thomas reined. 'And yours, I take it, is running a ferry.'

The cornet frowned. 'You'll answer respectfully, sir, or take the consequences. You're English? What business have you north of the Forth?'

'Feeding four thousand beggarly redcoats. I take it you'll not want to march half across Scotland on ammunition bread, and I'm buying cattle, so unless you've a desire to be lifting your hat before General Cope, lad, you'll not delay me with your damn fool questions.'

The cornet flushed, uncertain. The man looking down on him from the height of the tall Yorkshire had an air of confidence that was a little disconcerting. It was uncomfortable enough for a boy with less than two months service to keep in check four insolent dragoons without being ridiculed by a civilian. He had his orders — to picquet the ferry and detain all suspicious travellers crossing to the northward. But what did a suspicious traveller look like, anyway?

'You're commissariat? Then you'll have documents?'

'Documents? You suppose that beef cattle read documents?' Thomas scowled. 'Damn your eyes, boy — if you're to have rations tomorrow I've to drive a hundred head into Stirling before nightfall, and I'll not do it if I'm detained by a gossiping, shave-tail cornet!'

Behind them a dragoon sniggered, and the cornet flared. 'I'll remind you, sir, that I'm picquet commander here —'

'Picquet? You're commanding a *picquet*?' Thomas's eyes slashed at the slouched redcoats. 'Whose are they? Gardiner's? Damn' ploughboys masquerading as soldiers. It's a festerin' mercy they've only a few ragged peasants to deal wi' and not real military. Likely fifty lashes apiece over a gunwheel 'd knock some smartness into 'em —!'

The cornet whirled on his charges, red-faced. 'Dragoons — have a care! Sling ye' muskets and stand at ye' horses' heads! Make ready ye' links!' The redcoats, startled, jostled into line, and the young officer returned to Thomas. 'Now, sir —' But Thomas was edging his horse towards the scow, compelling the boy to step backward. 'Aye, an improvement,' he nodded, 'but you'll need to watch 'em, young man, or they'll have a halter on you —'

'Damme, sir —!'

'Damn nothing,' Thomas grunted. He was lucky. Festerin' lucky. The boy was raw. An older man would have had Thomas dismounted, baggage searched and identity established before allowing him to proceed, and for the first time in his life Thomas welcomed an acquaintanceship with inefficiency. 'If you're finished —?'

There was one thing more. 'I've orders to look for an Englishman, sir — a Jacobite — named Margery, late o' the 2nd Foot Guards —'

'I know,' Thomas nodded. 'Thomas Margery, Major. Deserted wi' regimental money and likely to be riding for the Pretender. General Cope told me himself. He's to be taken dead or alive — and dead'll save a lot of trouble. Well —' he sniffed, '— he'll not likely choose to travel by way o' Stirling and the British Army, *will* he?' Before the hesitating cornet could reply, Thomas kicked his horse forward and, followed by Isobel, descended into the waiting scow. The ferryman threw off the mooring line and reached for his pole.

'A moment —!' The cornet followed disconsolately to the sagging jetty, anxious to impress his watching men with some show of authority, but the scow was already twenty feet from the bank. 'Your name, sir? What is your name?'

'It's Major Margery you want,' Thomas shouted, 'not a collection of names.' The gap between scow and riverbank widened. He was struck by a sudden thought. 'When you reach Stirling, lad, you might question a traveller calling himself Patrick Campbell — if you meet him —'

'Patrick Campbell —?'

'Aye — a tall man, dark, riding a brown gelding — claiming to be a Scot, but more likely, I'd say, an Englishman with a shrewd tongue for an accent — and he was showing an uncommon interest in military matters. Patrick Campbell, d'ye hear —?' The scow was running into the shallows of the far side of the river, and Thomas chuckled. The boy would suffer agonies of indecision for the remainder of the day, not knowing whether to remain at his post or ride for Stirling in search of Patrick Campbell, and neither mattered to Thomas. He tossed a coin to the ferryman, and a few moments later the three horses were climbing towards the scattered cottages of Clackmannan.

Chapter 6

Clackmannan had the news but was unexcited. The issue would be settled, one way or another, far to the northward and westward. The villagers had watched the movements of redcoats across the river since dawn with a mixture of indifference and speculation, their loyalties divided. Too far south to be effected by clan disciplines or to suffer the raids of cattle-stealing Highlanders, yet — a rural community — they did not share the Lowland townsman's dependence upon trade across the border. True, any civil conflict was undesirable; for poor folk the consequences could only be discomfiting — higher taxes, higher prices, thieving soldiers. Four young hotheads, with more bravado than sense, had left in the hope of joining Lord George Murray, but two had already returned, a little sheepishly, after a chill night on the heather, and nobody really believed that the others would ever draw swords alongside the Athollmen. No, in Clackmannan it was wiser to remain at home and let fools fight who wanted to. There were troubles enough already without looking for more.

But Thomas had no intention of remaining in Clackmannan longer than was necessary to snatch a meal — 'four guid herring, breed, an' all the ale ye want f' saxpence,' — and to feed and water the horses. They weren't out of the wood yet; a fast-moving troop of dragoons from Stirling could still overtake them in a few hours, and he would feel easier when they were at least beyond the bounds into Perthshire.

They were a mile beyond Clackmannan, with the comforting barrier of the river on their left, when the child jolting against him began to whimper. He reined to a halt.

''Od's blood, Madam, I'm sorry. As you said before, you're not a dragoon, and I'm being damn' thoughtless. If you prefer, we'll turn back to Clackmannan, and resume tomorrow.'

Her face was flushed by the sun and her eyes weary, but she frowned back at him. 'You've not heard me complain, Master Margery. We're still too close to Stirling, and you know it. We'll need to put thirty miles between us and the English before we can ride easy, and I'll not be a burden — nor the bairn.' She turned to the child and spoke softly, scoldingly, in Gaelic. 'He'll not cry again —' she smiled, '— and I'll not resent being thought a dragoon. I wish I were, so that I could ride with you in King James's service.'

Women, Thomas considered, as they moved on, were fickle cattle and no mistake. One minute she was lamenting her clansmen's warlike temper, and the next she was brandishing a sabre. It was a damn' charity that English women weren't the same. There were places for women — the kitchen and the drawing room. Almost anywhere else they were a plaguy nuisance. And all children should be locked from sight.

They had clattered past a tall watch-tower on a hill and into a filth-strewn track between huddled cottages when Thomas realised that the road still clung uncomfortably close to the river, and here, too, was another ferry to the south bank. He could see redcoats on the far side — more dragoons — and cursed again. He should have struck northward earlier, and he was a fool for not appreciating that, as the upper reaches of the Forth narrowed, ferries, fords and even bridges would present themselves more often. Like Clackmannan, however, Alloa was little concerned. No English had crossed; they were intent on marching for Stirling, and there were several Alloa lads with bundles packed and impatient to be off to the Prince's army — if they only knew where it was. Perhaps Thomas could tell them. In the shadowed, earth-floored common-room of the inn, hazed by peat smoke and the day's cooking, Thomas and Isobel were surrounded by a throng of news-hungry villagers.

But they could tell little. Thomas had last heard that the Pretender — the Prince — was at Glenfinnan, likely a hundred and thirty miles away, and he might by now be anywhere in the wilderness between Fort William, Dundee and Inverness. 'You'll have bloody feet and empty bellies if you're thinking o' tramping the glens looking for the Stuart,' he warned a freckled youngster cleaning the tarnish from an old broadsword. 'And that rusty bodkin won't frighten a redcoat wi' a Brown Bess and a bayonet —'

Isobel's fingers were on his arm. 'Husband — if he's resolved, he must go. If you stay him, he'll hate you and himself for the rest of his life, don't you see?' She turned to the crestfallen boy. 'My husband, also, is riding for the Prince, but he has pistols and a sword, and he's well mounted. You're afoot, but Glenlyon's not too far for a braw lad, and the MacGregors will be out, and the Murrays. They'll not say no to a few more claymores. If an Englishman can fight for the Prince —' she glanced at Thomas, '— then no able-bodied Scot should be skulking at home —'

Festerin' —! Thomas simmered. She might not be a dragoon, but she was threatening to be a damn' successful recruiting sergeant — for the rebels. If he were a Scottish bumpkin, the vision of this flushed beauty with her earnest, tawny eyes, those perfectly-chiselled lips and a voice like defiant music, would — like another Joan — have sent him running for a sword and a horse. He cleared his throat. 'Mind you —' he began, cautiously, but the freckled boy was on his feet, and there were other thoughtful eyes resting on Thomas. A small, square man, greying, wiped his mouth with the back of his hand.

'We ken ye're English, an' ye guidwife's right. I were wi' the Earl o' Mar — we callit him Bobbing John — in the 'Fifteen, but it brought nae but tears. Aye, I've a sword an' a dag buriet under the hearth, and I sweared they'd stay there. But ye' guidwife's right.' He spat. 'Nae Englishman's fightin' fer me. I'll fight fer mesel'.' He whirled on a neighbour. 'An' there's others that kin fight, Duncan MacGreeve — them that sucked their fingers in the 'Fifteen, fillit wi' brave talk when the Earl Marshal's men rode through, an' then shouting huzzahs fer the wee German lairdie at the first sight o' red jackets —'

There was a sudden commotion, angry voices, oaths, denials, and a red-faced man with a flattened nose was shouting. 'Aye! Half of ye's Lowland dirt! Afeer'd o' the baillies an' redcoats. If the De'il himself came wi' brass buttons and a cocked hat, ye'd be cheering for everlasting damnation!' Isobel's hand, on Thomas's arm, tightened. 'Master Mar —' She halted, then, 'Husband — why not lead them to the Prince? And not just here! in every place there'll be men eager to march, but not knowing where, or how. You could raise a company — a hundred men, or more —!'

For a fleeting moment he thought that she had inadvertently presented him with the solution to his most critical problem. Although not relishing the idea of mustering supporters for Charles Edward, a company of volunteers at his back would mean a passport through rebel country and probably directly to the Pretender himself. It was a scheme worthy of even the devious John de Courcy. Then he shook his head. 'No. It would bring the military upon us within hours. There'll be detachments between here and the Tay — Inversnaid, Taymouth, and the forts of the Chain — and there'll be clans other than the Campbells who'll stand for the Crown, or at least not take sides. No —' he shook his head again, '— we'll do better alone, and so will they — in twos or threes.' To be caught by Cope's cavalry at the head of a foot-dragging rabble of Perthshire ploughboys could be disastrous. Isobel's face fell, and he compromised. 'Later it might be different, but not yet. We're still in redcoat country, and we can't afford to be waving flags and beating drums.'

Isobel sighed and then, reluctantly, smiled. 'A pity. You'd have made a fine show, on your big horse, and your pistols, and a hundred claymores marching behind you — and the Prince's standard curling in the wind.'

'Aye, and it'd take one of Cope's platoons precisely one minute, at one volley every fifteen seconds, to lay every damn' fool stark in the dust — and their claymores, horses and standards with 'em!'

'But think of all the lasses,' she suggested, 'love-sick for the handsome Englishman on the high, bay horse.' He snorted.

The inn had emptied, and a few minutes later they watched the first of the Alloa men turning northward from the village, two with swords and a third with a shouldered axe. Laughing, they shook their fists at the river before hurrying on, talking excitedly. Thomas shrugged. God help 'em. It was likely, however, that they would never reach the Pretender. Tomorrow, perhaps, like the Clackmannan lads, they'd be creeping back to their hearths. In any case, they were scarcely a threat to the fortunes of Johnnie Cope.

Despite the proximity of the river and the redcoats on the far side, Thomas had resigned himself to a halt until the following day, but Isobel was already preparing to continue. It was only an hour past noon, she said, and the horses not nearly spent. Six miles northward was Perthshire and the southern glens, the fringe of the clan country. 'The kilt and the pibroch, Husband —' She was using the title, artlessly, even when they were alone. Or perhaps she was not quite so artless. Did he detect the slightest emphasis on the word, to suggest she teased him? The word 'wife' stuck in his throat. Alone, he addressed her as 'Madam' — in company, without title at all. It was an embarrassment, but it would be only for a few more days — three or four — after which he could despatch her towards Inverness, and he'd be left with the only company he trusted — his own.

The afternoon was warm, and in less than an hour they overtook the three Alloa men who, their initial zeal expended and their boots and swords tossed aside, were asleep by the roadside. There were fields of barley and oats, or grazing cattle, on all sides, but these soon gave place to a rolling waste of thick grass, gorse and heather. The last isolated cottage of sod and unhewn stone was behind them, the last tethered sheltie, and before them stretched the wilderness.

So far, then — and at least while the weather held — the journey had not been painful, merely irksome. They'd find crofts and farmsteads, they'd been told in Alloa, before they reached the rugged Perthshire uplands. There was simple fare to be had, be it only oat cakes and milk, and they would usually asleep with a roof over their heads if they did not object to a peat-smoky loft shared with a dozen fowls and the reek of the midden heap at the door. At worst, there was the heather, wrapped in their cloaks — inconvenient, but nobody died of it, and there was good water. The Romans had marched here, and the Danes — and Perthshire homesteads had been burned and looted a hundred times by English marauders. Men had died by the claymore, by pike or musket-ball, but never from sleeping in the heather. Further north, beyond the Ochil Hills and the Earn river, there were mountains, and things might be different. People and conditions were poorer, harder — the 'Irish' of the North, that the Lowlanders feared more than they did the English. Travellers rode well armed, or with an escort. Better still, they moved from glen to glen with safe conduct assured by the chieftains, which no clansman would ignore unless he were a renegade or a Campbell, which meant the same thing.

And somewhere beyond that purple flush over the northern hills — far beyond — the clans were gathering under the red and white standard of Prince Charles Edward, the last feudal army in Europe. But where? Thomas was just beginning to appreciate the immensity of his task, first to reach the Pretender and then to kill him. The few obstacles he had so far overcome were puny in comparison with those he was likely to encounter during the next couple of weeks.

Against Thomas's chest the child Jamie was asleep, his dark hair splayed over his puckered eyes. Aye, the child's father was somewhere beyond there. Ranald MacDonald. What manner of man was he? Dark, that was for certain, a Highlander, and a quick-tempered rogue — or so MacDonald of Edinburgh had said. How did such a clod achieve a wife like Isobel? Godammit — it was none of his business. He pulled his hat over his eyes.

Chapter 7

He had the dark eyes of his Polish mother, a slightly aquiline nose, and shock of red hair that had never taken kindly to discipline. His slim build made him appear somewhat taller than he was, and he had the waist of a girl. Nobody had the courage to tell him that his interpretation of Highland costume bordered on the bizarre. His kilt and hose, of brilliant green, clashing painfully with a jacket of garnet velvet and a checkered bonnet, were, after all, French made — and the French could hardly be expected to know all the intricacies of Scottish dress. From henceforth, the Prince had ordered, all in the Jacobite army would wear the kilt — well-meaning, no doubt, but a nuisance. Many of the chieftains and lairds wore a kilt only occasionally, preferring the more practical trews, but, if the Prince said so, the kilt it had to be, whether for Scots, English or Irish.

They were wary of him still, and jealous of each other. He scarcely looked his twenty-five years, but had tried hard to correct the foppish French mannerisms that had contributed towards Boisdale's disdain for his cause. He rode well — better, indeed, than most of the Scottish gentry, and certainly better than John O'Sullivan, the theatrical Irishman who claimed a captaincy in the French service and who, for want of a more experienced alternative, was appointed Adjutant-General to the Prince's forces.

On the heather above Loch Sheil twelve hundred clansmen were camped — if camp was the right description for a situation that had neither tents, kitchens, baggage, horselines or picquets, nor even occupied the same site from day to day. Several light artillery pieces, without mountings, had been landed from the *Du Teillay*, with a small number of muskets, but most of the clansmen had brought their own weapons — a miscellany of firearms, swords, dirks and — for the ragged humblies of the third line — axes, scythe-blades and half-pikes. A hundred scattered fires trickled smoke skyward. Men sprawled, strolled, slept, and the Camerons' pibroch screamed, 'Ye sons of dogs, of dogs of the breed, come here on flesh to feed!'

But thank God for Lochiel's Camerons. The Prince's landing in Arisaig had hardly, as yet, set the Highlands afire. Following Boisdale, MacDonald of Sleat and McLeod of McLeod had declined the Prince's invitation to join what was, in their opinion, a forlorn and rash venture, and without the Camerons the whole business would have foundered before it had begun. Even now, twelve hundred made a disappointing muster-roll. There were promises from Scotus, Keppoch and Glengarry, but only promises —

By now Whitehall, Edinburgh and Stirling would know of the landing, and the wheels of retaliation, however slow, would be beginning to turn. The red-haired young man had no illusions about his enemies in the Highlands, and there was probably more than one English-paid kern within sight of Glenfinnan at this moment. In Paris they'd talked malevolently of a certain Sir John de Courcy, a ruthless snake of an Englishman, devoid of ethics, who would be sure to be devising every possible measure towards the humiliation of Scotland and her ally, France. But, i'faith, if the rebel army at Glenfinnan didn't double its numbers within the next two days, and treble them in a week, then Sir John de Courcy needn't stir from his lair in Essex.

The Prince trotted his horse slowly around the northern neck of the Loch, on the barely discernible track that reached for Kinlocheil. He liked to show himself, preferably unescorted, to his clansmen at least once a day, to demonstrate his confidence in them, and he was grateful to see a group of them rise from their fire, two hundred yards away, waving their bonnets in his direction. His bright green kilt must have been recognisable at four times that distance. He plucked off his own cap in return, held it high, gallantly. He was the Prince, heir apparent of James the Third, King of England, Scotland, Wales, and territories overseas. These brave, ignorant fellows were going to return the Royal Stuarts to their rightful inheritance, with or without the French, and shout it to Europe from the Palace of Holyrood-house and Westminster. That was, of course, if a few thousand more of them would come to Glenfinnan.

The clansmen referred to him as 'woor Charlie' and 'the Wee Bairn'. He would have liked a more masculine, more warlike, title, and perhaps time would produce one. The Stuart line was not renowned for battlefield prowess — not like the Camerons, 'fiercer than the fiercest', the proud Chisholm and the wolf-like Campbells. But thirty years would pass before nostalgic poems and ballads, written by fading, middle-aged Scottish ladies, would damn him for eternity as a romantic Prince Charming, the Young Chevalier, the Bonnie Highland Laddie. At this moment, however, at Glenfinnan, there was a knot in his belly that he knew was fear. True, these were early days, but already three powerful chieftains of the West had flatly refused to support him, and this wasn't the welcome he had been led to expect. Could he be mistaken about Scotland's desire for a Stuart king?

There was a distant shout, and he reined, turning in his saddle. From the westward, a half mile distant, another horseman was spurring towards him, gesticulating. He recognised the clumsy horsemanship of John O'Sullivan, and waited, his heart in his throat. There could be only one reason for O'Sullivan's haste — news. The Prince gazed up at the sky. Good or bad? Would today decide whether they re-embarked and crept like whipped schoolboys back to Paris —?

'Ye' Royal Highness —!' O'Sullivan's flushed face was twisted into the grin of a man who had important information to impart but wished to sustain the suspense of his listener. He tugged his horse to a halt, then paused, his eyes on the Prince. 'There's five hundred o' Glengarry on the march, so is Keppoch and MacDonald o' Glencoe. Clanranald has declared for ye, and the Duke o' Perth an' Lord George Murray —' The words tumbled breathlessly from his eager mouth. 'It's as we said. The clans are coming out, and there'll be more. In a week we'll muster five thousand. Fort William's as good as ours. Then the garrisons at Kilcumein, Badenoch an' Inverness. They'll not stand —'

The Prince allowed himself the luxury of a condescending chuckle. 'Not so quickly, Sir. Let us have sight of the clan standards first and, when we do, we shall raise my own and swear me Prince Regent.' He was choked with relief and he wanted desperately to be sick, but O'Sullivan must not know it. He drew a cambric handkerchief from a pocket and flicked at his sleeve. 'And that is all?'

'All?' O'Sullivan swallowed. 'Aye — there's news that King George has put a price o' thirty thousand pounds on ye' head —'

'Thirty thousand?' The Prince, his nausea under control, chuckled again. 'It's a flattering figure — so soon. We must reciprocate, but hardly so handsomely. Let it be issued that we, the Prince Regent, offer thirty pounds for the person of King George, delivered to our custody.'

'Thirty pounds?' O'Sullivan stared, then guffawed. A moment later he sobered. 'And one more thing. There's information from Stirling of Cope, who's preparing to move wi' four regiments o' foot, two o' dragoons, and Lord Loudon's bastard Highlanders, but no indication of his plans.' He paused. 'There's also a man recently departed Edinburgh with orders to kill ye.'

'Again? They tried in Paris, and Gravelines, and they still persist?'

'He'll not get far,' O'Sullivan said. 'Our people have him marked, and the English'll not hear more of him.'

Chapter 8

Below them, in the sunlight, the stone bridge over the Strath Tay was grey-white, partly obscured from view by clustered birches, with the river, forty yards from bank to bank, of silken cobalt veined with silver as the current streamed through the shadowed arches. It was a fine bridge for such a lonely setting, wasted in this wild fastness of hill and mountain, and it had cost four thousand pounds in English money. Behind it the valley's girdle soared to the sky, clothed in a tessellated plaid of olive, russet, saffron, emerald and purple, thick with firs, oaks, birches and broom. There was no movement and no sound, save that of rustling trees and the distant breathing of the river.

It was just as well, Thomas considered. This was divided, uncertain country — Atholl country. Beyond the bridge the twisting road would pass close to Blair Castle, the seat of James, Duke of Atholl, who was a loyal Whig, and it was probable that his tenants, willingly or not, would be King George's men also. But the Duke's brothers, Lord George Murray and Lord William of Tullibardine, had already declared for the Pretender, and were scouring the glens, forcing out the scattered clansmen on pain of burned thatch and ham-strung cattle. The half dozen wretched hovels of Aberfeldy, behind them, were silent and apparently deserted, and a ragged youth they'd seen on the road had run for the trees. Beyond the bridge, therefore, was the unknown.

'It's beautiful, isn't it?' Isobel said. 'Can you match it in England, Husband?'

His eyes were searching. The empty road, the birches, the five arches of the bridge, the road and the trees beyond. Husband, she'd said again. Damn everything. 'Aye,' he said slowly, 'we have beauty in England, too — at least, we think so.' It was plaguy quiet. It had been quiet since Perth, without giving him anxiety — until now, at Wade's bridge. He could not have said why, but there was something ominous about the narrow, empty road falling to the white bridge, the gentle river overflung by trees. He drew his pistols and checked their primings carefully. Isobel's eyes were on him. 'Ours is a softer beauty,' he went on, 'the

Downs, the hills of Devon, the Fens.' He looked up. 'You'd like Cambridgeshire,' he added, then wished he had not.

'You haven't seen Glen Moriston,' she said, but he was not listening.

His time was running short, and they had to cross. They had departed Perth only that morning — a town he'd had no desire to even see — after an eight-day frustrating, maddening delay following the strange sickness of their horses in Crieff. S'blood — he'd half throttled an ostler who cried innocence, swearing the oats were no different to any others, but the beasts were poisoned, that was certain, and the pack-horse dead by nightfall. The big Yorkshire, sweating, had covered the eighteen miles to Perth, and there refused to move another step. Thomas had searched the Vennels for new animals, but there was nothing other than broken-winded shelties that would hardly have carried him beyond the town limits. There was nothing to do but wait for the Yorkshires, starved and purged, to recover.

The business of the horses may have been an accident, but it was odd that all three had been affected and that other beasts in the same stable were not. In any event, they had lost eight precious days, and he rode now with his hand never far from a pistol butt. It would not have been difficult for a hard-riding man to reach Crieff before them, and perhaps be on the road ahead.

In Perth they had heard more rumours of the Pretender than of General Cope's movements behind them. There was hysterical talk of French landings, which he gauged to be nonsense, and the Prince, it was said, was sweeping north-eastward through the Locheil Forest towards the fort at Kilcumein and perhaps Inverness. That was logical, and Cope, in reply, must surely be moving northward from Stirling — which meant that Thomas and Isobel were somewhere between the two armies with the intervening gap closing daily.

Well, beyond the bridge, beyond Blair, he must abandon Isobel. She'd be on the fringe of her own clan country and a few guineas would buy an escort to take her on to Glen Moriston and safety, leaving him to ride hard for the forts of the Chain. It must be today.

'I'll lead,' he said, and kicked his horse towards the bridge. It was festerin' strange, he mused, how a woman's company could undermine a man's temper. That was why, Godammit, a soldier should never marry. The sight of red-gold hair in the candle-light, a snatched glimpse of white shoulders as she snuggled to the child against the wall, her cinnamon eyes on him, thoughtful and trusting, her cool hand when it accidentally met his — all these things sapped the determination of a man. It must be today. Tomorrow could be too late. He felt a hot flush rise into his face as he thought of Crieff — when, in the warm darkness, she had turned in her sleep to press against him. He had felt his belly contort, his throat choke and, with madness in him, he had reached for her thighs. They had opened to his hand and she had moaned. 'Husband —' He could have sworn that her eyes were wide and, terrified, he had turned away, slid from the mattress and descended to the chill, dawn air of the yard, the sweat cold on his chest and trembling. He had gone to the stable to bury his head in a tub of water, found the pack-horse vomiting, and had checked the Yorkshires from eating their fill.

Later, Isobel had given no sign that she had been aware of the incident, and the business of the horses had been a distraction but, since that night, the child Jamie had lay between them — Jamie, with shyness overcome, who chattered in Gaelic and infant English so that they both laughed, clutched confidentally at Thomas and toddled bravely in his wake at every opportunity. It was at odd, unexpected moments that his eyes met Isobel's, to find them already on him, calm and fathomless, that he felt afraid. Well, he'd been right. There was no place for a woman in his employment, and today would see the end of it.

Their horses' feet were clattering on the bridge, its causeway dusty and empty, flooded with hot sunlight — save for the long black shadows thrown by the obelisks that crowned the right-hand parapet, thrusting like sword-blades —

Thomas started. One of the shadows was *not* like a sword-blade. There was a curious abnormality at its base that no architect's hand had drawn. He pulled his feet from his stirrups, swung from the saddle and dropped quietly to the ground, crouching. His horse walked on. Isobel, startled, made as if to rein, but he put a finger to his lips and motioned her forward. Behind that far obelisk, he knew, was something which should not be there. If it were a man, he would be listening, waiting for the leading horse to come abreast of his hiding place — and the horses' feet on the stones had not paused. Thomas, drawing his pistols, ran forward on his toes, clinging to the parapet. He reached the near side of the obelisk and halted. A moment later his walking, riderless horse overtook him, and a yard from Thomas a man stepped forward with a raised musket, to stare for a single second at the empty saddle before a bullet smashed into his head.

It had all happened more quickly than Thomas would ever describe it, but there was no time to glance at the crumpled corpse. He thrust his spent pistol into his waistband, snatched at his horse's bridle and then Isobel's, hauling them to a halt. From the far side of the bridge there was a shout and then the noise of breaking foliage. The two bays were jostling, nervous, and he reached up to tear Isobel and the child unceremoniously from their seat, throwing them down against the stonework.

Their attacker, then, had not been alone, but it was possible that his confederates, if they were not within vision, would not know the origin of the pistol shot. He knelt, picked up the ready-cocked musket of the dead man, and laid his second pistol ready to his hand.

He had not long to wait. Sixty feet away, at the junction of bridge and river bank, a man emerged from the birches followed by a second and then a third. They were Highlanders, their kilts pulled between their legs to facilitate rapid movement, and each carrying a musket, claymore and target. Thomas could see them clearly, laughing as they ran directly towards him, and he raised his musket, sighting at the chest of the leader. He could not miss.

Then they saw him and, simultaneously halted in their tracks, mouths agape. He squeezed the trigger.

The musket-lock snapped, but nothing happened. He cursed, throwing the gun aside and reaching for his pistol. The priming of the musket, dropped by its dead owner, had been flung from its pan, and there was no time to renew it now. The three remaining Highlanders, recovering from their surprise, suddenly moved very quickly. Two turned to regain the cover of the trees, but the third gave a shout, bared his teeth, and came bounding forward, scorning to use his gun. He's either a brave man, Thomas considered, or a damn' fool — but it made no difference. His own pistol he could trust, and the heavy shot struck the Highlander high in the chest, spun him completely about, and hurtled him to the ground.

Thomas had lost sight of the others. By now they might be on either side of the road beyond the bridge. Isobel was huddled against the parapet with Jamie tightly held, but with her free hand grasping the reins of the two horses. Thomas had to reload, and quickly, but his powder flask and wallet of shot were on the saddle of his bay. He rose to his feet, steadied the restless horse, then unlaced the flask and wallet. With two reloaded pistols, and the musket re-primed, he could at least deny the Highlanders' approach — if they were still in the vicinity. He turned, and in that second saw the flash among the green foliage bordering the road. There was a vicious jolt and then a searing pain in his right leg above the knee and, helpless, he sprawled, swearing. Inches from him the iron-shod feet of his horse were hammering and chopping at the dust. There was a singing in his ears, and through a spitting haze he could see only blue sky and white, fleecy clouds. The powder flask had fallen from his grasp, and he groped for it blindly, but Isobel was on her knees beside him with a pistol in her hand, ramming home a charge, her eyes on the far bank. 'The musket!' he choked 'Prime the musket —!'

From a distance there was the sound of yet another musket shot. Isobel threw her body across his, pressing him to the ground, and he swore again. Isobel gasped. 'It's too late — they're coming!'

The pain in his leg shrieked, but he pulled himself to his elbows. The two Highlanders, with guns abandoned but with claymores drawn, had mounted the bridge and were approaching, half crouched and watching him warily. They were unkempt wolves of men, with pine-sprigs in the woollen bonnets pulled over the tangled hair that fell to their shoulders, ragged plaids and bare, mired legs. Seeing him half-risen, one of them uttered a contemptuous chuckle and both sped forward with swords raised.

But from behind Thomas there was another sound — of drumming hoofbeats and then a chilling howl — 'Cruachan! Cruachan!' A large brown horse, at full stretch, thundered on to the bridge from the road they had recently left, hurtling past, its rider low over its neck with a broadsword outflung and cloak streaming. Dust from the flailing hooves enveloped Thomas. The leading Highlander threw up his target desperately, but the charging horse smashed him aside like a straw doll. The second had already turned to flee. The horseman's sword rose high, and slashed — once, twice — and the Highlander was down, his legs jerking as if still trying to run, his head almost severed from his shoulders. Wrenching viciously to bring his mount to a halt, the newcomer whirled, plucking a pistol from a saddle holster. The first

Highlander was on all fours, dazed, and scrabbling at the stonework of the parapet. Seeing the threatening pistol, he held up a hand, weakly, but the ball struck him between the eyes, and he crumpled.

With an unusual litheness, the horseman slid from his saddle, strolled to the nearest corpse, and turned it with his foot. 'Blood-sucking MacGregors,' he muttered. Then he twisted his head and his face broke into a grin. '*Ah* — good-day to ye, Master Margery — and, o' course, Mistress Margery. I trust I find ye well?' It was Patrick Campbell.

Thomas stared at him. ''Od's blood, man — where did you come from?' He tried to pull himself to a sitting position, but nausea seethed into his throat and he fell back into Isobel's supporting arms. Isobel, with a glance at Jamie, seated in the dust and apparently unimpressed by the events of the last few minutes, looked up at Campbell. 'I never thought that I'd be indebted to a Campbell, but I am. You saved our lives, Sir, and if there is anything —'

'That you can do to repay me?' Campbell was still smiling. 'Well, I'll settle for a truce, Madam — but there are more important things — ye' husband's leg for a beginning.' He dropped to his knees. 'Ye're a fine shot wi' a pistol, Master Margery. Ye took ye' man at near fifty feet.'

'How did you —?' Thomas began again, but Campbell was cutting away the blood-stained fabric of his breeches, then frowning, sucking his teeth. Thomas jerked as the other's fingers probed. 'Goddam —!'

'Aye ye're right. Goddam it is.' Campbell nodded. 'There's a musket ball in ye' leg, and I'd say ye' thigh-bone is shattered. There's not much I can do for ye, Master Margery. It's a task for a surgeon.'

'A surgeon? I've no festerin' time to spare for a surgeon!' A shattered thigh? It was impossible. How long would a shattered thigh take to mend? 'If you'll splint and bind me, and put me in my saddle, I'll ride, dammit.'

Campbell snorted. 'Aye, I'll splint and bind ye, but ye'll never ride. Ye'll need a litter —'

'Litter! Have you ever heard of Benbow? He directed a battle wi' a leg broken to pieces by chain shot —'

'Aye, and if I remember right, they buried him after. Ye've got a vicious leg, Master Margery. The shot must come out, and that bone must be set — and soon — or there'll be gangrene for certain.' He paused. 'Another thing. Ye' blood is a bonny red, and ye can't afford to lose much more. We'll find a surgeon.'

'Where d'you suppose you'll find a plaguy surgeon in a God-forsaken wilderness like this?'

Campbell ignored him. 'Mistress Margery. If ye'll forgive me, I'd like to have ye' under-petticoat.' Isobel stared for a moment, then nodded and pulled up her skirts. Campbell returned to Thomas. 'Not such a wilderness as ye may suppose, Master Margery. We can't be more than ten miles from Atholl's estate, and I'll not believe that Duke wouldn't have a surgeon somewhere within reach.' He began tearing Isobel's petticoat into long strips. 'And now, Mistress Margery, if ye'll take my claymore and cut a few birch staves suitable for splinting —' Isobel was off without hesitation, and Campbell chuckled. 'It's the first time a Glengarry's ever run to do a Campbell's bidding!'

'You haven't said,' Thomas winced, 'what brought you here.'

Campbell shrugged. 'It's the King's highway. I should have been ahead of ye if it wasn't for a peculiar affair in Stirling — involving a cornet o' dragoons.' He grinned at Thomas. 'And I had no intention o' pulling ye' chestnuts out o' the fire, but I couldn't watch ye be killed — not by a filthy MacGregor, that is. All the same —' he was binding Thomas's thigh, '— for a cattle-buyer ye've a fine eye wi' a pistol — and for that matter, they're damn' fine pistols for a cattle-buyer.'

With Thomas's leg bound and splinted, Campbell fashioned a rough litter which was slung between the two Yorkshires. Then, pausing only to reload their pistols, he led them off the bridge, leaving the dead Highlanders where they lay. For Thomas the journey was a sickening nightmare. With every jolt of the horses, agonising, white-hot convulsions brought bile into his throat. The bindings on his leg were sodden with blood, and he cursed continuously — at Campbell, the MacGregors, and every rag-picking, ill-bred savage that had ever worn a kilt. He was still cursing when, weakened by loss of blood and delirious, unconsciousness overcame him. He did not feel the clumsy forceps of the half-drunken surgeon who also stretched and set his thigh — and had Campbell's dirk at his throat when he announced a desire to bleed Thomas further. Nor, during the fever that followed, was he aware of the gentle hands that bathed his sweating body, moistened his cracked lips, and soothed him when he tossed and ranted incoherently through the long hours of the night.

The following day the Pitlochry surgeon, returned from treating the colic of a neighbour's cattle, shook his head, hiccoughed, then gave as his opinion that Thomas could not be moved — or he would certainly succumb. A good bleeding was indicated, and probably an emetic. The leg, now — he rubbed his nose with a dirty finger — the leg might have to come off. The combination of shot-wound and fracture promised complications, and healing could be a long business, whilst a good, clean amputation would settle matters one way or the other. Campbell propelled him towards the door, but his face was pensive.

Isobel rose from the prostrate Thomas. 'Master Campbell —' she faced him squarely, '— it is time for plain talking, and I'll not be denied. What is your business with us? I am grateful — eternally grateful — for what you have done, but you were not at the bridge by chance. Your following of us was deliberate. Why? What is your interest in us?'

Campbell was plainly perplexed. He walked, frowning, to the window, then turned slowly. 'Ye have me, Madam, in a quandary. Ye can be assured that I intend ye no harm — else why did I endanger myself to save ye from the MacGregors? On the contrary — if ye'll forgive the impertinence —' he pulled at an ear, nonplussed, '— I'm concerned with ye' safety —'

'Then you're a Jacobite? A Campbell Jacobite? Or are you not really a Campbell?'

'No, I'm no Jacobite — and aye, I'm a Campbell.' He drew a deep breath. 'Y'see, I know ye' father-in-law, MacDonald — and I also know that ye're not Mistress Margery.'

Isobel flushed. 'I see.' She shook her head. 'No, I don't. If you're not a Jacobite —' She glanced at Thomas, insensible on the nearby couch. 'My hus — Master Margery — is riding to join the Prince, and the English have heard of it. We thought we had shaken off the redcoats, after Stirling — but why did the MacGregors try to kill us? And you —?' She hesitated. 'And another thing. The redcoat officer at the Clackmannan ferry said that he was looking for a *Major Thomas Margery of the Guards* —'

The perplexity had suddenly vanished from Campbell's face, and he grinned. 'Ah —' he nodded, '— it was the last part I didn't know.' His amused eyes remained on Isobel. 'If I thought all redcoats could shoot like that, I wouldn't hazard a pinch o' snuff for ye' Prince's chances.'

'You haven't explained,' Isobel insisted.

Campbell was thoughtful for several moments, then, 'It'd not help ye, because ye'd not understand, but I'll give ye my oath I've no ill intentions towards ye, and there'll come a time when ye'll know the whole story.' He paused. 'As for the other matters, well, ye must have guessed as well as I did that Master Margery was no cattle-dealer, and the fact that he's a deserted officer explains the Army's interest in him. They wouldn't have been so sensitive about any ordinary Jacobite.'

'And the MacGregors?'

He shrugged. 'There's no evidence to connect them wi' the Jacobites. It's just as likely they were moss-troopers, utilising the unsettled state of affairs to indulge in their favourite pastime — murder an' robbery. Still, there's need for being canny for more reasons than that. I happen to know that Johnnie Cope's column marches from Stirling tomorrow and it'll march this way. Aye, that means that there could be redcoats here in five or six days, which'll be damn uncomfortable — for Major Margery, and yeself as his accomplice. Ye'll have to move on wi'out delay.'

'But Master Margery can't be moved. The surgeon said —'

'The surgeon's a drunken oaf, and he'll detain ye as long as he thinks he can be paid. I'll not pretend that Major Margery might not die if ye move him, but he's certain to if he's still here when Cope arrives. It's a pity —' he thrust out his lower lip ruefully, '— that he'll miss his rendezvous with the Prince. He might regret that more than anything.'

'Yes,' Isobel murmured. She gazed at Thomas, his face flushed and moist, but breathing steadily. 'The fever's easier. I can't leave him here for Cope — not after all this. Perhaps — if we travelled slowly —'

'Not too slowly. Cope will have his patrols active, and there'll be people that have seen ye, ready to talk. But your two Yorkshires'll take the litter easy enough — and yeself and the bairn. One thing's in his favour. It's summer. If the snows were here, he'd never survive.'

'He'll survive,' Isobel affirmed, then she stared at Campbell, her eyes wide. 'But where? Where can I take him? A man with a shattered leg?'

Campbell gazed back at her without speaking, his brows rising. He grinned again.

Isobel's eyes widened even further. 'Glen Moriston?' she whispered. 'To my own clan country?'

'It must be nigh on a hundred miles,' he nodded, 'and none of it easy — but can ye think of anywhere else?'

Isobel shook her head desperately. 'The Glengarry are a jealous people, and Catholic. A married woman doesn't bring a strange man to the glen — and her husband absent —'

'Can ye think of anywhere else?' Campbell repeated.

'It's not possible. You know it's not. It's not the journey. Tell me anywhere — the far North if you wish, Mackenzie or Munro country — it doesn't matter. I'll take him. But not Glen Moriston. That wasn't agreed with my father-in-law, and he would never have asked it.'

'No,' Campbell glanced at Thomas, 'and nor would Major Margery, I'd wager. But ye can't leave him here, and the Prince's army will have no place for a man with a shattered leg. If ye abandon him in MacGregor country, wi' some crofter, he'll likely never be heard of again. They'd murder him for his clothes or sell him to the military as soon as ye turned ye back. And the Mackenzie and Munro are scarcely better — if he survived that far. It comes to one thing, Mistress. If ye care that he lives, then ye must take him to Glen Moriston. If not —' He shrugged.

Isobel drew a shuddering breath. The situation was one that had not been envisaged. Yesterday — she had sensed it in Thomas's demeanour — they would have parted company, and he would have ridden out of her life for ever, to the Prince, and perhaps to his death. Now it was decreed otherwise. She looked down at Thomas, his hair damp on his brow, his eyes closed. He was an Englishman, and she had departed Edinburgh with no liking for his ungracious company and anxious to be rid of it, but a woman couldn't play wife to a man for two weeks without something happening. It was inevitable — although she had fought the temptation — to make comparisons between him and Ranald MacDonald.

She understood Thomas now — as she had never understood Ranald. It was strange. Ranald was her husband, a dour man whose clumsy, self-gratifying demands left her empty and irritated, but resigned to the duty she supposed common to all wives. It had always been so, and women had no choice.

But she understood Thomas. No — it wasn't so much an understanding. Nothing so definite as that. It was an affinity, a relationship, that they both recognised, and which flared uncomfortably when their eyes met, and at every moment of trivial physical contact, when they laughed together over Jamie, and in the dark, strained moments before they slept.

She had, at first, experienced feelings of mild amusement, annoyance and self-reproach. She was a married woman with a child, she told herself, behaving like a young girl at her first trysting. When the Englishman had gone, she would forget him within hours. Her amusement, however, had disappeared, and her annoyance had become apprehension. When she addressed him, the word 'Husband' had seemed to choke on her lips, her heart raced, and she would contrive to speak only when he was turned from her, so that he did not see her flush.

And then Crieff. Had she been awake or dreaming? No, it was cowardly self-delusion to pretend that any of it was a dream. It was a madness, but she had come to him, hot with a wanting that she had never before thought was possible. She had felt his hands on her, and she had arched, splaying, knowing that until this moment she had been no better than virgin. 'Husband —' she had pleaded. It was now. He would take her, crush her under him, bruise her —

Then, inexplicably, he had twisted away, and the bed beside her was empty and cold. She had stared into the darkness, with shame quenching the madness in her, and dreading the daylight, when she would have to face him.

The poisoning of the horses had been a cruel blow, but it had at least reduced all other considerations to comparative unimportance, and Thomas, she was convinced, had been grateful to be free of her company as he searched unsuccessfully for replacement mounts. Her shame remained — of her own moment of immodesty, and of his disdain.

It should have ended yesterday, and she gone her way to Glen Moriston, to await the return of Ranald MacDonald with his coarse, black beard, his oaths, his bluster and his pride, to thirty, forty, years in a Highland glen, twenty miles from a cramped, muck-reeking Inverness, the only town she could expect to see again. Englishmen were rare — occasional redcoat officers hunting game, road surveyors, a packman or two. They were a foreign breed, tolerated by some, resented by most, welcomed by none — but here was an Englishman whom she had known for only two weeks, who, with Campbell, had saved her life and her son's.

Without her, now, it was likely that his days were numbered, but he would not meet with sympathy among the Glengarry folk, and she, in turn, would bring their indignation on her head.

There was her own father, Robert of Dundreggan, a fair man but hard, a pillar of the Church which distinguished sin from righteousness as sharply as black from white, who considered that women, in atonement for the errors of Eve, should be modest, submissive, and hidden from the eyes of others save at Sunday kirk. A man might bare his knees under a kilt, but the female form must be shrouded beneath a shapeless shift from neck to ankles. Women were weak and unwitting temptresses, and there were men enough ready and willing to be tempted. Babylon began at the Tay, and Lowlanders and Englishmen were subjects of Satan, who held infernal court at St. James's, in London. The younger clansmen might wink at each other behind his grizzled head, but never before him. He was still strong enough to fell a man with one pole-axe blow.

And the Reverend John Grant — a wheedling, lean-shanked man drained of sympathy and swift to condemn, an elderly bachelor long resigned to celibacy and embittered by a lifetime of prohibition. Unloved and incapable of love, he might have questioned even the morality of a marriage-bed were it not condoned by the Church.

And the Lauders, the Hossacks, and the Graingers? And when Ranald MacDonald returned —

Once, in Inverness, she'd seen a woman whipped at a cart-tail, for whoring — a young woman, thin-framed and ragged, and the townswomen had jeered and spat while the men watched, grinning and exchanging low-voiced obscenities. At the parish limits they had cut her loose and ordered her to be gone from the company of decent folk. There had been no pity.

But she owed Thomas Margery a life. And there was that other matter.

'I'll take him to Glen Moriston,' she said slowly.

Campbell nodded. 'Good. Ye'll not travel alone. I'll 'company ye to within sight of ye' chimney smoke, then leave ye. I'll hazard I'd be less well received among the Glengarry than the Englishman.' He laughed.

Chapter 9

At a later time Thomas's recollection of the journey would be vague, distorted, and torn with many gaps. He remembered pain — the long hours of jolting pain that, in the beginning, nullified all other senses, but which gradually diminished until it was only a throbbing ache. It was his right leg that hurt, he knew. It was splinted, and additionally secured, packed with spagnum moss, by Campbell. He recalled the incident at the bridge plainly enough, and Campbell's arrival. Then there had been oblivion. At least, there must have been, for his next period of awareness had involved a fretwork of green foliage passing across a sky, the noise of birds, a cool breeze on his damp face and, of course, the pain. He had closed his eyes again and, mentally, replayed the events he last remembered. The bridge, the Highlanders, the musket ball in his leg, Campbell — aye, and Campbell binding him with strips torn from Isobel's petticoat.

Campbell had mentioned a surgeon. Thomas couldn't recall one, but he retained a vague impression of cottage beams, a window, and a shaft of sunlight floating with golden specks of dust. He could hear the horses' feet now, clamp-clamping steadily, in rhythm with the swaying of the litter. He opened his eyes. The foliage was still there, and the air was cold and sweet in his nostrils.

He was alive then. Slowly, cautiously, he lifted his head. The litter on which he lay was slung between the two Yorkshires, the leader also carrying Isobel. Further ahead, on his brown gelding, was Campbell. Why was Campbell here? The track was flanked by trees, and below them, to their left, stretched a vast expanse of water, a sombre, leaden grey, its surface gently ruffled by the breeze, its shoreline rock-studded and deserted. Beyond the water were soaring hills, purple and olive, as forbidding and silent as the walls of some measureless cavern from the realms of Nordic mythology, resentful of the sun, wreathed in mist and jealous of their hushed shadows.

Neither Isobel nor Campbell, intent on the road, had observed his awakening to consciousness, and he lay for a long time piecing together fragments of memory, logic and supposition. His leg had been shattered by a musket ball — and it had received attention from a surgeon, that was plain. It might have been yesterday, or several days ago. Campbell must have arranged it.

Why Campbell? He had met the man at Kirkliston, again in Falkirk, and finally at the bridge. There were too many coincidences. Campbell's interest in him was no casual one, his appearances no accidents.

In that case, on whose side was Campbell? On the face of things a Campbell should be an enemy of the Jacobites, but that meant very little. MacDonald of Edinburgh, for instance, was spying on his own people, and a Campbell could do the same. By the same token Campbell had killed two Highlanders. The deed could be a reflection of his clan's traditional hatred of the MacGregors, or it could indicate that he was in the pay of the Crown or it could have been merely a Christian act. Then again, everything depended upon Campbell's interpretation of Thomas's own loyalties. How much did he know or guess?

Campbell, since Stirling, must have known that Thomas was being sought by the military. That meant that —

Thomas drew a deep breath. No, it was too complicated.

'Sblood — but a shattered leg! There was no avoiding that issue. How long would it take to mend? He'd always enjoyed good health, and minor hurts healed quickly, but there was no knowing what some rustic leech — probably never having seen a gunshot wound in his life — had done to his leg. There were plenty of surgeons whose ignorant bungling was more to be feared than the wounds they tended. Still — he was reluctant to admit it — there was something about Campbell that suggested he'd know the difference between good surgery and bad. Anyway, there was little Thomas could do about it for the moment but hope — for a rapid mending.

How rapid? Goddam, not in time for him to dispose of the Pretender before General Cope's column closed with the rebels. Cope must be marching in earnest by now, and his collision with the Pretender could only be a matter of two or three weeks, when Thomas would still be helpless on his back. De Courcy had said that Cope would be beaten, but Thomas still couldn't believe it. It was unthinkable that drilled troops could be beaten by a rabble of clansmen — like the man at the bridge who, with a claymore in his hand, had run against a levelled gun. Well, when the Pretender's clansmen met Cope's redcoats, they'd be facing whole regiments of levelled guns.

But Campbell had reined, and was now gazing at him. 'Ah — Master Margery. I'll not deny it's a comfort to see ye' eyes open.' He seemed genuinely relieved. 'Ye had us a mite worried for a while.' Isobel had twisted in her seat, smiling, but not looking directly at him. Campbell chuckled. 'How d'ye feel?'

'Weak as poor-house skilly,' Thomas said, 'damn' hungry, parched — and wondering what's festerin' happening.'

'Aye,' Campbell nodded. 'Wi' the blood ye've lost, ye're entitled to be weak — but it'll mend, and there'll be some colour in ye' cheeks in a few days. As for being hungry, well, we'll settle that in shorter time. There's an old abandoned bothy at the end of the Loch, and I've a fresh-killed rabbit that'll make fine roasting.' He paused. 'What's happening, did ye say? Yon is Loch Laggan. Wi' luck, ye'll both be sleeping in Glen Moriston tomorrow night, safe in ye' bed —'

'Glen Moriston!' Thomas jerked, then winced. 'Od's blood — what — ?' He shot a glance at Isobel, but her eyes were lowered. 'Dammit, man —'

'Wi' a broken leg, can ye think of anywhere better than being with ye' goodwife's folk?' Campbell enquired. 'Ye'll not be concerned wi' cattle-buying for a while.' He was grinning, his head to one side.

A mile further they halted, by a dilapidated, sod-built bothy long abandoned by some unknown crofter. Its roof sagged, and the flimsy door screeched on rusted hinges. Inside, the earth floor was thickly littered with ancient straw, feathers and fur fragments, the walls cobwebbed and crumbling. 'There's plenty o' worse places,' Campbell apologised. 'Anyway, as I said, tomorrow ye'll have ye' own hearth, and clean linen —' he glanced at Thomas, '— aye, ye could do wi' a shave.' He was wasting no time in preparing a fire and, with Isobel gone to the loch for water, began deftly to skin the carcass of a rabbit that had been tied to his saddle. He was humming softly.

On the litter, Thomas eased himself laboriously to his elbows. 'I haven't thanked you,' he said, 'for saving our lives — and for the business since. Those MacGregors were bent on murder.'

Campbell nodded, intent on his task. 'Aye, MacGregors are murderous cattle. Likely ye'll remember it in future when ye hear the Campbells maligned. The trouble is, ye only hear one side told — and it's always the Campbells that are bloody assassins, never Clan Gregor. Well —' he sniffed, '— ye have to be a bloody assassin to survive against men like ye met at the bridge.'

Thomas was silent for several moments, watching the motions of Campbell's practised knife. Then, 'Did you retrieve my pistols?'

Campbell rose to his feet. 'Aye, I did — and kept 'em loaded. They were too fine a pair to leave by the roadside, and there was always a possibility we'd meet wi' more trouble. As it was, we've seen naught to cause us concern.' He drew the pistols from his belt, presenting them to Thomas, butts foremost. 'Most clansmen o' fighting age have gone to join the Pretender, or are keeping hidden from sight to avoid Lord George Murray's recruiting parties and Johnnie Cope's dragoons.'

Very deliberately, Thomas cocked a pistol and presented it at Campbell's head, four feet away. Campbell stood very still.

'And now, Master Campbell, you will tell me a little more,' Thomas ordered, his voice quiet. 'We'll have an end to pretences. There's one way o' doing that — by putting a ball into your brain. That at least will mean I don't have to puzzle myself about you any further, and at this distance you'll agree I can hardly miss.' His eyes were narrowed in a pale face. 'And I will, b'God, if you don't explain yourself. You could have had me arrested by the military in Falkirk, or overtaken from Stirling, but you didn't. You could have let the Highlanders kill me, but you didn't. Those men were forewarned, and waiting just for me — nobody else, Master Campbell. They were Jacobites, not just moss-troopers. And somebody knew of me in Crieff — enough to poison my horses. You, Master Campbell?'

Campbell raised his dark eyebrows. 'That's scarce civil —'

The muzzle of the pistol moved an inch nearer and Thomas's finger on the trigger tightened. 'On your next word you'll live or die. I'll swear it.' He paused. 'Crown or Jacobite?'

Campbell's lips had frozen into a half grin, the humour gone. His eyes were uncertain, calculating. Within the cramped walls of the bothy there was no sound except the men's breathing. Thomas's unshaven face was hard, relentless. 'Well?' His pistol moved another inch.

Campbell sighed, then shrugged. 'Crown.'

'Aah —!' Thomas nodded slowly. 'The Crown.' But his pistol had not wavered. 'In Cope's pay?'

'Not exactly.' Campbell glanced down at the pistol, then back at Thomas. 'Ye'll not gain anything by knowing, *Major* Margery, and ye're an officer o' the Guards. Ye'd not shoot an unarmed man — not one who's saved ye' life.'

'You're wrong on all counts, Master Campbell. If you doubt me, try running for that festerin' door. I'll wager that before you reach it I've splashed your brains over the wall. And being employed by the Crown doesn't make you a plaguy ally o' mine. Who's pay?'

'Ye're determined, aren't ye?' Campbell shrugged again. 'Well, ye'll be surprised.' He leaned forward. 'Sir John de Courcy.'

Thomas wasn't surprised. It should have been plain to him before this. De Courcy was the only person anxious that neither redcoats nor Jacobites should wreck the assassination attempt on the Pretender.

'De Courcy,' he mused. 'Aye, it would be.'

'And now that ye know,' Campbell suggested, 'perhaps ye'll move that pistol a mite to the left. I loaded it meself.'

'De Courcy,' Thomas repeated. 'That means MacDonald of Edinburgh. What were your instructions?'

'To ensure that ye didn't turn tail on the task ye were given.'

'And if I did?'

Campbell drew a deep breath, and Thomas grunted. 'You needn't say it. You were to kill me.' Campbell was silent, and Thomas resumed. 'So you've been on my heels since Edinburgh. And the business of the horses at Crieff?'

'No,' Campbell said. 'Not that. There was no reason for it.' He sucked his teeth. 'It smells of Jacobite — and the affair of the bridge. It's plain they've knowledge of ye' intentions and meant to settle wi' ye.'

'How did they know?'

Campbell considered for several moments, then shook his head. 'I'd not guess. The Jacobites have their agents, same as De Courcy. They must have known of ye' errand as soon as ye did yeself — and moved quickly. The Crieff affair was meant to delay ye while an ambush was arranged further on ye' road. It could have been anybody. In matters o' political intrigue ye can't trust ye' own brother.'

'Or a father-in-law,' Thomas added. 'Donald MacDonald.'

'Aye —' Campbell conceded. He scratched his head. 'Aye, it could be. I've worked wi' MacDonald for years, and he must have held my life in his hands a dozen times, but that's not to say he couldn't be paid by two masters. If that were so — and I'm not saying it is — he could ha' played a double game wi' yeself. One man to see ye succeeded, and the Jacobites informed to ensure ye were stopped. Either way, he wins.'

Thomas lowered his pistol. 'It's becoming clearer, Master Campbell, a little clearer. What would have happened if you had been compelled to kill me — or the Jacobites stopped me? Were you also to attempt to remove the Pretender?'

'No.' Campbell frowned. 'MacDonald didn't say so. It's plaguy odd, ain't it? Ye'd think —'

'You'd think, with all the trouble de Courcy's taken, that you'd have more to do than just dig my grave and return to Edinburgh, eh? For that matter, I'd say you're as well qualified to kill the Pretender as I am — but it didn't seem to occur to MacDonald.'

'Or de Courcy?'

De Courcy? It was surely impossible that Sir John de Courcy was playing a double game? There were Jacobites in England — in London — to be sure, and possibly in high places, but if their ranks included men like de Courcy, who held the confidence of Lord John Avershaw and Mr. Pelham, and —

Godammit, if de Courcy could be a Jacobite, then so could Avershaw and dozens of others, all sitting on the fence, supporting both sides until one or the other emerged as clear master. Yet Thomas couldn't believe it of de Courcy, of all people. The old knight had too strong a hatred for the French — or was that a subterfuge?

Campbell must have read his thoughts. 'Ye just can't tell, Major. The minds o' ordinary men like yeself and me don't cope easy wi' these festerin' machinations. But I'll tell ye one thing — if it's a consolation. I'm no Judas. I take English — Hanoverian — money, and nobody else's. The only thing the Jacobites'll give me is a swift hanging.'

'And you were skulking behind, ready to do murder.'

Campbell's reply came immediately. 'If ye suppose I'm going to apologise for that, ye're mistaken. Remember, Major, that ye were going to murder Charles Edward —'

'There's a difference. It was a military necessity —'

'Ah —!' Campbell's eyes widened. 'Aye, o' course. I didn't see it that way before. When a common Campbell pistols a man, it's murder, but for an officer o' the Guards it's a military necessity.' He nodded gravely. 'Aye, ye can learn things all the time: It must be the same wi' stealing. A threadbare humblie steals bread to feed his starving brats, and hangs. The laird's son can plunder, burn an' rape — and he's just a braw young blade.'

'There's still a difference,' Thomas accused. 'Charles Edward is an enemy of my country and likely to be responsible for the deaths of thousands of Englishmen. I'm not concerned wi' the rights and wrongs. I'm English. You're a Scot, and you've sold yourself to destroying your own royal line —'

'Not my royal line, Major,' Campbell retorted. 'And nor Scotland's. It's all a damn' pretence. There's a midwife's story, told on oath, that's been handed down among my people for nigh two hundred years — and I believe it — which says that King James the Sixth o' Scotland was no child of Mary Stuart. Aye, ye made him King o' England, and thus ye' House of Stuart. But the child o' Mary and the Earl o' Darnley was stillborn, and the body bricked into a wall of Edinburgh Castle — where it likely still is. And the brat that survived —?' He shrugged. 'Whoever's it was, ye can be certain it was substituted wi' the knowledge of Douglas o' Lochleven — and James had the hair and skin o' that black breed, not the fairness of Mary and Darnley.' He snorted. 'Mix Douglas blood wi' French, Spanish, Polish — and the likelihood of a second substitution by the grandson o' the first, and ye' royal line wears a mite thin, Major, wouldn't ye say?'

''Sblood —' Thomas snorted, '— there's similar stories told about every damn' royal house. If you believed them all, there'd not be a crowned head in Europe that wasn't sired by a coachman or whelped by a scullery-maid — and every royal midwife with a bushel-size warming-pan kept ready. But, dammit, I'm not concerned. Does Isobel MacDonald know anything of what you've told me?'

'No. She's convinced ye're Jacobite and riding to lay ye' gallant sword at the Pretender's feet.'

There was the sound of Isobel's and Jamie's voices beyond the door, and Campbell added hurriedly: 'But she knows ye're a deserted officer o' the Guards, and she knows that *I* know she's not ye' wife —'

The damn' business was getting complicated again. With a canteen of water, and with Jamie trailing, Isobel allowed her eyes to flicker from Thomas's pistols to Campbell. She frowned, but Campbell was already chuckling. 'Aye, I've not seen better pistols in Scotland, and I've always reckoned Edinburgh gunsmiths as good as any in Europe. Coutts o' Houndsditch, did ye say? If I ever come by a fortune I'll be having a pair o' the same.'

Thomas and Isobel ate in silence, each studiously avoiding the gaze of the other. It was Campbell who talked, irrelevantly, of the merits of beef against venison, of fishing for salmon, glanders in horses, and chiding Jamie for not picking clean his bones. With the meal finished, Isobel held the head of the lead bay as Campbell, with difficulty, reharnessed the litter. Thomas, his belly satisfied and already feeling stronger, swallowed an oath. He was angry at his own helplessness and curiously ashamed that Isobel should witness it. There were other questions he wanted to ask Campbell — about Glen Moriston, and Campbell's intentions, and the Pretender and Cope — but not in Isobel's presence. He was beginning to feel that there was a new conspiracy between Campbell and Isobel, that he was being excluded from their confidences, and he was heartily sick of conspiracies. Besides — it was a grudging concession — Isobel's company was no longer exclusively his. Campbell was an interloper and had taken charge of matters, to Thomas's resentment. Thomas was dependent on him, without choice.

He lay, sulkily brooding, as they moved westward above the loch, his eyes on Isobel's straight back and her curls gambolling in the sunlight. This was a pretty pass, and no mistake. 'Sblood — he had no business here in the first place. At the head of a company of Guards, with the grenadiers forward, the damask colours streaming and the drums roaring, he would know exactly what to do. Load, prime, present, and fire — powder smoke stinging the throat, bayonets rippling like silver corn, and the tramping redcoats, shoulder to shoulder, sweating, swearing —

He winced as the litter jolted suddenly. Campbell had halted, raising his hand in warning, and Isobel, too, had reined. Then Campbell, peering ahead, pointed. 'Highlanders,' he said.

Thomas raised himself. Scarcely a mile further the road climbed to a ragged crest and disappeared into a blanket of firs, but not before it traversed a broad stretch of open heather — and crossing the heather, moving almost parallel to the road, was a long, untidy file of men and horses.

There were thirty, perhaps forty of them, and Thomas could see the plaids, the claymores and targets slung over drooped shoulders, the bare, dusty legs. There was little semblance of order. In the van several rode small horses, stirrupless, with feet almost trailing the ground, and the column straggled, broken into groups of four or five, the men walking with no great enthusiasm. One of the mounted men carried a banner, but the flag hung listless on its pole, its insignia obscured.

'Who are they?' Thomas asked.

Campbell shook his head. 'I'd not say at this distance. They're tired, and they've had a long tramp — thirty miles, likely. And from the North-east. They could be Fraser, or Glengarry —'

Glengarry? Isobel sat motionless in her saddle with Jamie before her. If that column of tired men were Glengarry, then Ranald would almost certainly be among them, his boasted broadsword whetted, his cheeks dark with stubble and his eyes truculent — tired or not. There'd be other men — Bald Ewen, and Morton, and Cluny — and would her father, Robert of Dundreggan, have marched with his clan? If one of those tramping Highlanders turned his head and saw the little group of horses in the glen below — They sat in silence, unmoving, until Campbell drew a deep breath and cleared his throat. The last of the clansmen had vanished into the tumult of trees on the skyline, leaving no sign that they had passed. 'We're damn' lucky,' he said. 'A few minutes sooner, and we'd have ridden into them —' he grinned, '— and that would've meant a deal of explaining, for each of us.' He gazed at the road ahead. 'They're making for Loch Lochy, so we can take it that the Prince is somewhere in that vicinity — a mite close to Glen Moriston for comfort. Still —' he shrugged, '— there's Johnnie Cope behind us, so we can't turn back, nor stay still. We'll have to gamble on there being naught but women, bairns and old men when we reach ye glen.'

Women, bairns and old men, Thomas simmered. And an Englishman with a broken leg — while Cope's regiments were grappling with the rebels, perhaps in these very glens. If the clansmen he had seen a few minutes ago were typical of the Pretender's forces — undisciplined, without picquets or formation, without the slightest understanding of battlefield tactics — then Cope would scatter them like chaff in a wind, and then the pitiless slaughter would begin. If the Pretender was taken alive he would constitute an immediate embarrassment to King George and his ministers. If he escaped he would remain, as de Courcy said, a pistol held at the head of England. And Thomas Margery would be nursing a broken leg among the women, bairns and old men.

He did not quarrel with Campbell's decision to turn abruptly northward, away from the direction of the clansmen's march, but the new track followed a narrow defile, soft with a thick carpet of pine needles that deadened their horses' feet and twisted, climbing steeply for more than an hour, until suddenly it emerged onto the high summit. Behind them, far below, was ashen Loch Laggan, and they could just see the shingled roof of the abandoned bothy. Ahead was a vast and spreading panorama, a magnificent marquetry of mountain, heather-covered moor, narrow glens in shadow from the setting sun and, distant northward, the sheen of further water stretching beyond sight. 'Loch Lochy,' Campbell grunted. 'Fifteen miles further is Fort Augustus and Loch Ness — and on the far side of the Fort is Glen Moriston. That's where we'll be tomorrow, Major Margery — all being well. I'd not say that the Glen is the safest place in Scotland for ye, but —'

His gaze had gone beyond Thomas. 'Goddam,' he muttered, 'we *must* be in Glen Moriston tomorrow.'

Isobel had turned in her saddle, her face pale in the soft evening light and her white teeth biting on a lip. Thomas snorted angrily. 'Fester it, man! What are you staring at?' In this damned litter he was as helpless as a cradled infant.

'Dragoons.' Campbell muttered. 'Johnnie Cope's dragoons. They've reached the bothy, and lighting bivouac fires.' He laughed ruefully. 'I didn't think those snivelling bog-irishmen would've reached this far so soon. Mind ye, they're only advance picquets. Cope will be swilling port in Dalwhinnie, I'll wager — a day's ride back.' He pondered for several moments, then shrugged. 'Well — that's slammed the plaguy door behind us. It's Glen Moriston for ye, Major. Tomorrow. Or a musket ball.'

Chapter 10

Edward Burt, private soldier of Lee's Foot, probed his aching mouth with his tongue and cursed. In Stirling or Falkirk — if he had fourpence, which he did not — he could have swilled his decayed and throbbing teeth with a pint of raw gin, but in this God-forsaken wilderness there was nothing but weary miles of dusty road, mountain and heather, relieved only by occasional clutters of mean cottages peopled by surly natives with nothing to offer the passing redcoats except scowls and indifference. There was nothing to loot, even if there were any opportunities to do so.

The weather was warm, and under his heavy scarlet he was sweating, with the dye staining his wrists and the tight leather stock rubbing the skin from his neck. His pipe-clayed cartouche pouch slapped monotonously against one leg, his hanger and bayonet against the other, and he could smell his own warm sourness as well as that of his tramping fellows.

Well, Burt considered, the Scottish glens were likely better than the Gambia, the Carolinas, or Madras — and what fighting was about. At least, that was what Edward Burt had been told. Neither he nor any of Lee's had fired their eleven-pound muskets in anger. Fester it — Burt hadn't even fired more than a score of times in practice. The drill manual decreed that recruits should not be released from training until they could load and fire fifteen times in three and three-quarter minutes, but none of Lee's platoons — raised only four years earlier — could have nearly achieved this standard.

Precise marksmanship, of course, wasn't important in the field. The infantry's object was to provide a dense and continuous curtain of fire whilst advancing, or when receiving an attack and, with the enemy suitably mauled and shaken, it was the bayonet — the queen of the battlefield — that usually decided matters.

The pain in his fevered gums flared. Christ —! When this rot-gutting campaign was finished he'd find a surgeon, who might do something. And the campaign wouldn't take long. He had twenty-four paper-wrapped cartridges in his pouch, and he'd wager he'd not need the half of them. He'd be surprised if the rustic clansmen would wait to receive one volley. If it wasn't for the torment of his teeth, it might have been an amusing diversion.

Somewhere ahead a solitary drum was tapping, half lost among the screeching wheels of the caravan of wagons behind. Those wagons carried a thousand stands of arms for distribution among Highlanders loyal to the Crown — in Private Burt's view an unnecessary business. The infantry could deal with the rebels easily enough. It was doubtful whether even the dragoons — mostly illiterate Irishmen — would find employment. Edward Burt could write his own name, and considered himself literate.

The wagons also carried rations — cheese and ammunition bread for the men, beef for the officers, and General Cope's wines. Burt had not yet seen Johnnie Cope, but neither had he heard any criticism of the man. He was likely to be no better nor worse than any other general officer — as remote to a private man as the Shah of Persia. Cope was an easygoing man, it was said, with battle-command experience — the latter fact indicating that he would be ludicrously superior to the patchwork staff that the Pretender was likely to muster.

And who was this Pretender? Edward Burt's knowledge of the whole affair did not extend beyond the rumours and exaggerations of billet and barrack-room. Oddly enough, he had seen King George in London, before his enlistment a year earlier — a portly little man with bulbous eyes and a reputation for possessing a voracious sexual appetite. Cripes — why not? If Edward Burt were King there'd be no shortage of perfumed, creamy-white ladies in the royal bed. None of your well-ridden tavern sluts for a King, when a beckoning finger could have a dozen duchesses unlaced and ready. It was an intriguing thought.

Aye, Burt had a grudging admiration, albeit tinged with envy, for a man who used his opportunities. This Pretender — this Frenchified Scot who had proclaimed himself Prince Regent — was he likely to improve the lot of Private Burt? He had enlisted in London twelve months ago for a bounty of four pounds, and eightpence a day thereafter. A labourer's pay was ninepence. He remembered nothing of the four pounds after he had awakened with a reeking head the following morning — but likely the recruiting sergeant did — and his daily eight pennies were reduced to two by deductions for uniform, linen, and other necessities imposed by his officers. He had spent weeks polishing the browning from the barrel of his musket — specifically applied by the Minories manufacturer to prevent rust and avoid glare — because a shiny musket made a braver show. It was still, however, the finest infantry weapon in Europe, in the hands of well-drilled soldiers. The French had already painfully learned that.

Burt seldom had the opportunity, and still less the inclination, to bath, but he kept his own hair tied and clubbed on his neck, his equipment thickly pipe-clayed and his gaiters unspotted — on pain of ruthless flogging. His officers treated him with contempt, civilians despised him, and only the lowest of women would consort with him. This didn't concern Burt unduly, and he hardly thought about it. It had always been so.

Somewhere to the rear, far behind Private Burt, there would be the sutlers' wagons, stocking ale and spirits, linens and hose, foodstuffs to supplement the army rations of cheese bread and skilly — and hard-mouthed wenches. It was gin he wanted — raw gin to soothe the fire in his inflamed gums and give him, for an hour or so, that rosy haze of semi-intoxication through which the rigours of army life could be viewed with less repugnance. But he had no money, fester it. Neither would there be any tomorrow, or the next day. And no sutler's credit on an active campaign. Dead creditors didn't pay tallies.

It was possible — if the redcoat lobsters drubbed the Highlanders well enough — that Johnnie Cope would show his gratitude with an issue of rum. A decisive victory could earn Cope a peerage, and that was worth an anker or two of Jamaica. Well, the Highlanders would be drubbed. Lee's Foot were no Guards regiment, but they knew too much for a few half-starved clansmen and their rusty claymores. Private Burt knew his drill well enough. The infantrymen would wheel into line — two ranks shoulder to shoulder, with a third of file-closers in the rear ready to take the place of casualties. Not that the plaguy clansmen were likely to inflict many casualties on the English line before the concentrated musket-fire tore them to bloody rags. The few reeling survivors would be swept from the field with the bayonet, and finally sabred into the ground by pursuing dragoons. That's how battles were fought. Burt chuckled, then winced.

Pox rot these cankered teeth. It was gin he wanted — or Johnnie Cope's rum.

If they could meet the Pretender's rabble tomorrow, say, the whole festerin' thing would be over in an hour, and he'd be swilling his teeth in rum.

Since Crieff, Cope's column had been accompanied by Lascelles's Dragoons, now on outguard patrol ahead and to flank. They were probably in Glen Garry now, driving in the local people for news of the Pretender's movements. Yesterday, by Wade's bridge over the Tay, the sweating redcoats had seen the corpses of four Highlanders, bloating in the sun and attracting flies — rude looking fellows in soiled plaids, muddied knees and unkempt hair. Three had been shot, one sabred — they must have been surprised by the dragoons and ridden down in seconds. What had happened would happen again, on a much vaster scale, if the rebel army could be made to stand. Edward Burt felt for his bayonet scabbard. It was a festerin' mercy there was no artillery to claim the honours, to sneer that a battle needed gunners to tear the heart out of the enemy before the footstumbling infantry could sweep up the remnants.

The agony of his jaw blazed again. He swore viciously.

*

High on the Druim Fada, Ranald MacDonald was also sweating after the long climb that had left all possible pursuit far behind. The breathless boy who had overtaken them that afternoon had told of English dragoons passing through Glen Spean, only eight miles back, and that could mean that Cope's main force was not far behind. He — Ranald MacDonald — was eager for a trial of strength with the dragoon patrol. It would be a fine thing to join the Prince with a victory already under their belts. The others, however, less belligerent, had chosen caution, and the thirty-six Highlanders turned westward.

They were all from Glen Moriston, but they were 'broken men' — not blood-tied to the Glengarry, and owing their place on the rent-roll to marriage or other reasons. Young Angus Og, the Chief's son, would be leading six hundred native men from Knoidart within the next few days, and Ranald MacDonald would carry the clan's promise to the Prince. The pipes were screaming in the Glen, the torches burning through the night, and every man and boy fit to carry weapons would be marching to teach the English that no pipe-clayed Hanoverian puppets could tread Scottish soil with impunity.

Around Ranald were his nearest neighbours of Inverwick — his own brother John, Gregor MacGregor, Bald Ewen, the brothers Hugh, Alexander and Donald Chisholm, Cluny Grant and Alexander MacDonell — all braw young men, easily swayed by Ranald's rhetoric. They'd taken to the heather before, on many a moonlit night, more often in bravado than serious intent, but they knew each other well, and there would be no drawing back when the testing time came.

Not all had leapt to arms when the news came. Ranald's own father-in-law, Robert of Dundreggan — the pompous old babbler — had counselled patience. The Chief would decide, he had said, and the Chief's appointed would lead. There was an allotted place for every man — the henchman, the bard and the piper, the bladier and the gillie, then the clansmen, tacksmen and humblies. The Chief must decide, ranted Robert of Dundreggan, but Ranald had laughed at the angry grey-head.

Ranald MacDonald had scant regard for the Glengarry. He had come as a lad from the West, to a marriage arranged by his father. He spat disgustedly. It was a mistake, that marriage. Aye, she was bonny enough, and his loins had trembled when he'd first seen the whiteness of her. Besides, there had been a handsome marriage portion — the farmstead and acreage at the joining of the Moriston and Doe rivers. Any other man would have counted his blessings. Any, that is, except Ranald MacDonald. There were quicker ways to make money than scratching the earth with a wooden plough.

Isobel had not been his first woman, nor — he sniffed — his last. Women were easy come by if you had the manner, and he did. There were few wenches who did not breathe a little faster when they saw the swashbuckling, black-bearded Ranald MacDonald. He had taken his wife on their marriage night, determined that she should know who was master thereafter, but she had lain like a cold fish, unresponsive and silent, until his strength brought tears to her eyes. It was a minor satisfaction, but he preferred red meat — the lusty farm-wives with thick thighs and their bodies smelling of the byre, who returned him as good as he gave. And no braw lad should be tied to one woman.

There was another thing. He'd had no schooling, but his wife could read and write — a degree of superiority that incensed him, provoked him to animal rudeness when he grasped at her in the darkness. But she had never wept since the first time.

Then the child had come — Jamie — a sickly child. Ranald had sworn it was because of Glengarry blood, and he swore because fatherhood was not for him. The wild young men of the Glen were sceptical of the leadership of one who was married and a father. It reeked too much of rooted respectability. So he had not demurred when Isobel had accompanied the child to Edinburgh. He was well enough without either, and he could please himself where he spent his nights.

When the fiery cross had come through the Balmacaan Forest, trailing its blood-stained rag, it had presented a heaven-sent justification for avoiding approaching storm-clouds. Jeannie MacDonell, fifteen-years old sister of Alexander, was with child, and in a month she'd no longer hide it. Aye, she was a strapping lass for her years, and she'd given sweet and eager amusement in the heather below the Black Cairn, but she had no husband to blame for the brat. A bastard in the Glen meant more trouble than even Ranald MacDonald cared for. Vinegar-voiced John Grant would screech hell-fire from his kirk pulpit, Jeannie would be whipped in public, and the MacDonells would be seeking a blood-letting. No time, then, to wait for the old Chief to leisurely call out the clan. Ranald had harangued his wild ones, jeering at the lukewarm, and had tramped, breathing damnation to the English, with a bigger following than he had anticipated. He might never see Glen Moriston again — a pity, but better than a dirk-thrust through the heart. And Jeannie's fate? That was a pity, too — but he'd not be there to witness it.

He had time, now, to consider the immediate future. He had thirty-five strong fellows behind him, all with claymore, dirk and target, and more than half with muskets. They were broken men, with less than usual clan loyalty, although several had family ties among the Glengarry and would choose to return when their business was finished. Still, a good showing before the Prince could earn Ranald a title and position, when he could thumb his nose at the Glengarry — and his impassive, superior wife. Failing that, there was gainful employment for a band of well-armed men on the fringe of the Lowlands, more gainful by far than a patch of starved soil and a few sheep and goats.

And not only the Lowlands. There was England — like a fat, sleek cow waiting to be milked. Ranald chuckled. What were Cumberland women like? Well-fed and plump, he'd wager, like English cattle, and not resisting too far a handsome rogue from across the Border. Aye, moss-trooping offered possibilities — but first there were the redcoats.

He'd seen enough of redcoats to know that, despite their arrogance and their laced hats, they were no more than mortal. In the vicinity of the Forts, in Inverness, and once on a visit to Dundee, he had watched them drilling like clumsy marionettes jerked by strings. True, there was something to be said for training fifty men to fire simultaneously but, faith, it meant that the nimble-fingered men must wait for the laggards, and he'd wager he could load and fire three times to an English platoon's two. But clansmen didn't take easily to drilling, or to exchanging volleys at seventy paces. The claymore it was that would shatter the cattle-like English, and their little bodkin bayonets wouldn't save them. And who was this General Cope? Nobody had heard of Cope.

Aye, he remembered Dundee well — where the Scots wore trews and coats, and turned up their noses at anyone or anything that didn't follow the English fashion. Seeing his kilt and bonnet, they had called him an Irishman, and a tavern wench named Elspet had laughed condescendingly at the way he spoke. He'd find what he wanted, she sniffed, among the tinklers huts towards Glamis. The tinklers weren't fastidious. Well, the Dundee burgesses would whistle a different jig when the Highlanders were masters, and Elspet — if she were still there — wouldn't be so fastidious either.

Chapter 11

For an hour Patrick Campbell had stood motionless at his horse's head, staring into the glen below and watching for movement among the several scattered cottages. One of them, Isobel knew — and she could see it clearly — was her own. Like Campbell, she had watched intently, her throat clogged, but there was no smoke from the chimney, no sign of movement, and the meadow was empty of livestock. If there were occupants, they kept no fire burning for cooking and, with dusk now turning to darkness, they lit no candles. The cottage had the air of long neglect. Ranald, she knew, would not have weeded her herb garden, scythed the long grass clawing at the wall, or white-washed the byre. She could close her eyes and easily imagine herself standing at the low door, alone with the rustle of the waterfall and the scent of wild flowers — as she had so often been alone until Jamie came. From the door she would see no other cottage — only the high brae, the heather, and the twisting river whose constant noise she was never conscious of until she left the glen. She could hear it now, faintly, and her throat swelled again.

Campbell stirred. 'I'll hazard it's safe enough.' He reached for his horse's bridle.

'You said you'd take us within sight of my chimney smoke,' Isobel reminded him. 'There's no need to come further. If you were discovered —'

'But there's no chimney smoke yet, Mistress. Ye'll need a fire lit, and the litter's too plaguy clumsy for ye to manage alone — as well as the horses. There's enough for ye to do wi' young Jamie an' the Major. Besides —' he grinned, '— I couldn't let ye ride into the glen wi'out being satisfied it's safe. 'Specially in Glengarry country —'

'I've got my pistols,' Thomas said.

'Aye —' Campbell nodded doubtfully, then shook his head. 'No. I'll see ye settled, Major, before I leave ye. There's not likely to be anything to cause ye concern tonight. It's tomorrow, when ye' neighbours see ye' smoke, that ye'll be having visitors — and I'll confess I'm not anxious to be introduced.'

He led them cautiously down the braeside, seeming to have eyes like a cat in the darkness. Twice he halted them, listening, and Thomas's hands, gripping his pistols, were slippery with sweat before they reached the cottage looming grey-white in the gloom. The noise of the waterfall was louder. This, then, was Glen Moriston — and he couldn't see more than a few feet of it. This was Glengarry country. He'd had little else to think about for two days — Glen Moriston and Isobel. His exchanges with her during that period had been scanty, and usually in Campbell's presence, but he was aware that her decision to harbour him, an Englishman, among her own people could have ugly consequences. He had argued that they should leave him with a surgeon in Inverness, or find an inn where a surgeon could give him occasional attention, but they would have none of it. A lamed Englishman, Campbell said, alone in a Scottish town when emotions were running high as a result of the rising, might fare badly at the hands of both Jacobites and Whigs. Thomas knew what he meant.

Unharnessing the litter and compelling it through the door was a clumsy business in the dark, but it was managed, and Campbell disappeared to lodge the Yorkshires in the byre — where perhaps there was fodder — and fetch water from the burn. Inside, Isobel lit candles.

'It was once scrubbed and neat,' she apologised, 'but I've never met the man who could keep house.' There were cold ashes in the hearth, the floor was muddied, and dust lay everywhere. 'Least of all Ranald MacDonald,' she added. 'But it will be set right tomorrow.'

And tomorrow, Thomas considered, would bring other problems.

The kitchen was reasonably stocked, with flour, oatmeal, a flitch of bacon, bread hardened but eatable, cheese, a jug of milk barely soured, and a small cask half filled with ale. Ranald MacDonald, then — wherever he was — could have departed only within the last two days. His bullet mould and a worn flint lay on the table among a scattering of black powder, but his weapons were gone, the loose bricks over the hearth, behind which his musket had been hidden, still awry.

Campbell, re-entering, was fastening his cloak. 'Ye' horses are settled,' he said, 'and there's naught else I can do for ye, so I'll take my leave —'

''Sblood, man —!' Thomas snorted. 'You'll not ride tonight? There's time enough at dawn —?' Isobel, kneeling at the hearth, rose to her feet.

'You're welcome to my roof, Master Campbell,' she offered, 'now, or at any time.'

Campbell shook his head. 'My thanks, Mistress, but I'll need the darkness to make clear of ye' clan's country. It's no place for a Campbell in these unsettled times, and ye' menfolk aren't likely to ask for an explanation before they put a festerin' pistol ball into me. But I've a good horse, and I'll fare well enough.' He smiled roguishly. 'It'll not be the first time I've cheated the Glengarry.'

'But at least you'll eat?'

'If it pleases ye, I'll take a handful o' bread an' bacon wi' me, Mistress. I've a need to be twenty miles from here by first light.' Westward to the Pretender or eastward to Cope? Thomas wondered. With Isobel out of earshot, fetching the food, Campbell spoke quickly.

'Ye' pretence to being a Jacobite is ye' best protection, Major — unless the military come this way, then I've naught to suggest. And remember — the Glengarry might suffer an Englishman, but they'll not tolerate familiarity wi' a married woman —'

'With a broken leg?' Thomas grimaced. 'Goddam —!'

'Ye'll be on ye' feet in five or six weeks, Major. After that —'

But Isobel had returned, with bread and bacon bundled in a kerchief. 'It's a petty reward for what you've done, Master Campbell. Is there nothing else?'

Campbell was thoughtful. 'Aye, just one thing, Mistress. I'd consider myself well rewarded if ye'd think better of my people, and likely teach ye' son the same. Scotland needs an end of feuds and jealousies if she's to convince others that she's not a land of savages, to be used as a pawn between power-seeking politicians. We must stop wounding ourselves and stand under one flag — whatever its colour.' He grinned. 'And having said that, I'll bid ye both adieu.' He doffed his hat, turned, and vanished into the night.

Thomas was perplexed. Campbell had said nothing about the Pretender. Did he — Campbell — intend to resume the assassination attempt? There was time still for Campbell, but none for Thomas, before Cope's forces met the rebels — just time for the clansmen to scatter. There might still be blood spilled, but hundreds would be saved and, equally important, the Pretender would be dead and the French confounded. Aye, and it would mean the return of Ranald MacDonald.

Isobel, himself, and Ranald MacDonald. He had been harbouring the thought for days, unwilling to face it fairly. Now, at least, he did not have to share Isobel's company with Campbell, nor be subject to the man's decisions, however valid. He was his own master.

'Od's blood —! Why did he resent Campbell? The man was civil enough, whilst without his involvement Thomas would have been dead at the bridge, and Campbell's behaviour since could scarcely be faulted.

No, it wasn't Campbell. It was Isobel. At least, it was jealousy because of her. Dammit, there was no point in pretending otherwise to himself. It was incredible, but he wanted another man's wife. Thomas Margery, the implacable bachelor, was enamoured of the wife of a Highland clansman! In London, or even Edinburgh, he would have dismissed the possibility as ludicrous, but there it was.

Well, he could abandon immediately any illusions this madness might generate. Isobel supported the King's enemies, and was married to one. She was fifteen years younger, and from a world completely different to his. She could never be a lady of St. James's any more than he could become a Highlander, and if she ever learned his secret she would detest him for his duplicity. When all that was said, what could he offer any woman? In a few days Sir John de Courcy and MacDonald of Edinburgh would be aware that he had failed or refused his task, and there would be men like Campbell hunting him. Would it make any difference if they knew that his failure was not of his choosing? Probably not. Cope would shatter the clansmen and, almost certainly, take the Pretender. And that was it. King George didn't want the embarrassment of a Stuart in the Tower. King George wanted him dead, at the hands of someone as remote from him as possible — and that someone silenced.

Isobel had brought him food. 'I'll lay a bed in the loft for Jamie and me,' she said. A simple ladder served a dark aperture between the beams above him. She saw his frown and smiled. 'Not even the Minister will claim that you climbed that.'

'The Minister?'

She nodded. 'The Reverend John Grant of Urquhart. He has a keen nose for sin, and you can be certain he'll be searching for a scent when he learns of our coming.'

Thomas groaned. 'It would have been better if you'd taken me to Inverness. I'd not have you suffer embarrassment on my behalf — especially from a sanctimonious cleric —'

'I'll not suffer embarrassment, and I've nothing to be ashamed of,' she retorted. 'Better sour words from the Minister than leave you among strangers. Your leg will heal, and you'll be wanting to join the Prince, but by then Inverness might be in English hands.' She added a log to the kindling in the hearth to hide her face from him. 'You'll be safer here.'

After several days of jolting road, Thomas fell into sleep quickly, the warmth of the fire on his face and his leg, for the first time, no longer giving hurt. The enigmatic Campbell, he supposed, was riding his brown gelding by moonlight, on some distant, twisting bridle track. Was he to be trusted? It was true that he could have disposed of Thomas a dozen times since the affair at the bridge, and had not, but there might be good reasons for deferring the deed or delegating it to another. Would dawn find the Scot at Cope's headquarters, telling all? Fester it — it was a time-wasting conundrum.

He awoke to the clatter of a cooking pot within a few feet of him, realising, guiltily, that the sun was high, the birds singing over the whisper of the river beyond the window. Isobel was at the hearth, blowing new life into the embers of the fire, her lips pouted. He watched her idly until, satisfied, she rose to her knees and frowned at him.

'All men are lazy cattle. Do you know it's eight of the morning, and you still sleeping?' There was a smudge of soot on her cheek. 'There's porridge for you — when you've shaved that black beard, Master Margery —'

'Master Margery? You've forgotten I'm your husband?'

She turned back to the hearth to lift the pot to the flames. 'Not in Glen Moriston. Didn't I tell you I'd never have an Englishman for a husband? That I'd sooner be wed to a heathen Turk?'

'Ah, but you meant an *English* Englishman,' he reminded her. She frowned again. 'And there'll be cold water for your shaving,' she pronounced.

He had little enthusiasm for porridge and even less for scraping the beard from his cheeks with cold water from the burn, but he was hungry. 'That's a deal better,' she approved, surveying his scoured face. 'And since you refused my good porridge in Edinburgh, you'd best have bacon. But don't think you'll always be spoiled —'

She had halted in mid-sentence, listening, her head to one side and her perturbed eyes on the casement. Thomas could hear nothing beyond the rustle of the river, the birds' chatter, and the occasional mutter of the fire in the hearth. 'What is it?'

'Horses,' she said. She went to the casement. Thomas reached for his pistols. Isobel drew a deep breath, resigned. 'It's my father,' she whispered, 'and a gillie.' She turned, seeing the pistols in his hands. 'No, not that. There'll not be bloodshed in this house.' She walked to the door and opened it.

From a short distance Thomas heard a stentorian shout followed by a greeting in Gaelic. A horse whinnied, and then the doorway was filled by the figure of a man, holding Isobel by her shoulders and kissing her brow.

Robert of Dundreggan was a big man, of possibly sixty years, his white hair — still showing evidence of its original copper red — tied by a ribbon into a long queue over his shoulder. Under his bonnet, trimmed by a curled feather, his face was tanned and hard-muscled, his eyes the same cinnamon as Isobel's. He wore tartan trews and a plaid that fell to his calves. He carried no weapons.

For a brief moment Dundreggan was smiling, holding Isobel at arm's length, his speech incomprehensible to Thomas but good-humoured. Then, seeing Thomas, he suddenly jerked into stiffness and his eyes narrowed. His right hand fell to his waist, but found no dirk there. He pushed Isobel to one side.

Isobel spoke quickly, again in Gaelic, but Thomas caught the names 'Margery', 'MacDonald' and 'Aberfeldy' as Dundreggan's eyes flickered coldly towards him and then back to Isobel. Annoyed at being the subject of a conversation he did not understand, Thomas eased himself to his elbows. 'If your father understands English, I can speak for myself.'

Dundreggan nodded slowly. 'I have the English.' His voice was hard, challenging, 'And ye can talk for yesel'.'

'My name is Margery — Thomas Margery — late Major of His Majesty's 2nd Regiment of Guards, now posted as a deserter and renegade. I am in your glen, Sir, as a result of injury, not by choice. Your daughter will perhaps tell you that it was my wish to be taken to Inverness, but by her charity I am here. You have my word that I intend to leave as soon as I can sit a horse.'

Dundreggan was silent, his face showing no indication of his thoughts. Then, 'My daughter has said that ye saved her life, and that of my grandson — and that was how ye' injury was suffered.'

Thomas shrugged. 'It's probable that our attackers intended to kill me, not your daughter.'

'It is possible, but the outcome would have been the same. They would have left nobody to tell tales. We shall demand a rendering from the MacGregors.' He was silent again, for several moments, regarding Thomas sombrely. 'I'll not give ye my hand, Englishman. I've no friendship for ye, Jacobite or no, but I owe ye at least sanctuary while ye' injury mends, and ye'll not suffer harm of my making. Moreover, any among the Glengarry that lift their hands against ye will lift them against me also.'

'I'm grateful, Sir.' Thomas resented the condescension in the other's manner. 'But I'm not entirely crippled, and any of your people who want to play Mohock may get themselves stung. I'm more concerned for your daughter, and I've no desire to be responsible for any prejudice.'

Dundreggan's lip curled, but whether in smile or sneer it was impossible to guess. 'There might come a time when ye'll be required to make good ye' words, Englishman — but not while ye're disabled. I'll own that I'd prefer to see ye elsewhere than in my daughter's house — wi' her man away — but I'll not make a dispute of it. Ye may take my oath that there'll be no slandering talk in Glen Moriston or Glen Urquhart wi'out I hear the justice of it — and either the chatterer will pay for the lie, or yeself for its truth.' Abruptly he turned his broad back and spoke in Gaelic to Isobel for several moments, his hand placed lightly on her shoulder. Then, without a second glance at Thomas, he strode through the door.

'Your father doesn't waste conversation,' Thomas grunted, puzzled. 'After all these months' absence, didn't he want to talk with you — and see his grandson —?'

Isobel shook her head. 'Not in the presence of a stranger, particularly an Englishman.' She was apologetic. 'You see, he was out in 'Fifteen, and he had a younger brother taken at Sherrifmuir who was afterwards hanged and disembowelled. He's never disputed the justice of it, but neither has he forgiven the English. He's a hard man, stern — but not unjust. And Dundreggan's word is better than a magistrate's paper. Though it chokes in his throat, he'll not break his oath.'

'And your husband?'

'He led off a party of broken men to join the Prince, three days ago. The other clansmen marched yesterday, under Angus Og, the Chief's son.' She did not elaborate. 'My father has taken our sheep and kine to the Inverwick fields until the men return. He will also have a fresh stock of foodstuffs sent, and arrange for a doctor from Inverness to examine your leg. So you see —' she smiled, '— he is not an ogre.'

Thomas chuckled ruefully. 'Faith — I'll never understand you people. You're full of contradictions. Likely your Reverend John Grant will prove to be a white-haired old saint who'll scold me for not attending church and then give me his blessing.'

'No.' Isobel pulled a wry face. 'That I can promise you. The Reverend Grant might refrain from direct accusation, but he'll leave no doubt of his meaning in the minds of the Glen. He's an intolerant man, with little sympathy for the frailties of ordinary people.' She paused. 'And women must still atone for the sins of Eve.'

'Aye, we have them in England, too,' Thomas nodded. 'Well — we'll see.'

The day passed, and the next, with the weather bright and sunny save for a brief shower that scarcely dampened the heather. Robert of Dundreggan, true to his word, had sent a cart with victuals, but did not accompany it, and on the second day a dusty surgeon arrived, ahorse, to probe Thomas's leg, sniff it, and pronounce that it was healing satisfactorily. He brought, also, news of military activity. On the road from Inverness, he said, just southward of Fort Augustus — and scarce five miles from Glen Moriston — he had seen the marching Highlanders of Prince Charles. It had been a rare sight, with the clan banners and the pipes, and all in fine fettle. General Cope, it was said, had turned away from Fort Augustus and seemed to be making for Inverness. There'd be a battle, sure enough, and the doctor had no desire to be elsewhere but between his own walls. He departed in less than fifteen minutes.

Thomas's spirits plummeted. He had foreseen the probability of an action between Cope and the Pretender, but there had always been a flimsy hope that something — he could not suggest what — would happen to delay it. Additionally, everything about his mission had been so completely unreal, so unconvincing, until the ambush — and even then he had found it difficult to believe that his situation was anything but absurd. Now, however, the Pretender's rebels were marching within five miles of him. In an hour he could be within sight of the Highland column. Tonight, when they'd lit their fires, and half of them asleep, a swift gallop through the picquets — if there were any — and a well-aimed pistol shot could see the matter finished. Then spur for the darkness, sword slashing — and there was a reasonable chance of reaching safety.

Only five miles — and he was helpless.

Festerin' blood — but was he? There'd been numerous soldiers and seamen, with ghastly wounds, who had continued fighting until drained of life-blood. His father, Adam Margery, had spoken of the murderous assault on the Schellenberg, in which his own Foot Guards had marched, unfaltering, through a storm of canister, of the dead infantry at Blenheim, lying where they had stood firm, in ordered ranks — and there was Benbow, who had remained on his quarterdeck with a leg smashed by chain shot, directing a battle as though nothing untoward had happened. Could he — Thomas — muster that sort of iron courage? It was easier, perhaps, in the white heat of battle, surrounded by comrades and drunk with derring-do. It was easier, perhaps, because there was little choice. A severe battlefield wound almost certainly meant death anyway, and a man might as well die fighting as bleeding into the dust or under a surgeon's knife. Aye, it was easier.

He reached for his pistols and powder-flask, re-primed, and blew off the loose powder thoughtfully. Isobel watched him.

'I'd be grateful,' he said slowly, 'if you'd saddle my horse.'

She was silent, then, 'Your *horse*?'

'Aye, and wi' these pistols holstered. Then, if you will, you'll help me to mount. Likely you'll need rope.'

She stared, unbelieving. 'You want to ride a *horse*, with a broken leg?'

'I'll wager I'll not be the first. I can't lie here like a lame old woman while Charles Edward is only five miles away.' He began to ease himself to a sitting position. 'If you can lash this damn' leg between withers and shoulder, I'll ride — fester it —'

'Ride?' Isobel tossed her head scornfully. 'Five miles? You'll not ride five yards. And why? Do you suppose the clansmen will throw up their bonnets and cheer for an Englishman with a broken leg?' She was damn' beautiful, Thomas reflected, when she was angry. 'If you'll not help,' he returned, 'I'll manage for myself.' His leg was beginning to hurt.

'Either you've a fever, or you've taken leave of your wits,' she retorted. 'One sword more or less isn't going to win the Prince's battle for him, and you'll do him better service by staying here until you're mended. Cope's army isn't the only one to be fought. There'll be others — and you'll have your fighting.'

Thomas put his sound leg to the floor, and the pain of his wound suddenly flared. 'Damn you, woman —!' he gritted. 'Fetch the horse!'

'No!' Her eyes were hot with anger, her cheeks colouring. 'You'll not!'

''Od's blood —!' Thomas snarled. 'I'll not let any goddam housewife tell me I can't sit a plaguy horse —!' He pulled himself upright, then lurched, gasping, as his trussed leg exploded with excruciating agony. He fell back onto the litter, sickened, his teeth clenched. 'Christ —!'

The next moment her arms were around him, his head cradled against her breast and her lips pressed to his brow. She was crying. 'You can't — my love — don't you see —?'

The red haze before his eyes cleared, and he could feel the wetness of her tears on his face. 'Isobel — damme —' He reached for her.

There was an interruption. 'The curse of the Lord is in the house of the wicked!' A reedy voice spoke from the open door. 'And a whorish woman shall be an abomination in the sight of the Lord!'

Chapter 12

But the battle between Cope and the Pretender, which yesterday seemed imminent, had not taken place. Cope had turned away, ignominiously, to Inverness. It was not that he feared meeting the Pretender; rather the reverse. He suspected that the rebels would wish to avoid an encounter, to slip past the slow-moving redcoats into the unguarded Lowlands and the Border. And Cope was ill-equipped for a campaign of march and counter-march. He had barely three days' rations remaining, and his Highland irregulars had been melting away — many going over to the rebels. His dragoon horses, too, were in poor fettle, untrained and recently from grass — and clearly unfit for the rigours of the field. He needed supplies, and time to regroup his straggling column. It was an embarrassment for an English general to decline battle with a few barbaric clansmen, even if his own force was composed of the dregs of the Army, but he had little choice. Inverness it had to be.

The sweating, dust-plagued column crawled, like a monstrous, scarlet snake, northward through the Slochd Pass. The men were footsore, brushing aside the swarming gnats and floating thistledown. The colours were covered, and the hautboys and fifes had been silent for days. Only an occasional drum tapped out the weary step on the rutted road. Still, Johnnie Cope was taking them to Inverness. They might be paid in Inverness, and for Edward Burt, at least, that meant the soothing balm of gin on his throbbing gums and a night of drunken sleep immune from pain. And doxies — but the gin first.

There'd be spit and pipeclay as well, that was certain, but rather that than these endless Highland roads which climbed and twisted, leading to nowhere. Who wanted to fight over this damn' wilderness? The plaguy porridge-guttling Scots could keep it, so far as Burt was concerned. Mind you, as he'd said before, it was likely better than the Carolinas or the Cape Coast — but the black heathen could keep them, too.

It was scarcely more than a year before that Edward Burt had succumbed to the cajolery of a recruiting poster which declared that 'all those who prefer the Glory of bearing arms to any servile mean Employ, and have Spirit to stand forth in Defence of their King and Country, against the treacherous Designs of France and Spain, in the 55th Regiment of Foot, commanded by Lt. Col. John Howard Lee, let them repair to the Temple Gate House where they shall be handsomely Cloathed, most completely Accoutred, and treated with Kindness and Generosity.' He had been handsomely clothed in cheap red bowdy that had shrunk in the first rain and stained his neck and wrists, pewter buttons, red breeches and white worsted hose. For all these, and including his belt and side-arms, spare shirts, neck-cloths, breeches and shoes, he had to pay his Colonel — and contribute towards the maintenance of Chelsea Hospital, where he would 'receive succour from the fostering hand of a generous country' in the event of being maimed in battle. The kindness and generosity of his officers were tempered by the lash, the 'black hole', and the gallows. What remained of his pay after he was free of debt — called 'net off reckonings' and amounting to £2. 8s. per annum — was often as much as a year in arrears. Funds for widows' pensions were accumulated by setting aside the pay of one fictitious man allowed to each company.

Burt's understanding of the movements of the Army in which he served was negligible. He simply marched where he was led and left reasoning to his officers. But Cope's apprehension, despite the embarrassment, was not unjustified. The French war had drained England of troops, and if the Pretender's Highlanders reached the Border they could swarm into England almost unopposed. In Cumberland and Westmorland there were only 600 men with arms 'extremely bad'. Lancashire could muster only three regiments of militia and only one officer who knew how to form a company, and 'no man trained or exercised since King William's time.' Chester Castle was defended by seventy-five time-expired veterans without ammunition or stores, and Durham Castle, too, had neither arms nor ammunition. Cope had to be very, very cautious.

None of this concerned Private Burt. He couldn't think beyond tomorrow, Inverness, and gin. Mind you, he could seek out the regimental surgeon; there was a deduction from his pay for medical services — or let a local barber's apprentice practice on him — but gin was more convivial. A pity about Johnnie Cope's rum. 'Od pox these festerin' Highlanders! Why didn't they stand still and be shot to shreds? He wiped the sweat from his face with the back of a grimy hand.

*

Secretly relieved, Charles Edward made a show of restrained disappointment at Cope's reluctance to take up the gauntlet, annoyed at O'Sullivan's bluster that the rebels had achieved their first victory. The Prince was not unacquainted with the fluctuations of campaigning, and it was stupidity to interpret an ordered withdrawal as a defeat. Still, the Highlanders were jubilant, and for the occasion he donned a blue sash embroidered with gold, a green velvet bonnet with a white cockade, a periwig over his red hair, and a silver-hilted sword. If for nothing else, Cope's withdrawal was good for morale.

But it was good for something else. By his march to Inverness, possibly in the hope that the rebels would follow, Cope had done the one thing he should have strenuously avoided. He had left open — even though temporarily — the door to the Lowlands. O'Sullivan, anxious to further prove his success as Adjutant-General, urged that Cope should be pursued and forced to fight, and drew up an order of battle for that purpose. 'Cope's dancing backwards! A Dettingen man, is he? The little man in St. James's will be tearing his wig when he learns that three thousand of his redcoats are running for their lives! Smash Cope, and there's naught more than a corporal's guard left in Scotland!'

It was a temptation. True, the rebel army had swollen considerably since the desperate days at Glenfinnan. Lochaber's Camerons had been joined by the MacDonalds of Clanranald, from Morar, Moidart and Knoidart, the Glengarry of Glencoe, and three hundred Appin men with their oak-sprig badges and their clan standard — a yellow saltire on a blue field. There were MacLachlans, Robertsons, Menzies, and three or four score unattached and broken men who had drifted in by fives and tens at every halting-place on the march. Aye, it was a temptation, but the Prince needed still more men and better advice than O'Sullivan's before he faced Cope. And Cope would keep for a few weeks. A march on Perth would be better. At Perth there'd be Lord George Murray and James, Duke of Perth, and the substantial following they had mustered. Then Edinburgh. That would make the little man in St. James's tear his wig.

The clansmen turned southward. The wild ones among them would have preferred Inverness and Cope's bonnie wee redcoats, but there was an equal number who had no more regard for Charles Edward's cause than that of King George. They knew nothing about either, and they had left their homes only because their chiefs had ordered it. Nobody refused the chief if he valued his roof, his cattle, or even his life. To an impoverished crofter scratching a meagre living from the thin Highland soil, or grazing a few gaunt kine that he could not afford to kill for meat, it didn't matter much who called himself King in London, four hundred miles away. There were still some, too, who remembered the failure of the 'Fifteen, and had no more confidence in the present adventure. Besides, how would the women and the old men fare in the glens during the Winter? Inverness or Perth, it didn't matter, so long as the affair was finished with quickly.

Many of the thirty-five men who had followed Ranald MacDonald from Glen Moriston had trickled away to join the larger clan groups, and several had crept back to the Glen, tired of his continuous swagger and arrogance. He had put an eagle feather — the mark of a chief — in his bonnet, and talked with the aloofness of a laird, when everyone knew he was no better than they — a broken man with nothing but the farmstead that formed his wife's dowry and entitled only to stand in the third line of the Glengarry. He had sworn and ranted when the order to turn to Perth was received, bragging that he'd lead a band of braw lads to Inverness himself, if any would follow him — and he was confident that none would.

If the truth were known, Ranald MacDonald was more than pleased with the prospect of Perth. It was that much further from Glen Moriston. Yesterday they had been only five miles from Inverwick, and it would have been easy enough to slip away. Alexander MacDonell had, with a stolen flitch of bacon and a peck of flour for his family, returning before sun-rising. He had said nothing of Jeannie, so it was clear that the wench still kept her pregnancy secrecy. Ranald had near choked with apprehension. But MacDonell had reported seeing smoke from the chimney of Ranald's cottage. Did that mean that his haughty wife had returned from Edinburgh? He toyed with the possibility of surprising her with a sudden appearance and giving her a reminder of his husbandry that she'd not forget for many a month, perhaps even throwing in her face his preference for a fifteen-years-old farm wench over the daughter of Dundreggan. It would have given him pleasure, but it was not worth the hazard.

Better Perth — and perhaps Dundee. They'd not send him to the tinklers' huts in Dundee this time.

Chapter 13

There was a long shadow reaching towards them across the floor, and the narrow door framed a figure in black home-spun, a hat like a pipkin lid and clumsy shoes. The man was a beanpole, with his well-darned hose wrinkling on his lean calves, his cheeks and eyes sunken. His hands, protruding from frayed cuffs, were knotted tightly across his middle. 'Woe unto her that is filthy and polluted!' he repeated. 'She hath done violence to the law!'

Isobel rose to her feet. She hesitated, then curtsied. 'Welcome to my house.'

The Reverend John Grant advanced two paces. 'Ye' house, ye say? It has the manner of a brothel.' He glanced about him. 'And where is the child?'

'He is still sleeping.'

'So while the grandson of Dundreggan sleeps, and his father gone to the war, his mother fornicates with a man of our enemies. Is this the way of the Glengarry?' He shook his head grimly. 'The married woman that takes another man under her roof has already succumbed to sin. It was plain enough to me — and I have the evidence of my own eyes. Do ye know our custom with a lewd woman, Mistress?'

Isobel drew a deep breath. 'There's no lewdness here, and Master Margery is a friend of our people —'

Grant had unclasped his hands and held one aloft to silence her. 'I have been told, and I am here to see for myself. Ye' father was blind, but I am not.' He sniffed. 'A house of iniquity is no place for a child who will one day be the Master of Dundreggan and Bailie of Inverwick. I shall demand that he be removed from ye' influence — and ye, Mistress, will answer for ye' harlotry in a manner ye know of.'

It was not until that moment that Thomas saw the real anger of which Isobel was capable. She stiffened, her copper hair tossing, her eyes wide, blazing with sudden fire. Every inch of her was taut, tensed like a cornered wildcat, her head high and her breasts rising and falling furiously. 'Take Jamie?' she lashed. 'You'll not take him from me — nor will anyone else, Minister. And there's naught in this house to cause him harm save your lecherous mischief and the filth of your tongue. Yes, Minister, I know your custom with a whore — or any simple wench who has yielded to a man's coaxing. Her head shorn, a whipping at a cart-tail, and banishment. If that is the teaching of God, then I'll choose the ignorance of the heathen.' She walked to stand by the door. 'You've out-stayed your welcome. Take your fine gospel to your own pulpit. It's not wanted here!'

Grant swallowed, then drew himself up. 'I'll not tolerate insolence, woman, and God is not mocked. Ye'll not be so brazen when the whip is laid on ye.' He glared at Thomas. 'And this — this —'

'Blackguard.' Thomas suggested. 'And if I had two sound legs, you'd find yourself kicked through that plaguy door. But there'll not be any whippings, Master Minister — least-ways, not if you value your life.' He laid his two pistols on his folded cloak. 'I'll question whether you'll attempt the business yourself, but you'll explain to your disciples that two of them must die before anyone lays hands on Mistress MacDonald. I've a feeling that the prospect might dampen their fervour.'

Grant's thin face had yellowed. 'Ye'd offer violence to the Church — ?'

'Aye.' Thomas nodded. 'What else would you expect from an English cut-throat?' He picked up one of his pistols. 'And sooner than you'll relish if you don't —'

But the Reverend John Grant had already turned for the door. Safely beyond it, he halted. 'The house of the wicked and the proud shall be overthrown!' he shouted. 'There will be a reckoning!'

Thomas aimed his pistol at the sky he could see through the open door, and pulled the trigger. The gun roared, and Isobel put her hands to her ears. From outside came the sound of hastily retreating footsteps. Thomas laughed.

There was, however, no similar reaction from Isobel. She eyed him gravely. 'There could be a serious outcome. He might have been cautious about denouncing me because of my father's standing, but now he can complain that you attempted to murder him.'

He snorted. 'Good. Then it'll discourage any other meddling scandal-mongers.'

'It won't discourage the Provost of Inverness if the Minister lodges a complaint, and you can't shoot at law officers.'

'With a battle brewing on his doorstep, I'll hazard the Provost of Inverness will have more pressing matters to worry about than the reverend minister's bleating. Grant can go to damnation. I'm more concerned about you —' his eyes sought hers, '— and what you said.'

'Said?' She was closing the door and lowering the securing beam into its sockets, her back towards him.

'Aye.' He had to know for certain. He was a damn' fool, but he had to know. He was a damn' fool. 'You were saying something — when Grant came —'

'I don't remember. Some foolishness to keep you from hurting yourself.' She glanced at the ladder to the loft. 'Jamie must have slept through the noise of your pistol, but it's time he was wakened.'

'It didn't sound like a foolishness.'

'But it was. And the Reverend Grant was right in one thing. My husband has gone to the war, and you're here.'

'It's a situation that would have been avoided if Campbell had taken me to Inverness. But it can be mended, if your father would send two men to manage the horses, and I've money to pay. You'll have spiked Grant's guns, and likely your father will be better pleased.'

He doesn't understand, Isobel thought, that it was not herself she was concerned for. Inverness wasn't like London with its ordered society, its magistrates and Bow Street officers. It could be in Cope's hands today and the rebels' tomorrow, and Thomas would be helpless if faced with either.

'You've mentioned your husband only once before,' he was insisting. He hadn't been mistaken, dammit. 'Do you love him?'

Her eyes were pleading with him. Don't, they were begging — don't, please — this is wrong.

'He's my husband,' she said defiantly, 'and Jamie's father.'

'That's not the same thing. Do you love him?'

'To whom else should a wife give her love?' She refused to be drawn. 'It's a husband's right.' She might have protested that her marriage was not a subject for his curiosity, but dared not. It was she after all, who had provoked him. 'Whatever the Reverend Grant thinks now, I'll not allow him cause for further reproach.' And that, her eyes added, is the answer to the question you mustn't ask.

But he was not to be impeded so easily, i'faith. When you'd fired the first volley, you didn't pile arms and wait for the opposition to reform. You kept reloading and firing until they broke, and when they broke you made them rim — and when they ran, they were beaten.

He fired his next volley. 'You didn't bring me to Glen Moriston just because I had a musket-ball in my leg. And I had no injury in Crieff.' He paused. 'There was another reason in Crieff.'

He watched the flush flood into her cheeks and her white teeth claw at her lip. Now, he thought — another volley and she'd break. My love, she'd said, with her arms about him. My love —

But he couldn't. She was gazing at him as though he had struck her in the face. Then she choked. 'I was ashamed,' she whispered. 'Ashamed.' She cradled her burning cheeks between her hands. The next moment, sobbing, she ran for the ladder reaching to the loft.

He lay back on his litter. Goddam — he still didn't understand women. It had been she who, on two occasions, had made an overture which hardly suggested a devotion for her absent reaver of a husband. He'd heard tell of women, both married and spinster, who took pleasure in baiting a man, whetting his appetite, but taking care never to yield. Men had a contemptuous name for them. Was Isobel one of these? 'Sblood — what was a man expected to do?

Now it was likely there'd be some unpleasant developments. Even if Grant didn't carry a complaint to Inverness, he'd be sure to run tale-telling to Dundreggan. Festerin' blood — how had he, Thomas, entangled himself in this ridiculous predicament, hundreds of miles from home, friendless and outlawed, with a broken leg — and not an item of it of his own choosing or fault? Any dramatist who put the story to paper would be jeered for his absurdity. Damn de Courcy and his inextricable schemes! At this moment, in Halstead, the portly old fool was probably swilling his madeira with a complete indifference towards the plight of his protégé in Scotland. Or was he still weaving his senile conspiracies for Wolfe, and Howe, and — who was it — Clive?

When Isobel reappeared with young Jamie she was calm, her face expressionless. She did not speak unless compelled to, and then as briefly as possible, her eyes lowered. Thomas suspected that her occasional activities outside the cottage were deliberately prolonged, and he swore again. It was painful to contemplate weeks of confinement with an uncommunicative woman and an infant with a vocabulary of scarce more than a dozen words. Inverness couldn't be worse, and even the company of Patrick Campbell would have been welcomed. Still, there'd be company soon enough, he'd wager. Robert of Dundreggan would be breathing Gaelic fire and demanding satisfaction for the impeachment of his tiresome honour. Well — it would be a diversion.

The day passed, and it was during the afternoon of the next that the diversion presented itself — but it was not in the shape of Robert of Dundreggan nor the officers of the Provost of Inverness. It was a plump and ruddy-faced girl of some fifteen or sixteen years, her naked feet peeping from below her skirts and a worn plaid cowl-like over her head and shoulders. Seeing Thomas, she would have fled had Isobel not descended from the loft. There followed the inevitable exchange in incomprehensible Gaelic, with the girl shooting nervous glances at Thomas. Isobel, for two days devoid of emotion, had coloured. She spoke angrily, her words tinged with scathing, until the girl lowered her head and began to weep. Isobel turned away impatiently, then relented, and stood motionless with her lips pursed and thoughtful.

Thomas, intrigued and irritated, raised himself to his elbows. 'Damme —!' The girl burst into a fresh paroxysm of sobbing, and Isobel silenced her sharply.

'This is Jeannie MacDonell,' she said slowly. She was gazing at the wall above his head. 'She's fifteen years old, not even promised, and she's with child.'

Thomas raised his eyebrows. 'Aye, it happens.' The girl was buxom enough for fifteen, he mused, and could have caught many a man's eye. There were loose fish, then, in even this convention-ridden community — and that being so, the threatened discord subsequent upon his own relationship with Isobel paled into insignificance. 'The Reverend John Grant's going to laugh like a festerin' pantaloon.'

Isobel ignored his sarcasm. 'She's told nobody else, but she can't hide it much longer.' She allowed her eyes to fall to his. 'You don't know what this means. Her family will disown her. She'll be arraigned before the kirk, and the elders will publicly pronounce her a whore. They'll shear her hair, tie her to the tail-board of a cart and whip her to the bounds of the Glen, where she'll be cut down and warned never to return. If she's fortunate she'll die in the heather, quickly. If not, she'll crawl like an animal —' She shrugged. 'That's why she's here. She has no father, and the man of her house is her brother, Alexander MacDonell, who's gone to the Prince. When he returns — and knows — he'll swear for the death of the man who insulted his name.'

'Well,' Thomas conceded, 'at least that's one thing Grant can't blame me for, 'though I'll wager he'll have his suspicions.' He frowned. 'Why has she come here? She'd do better to find the kern who fathered the brat. There's naught —' There was something in Isobel's face that halted him in mid-sentence. 'Who is he?'

The girl Jeannie obviously possessed some knowledge of English, for she immediately cried out protestingly, as if to forbid Isobel's answer. Isobel drew a deep breath. 'Ranald MacDonald,' she said firmly. 'My husband.'

Thomas stared. There was a warped piquancy about the situation that, for a moment, tempted him to laugh, but he resisted it. It was not the time for cynicism. 'I see,' he nodded. The girl, now that her predicament was exposed, was gazing at him as if he were about to offer some miraculous solution. 'I'll concede there's a certain logic in her coming here,' he went on, 'but what does she expect?' Jeannie MacDonell wasn't the first wench to find herself paying a high price for a few tumbles in the heather.

'Expect?' Isobel's eyes had returned to the wall over his head. 'She doesn't know. Ranald's not here, she can't confide in her own people, and each day she's terrified that someone has whispered to Reverend Grant —'

'Grant? Is that damn' spindle-shanked hypocrite the lawmaker in this glen?'

'The Chief is the law-maker, and the law allows no charity to whores. The Reverend Grant makes doubly sure.' She paused. 'The clans' laws are harsh, and vengeance is cruel. It must be so, or the people of the glens would never sleep secure. But I can't let someone be whipped to her death because of the lust of my husband.'

Well, women were publicly whipped in any English town for considerably less than whoring — aye, and transported to the Americas — but it was a brutal custom, and he'd not willingly see a wench of fifteen years a victim of it. Still — 'You owe her nothing,' he suggested. 'If you can't send her away, can you hide her here? And when she bears her brat, what then?'

'I don't know.' Isobel's voice was strained. 'No — she can't bear her child here. Even if it were possible, I couldn't —'

Jeannie MacDonell burst into another turmoil of weeping. 'Am I malicious?' Isobel whispered. 'You see —'

'Damme, I've no opinion — but you're not responsible for your husband's knavery.' He considered. 'There must be scores of brats born to unmarried wenches — aye, and gentlefolk. They don't all get whipped by the parish and flung into the street, do they? What happens to a chamber-wench that's been in the master's bed?'

She shrugged. 'A few guineas would see the girl delivered discreetly, and then settled where she'd not be an embarrassment. But this is Glen Moriston, not Edinburgh — or even Inverness.'

'But if she were in Inverness,' he persisted, 'it could be managed?'

Isobel nodded doubtfully. 'Yes, it probably could.' Then her face fell. 'But she'd have to leave the Glen now, before someone notices and begins to gossip. It will be five — six — months before she's brought to child-bed, and a rustic wench, with child, won't easily find employment among townspeople —'

With his thumb, Thomas tore apart the stitching at the waist of his breeches. 'Would twenty guineas be enough?' It was his reserve. He had little else left.

'Twenty guineas?' Isobel stared. 'It's enough and more. With twenty guineas she can live like a duchess.' She shook her head irritably. 'She doesn't deserve it.' Jeannie MacDonell's tears had miraculously ceased, and her eyes, on the gold, had brightened. She wetted her lips.

'Then she can go to Inverness,' Thomas decided. 'The money will pay for lodgings and food, and a midwife when the time comes.' A labourer with a family earned, at best, ninepence a day; twenty guineas was a fortune for a girl of fifteen. 'Is there a carrier who could take her?'

'She'll walk!' Isobel flared. 'It's scarce more than ten miles, and she's sturdy enough.' She turned to speak to the girl in angry Gaelic, but Jeannie MacDonell had already gleaned the sense of the exchange. Flushed, she nodded happily, unable to tear her eyes away from the tumble of golden coins that Thomas held in his hand. 'She's more than willing,' Isobel said. 'For a wench that tends cows from four in the morning till dark, knows nothing better than fried oatcakes, kale and porridge, never had shoes to her feet or a shift without holes, she's impatient to be a fine town lady.'

Thomas grunted. 'Well, twenty guineas'll not go far if she wants a carriage and pair. You'd best warn her to be cautious —'

Vigorously, Jeannie MacDonell nodded again. She was a canny lass, she asserted, born to stringency. She knew the value of every farthing, and the English gentleman's guineas wouldn't be squandered. The Glen would hear nothing further from her, and she'd not bring shame to Isobel MacDonald. If she were pressed on the subject of her bairn's paternity, she'd blame some passing gypsy, some drunken redcoat. In Inverness she'd be safe from the Glen and Reverend John Grant — and there'd be no trouble. She took the money eagerly, curtsied her thanks and, with a final, almost triumphant glance at Isobel, fled for the door.

Both Thomas and Isobel were silent for several moments, then Thomas laughed ruefully. 'That's one trouble less — and I'll wager she'd be satisfied to have fifty brats, at twenty guineas apiece.'

Isobel brushed back her hair from her brow. She was trembling from a mixture of anger and bitterness, of humiliation at the thought of Ranald MacDonald's lusting with a farm wench — for whom a handful of guineas was generous compensation for a bastard infant. Had it happened here — in the cottage? On her own bed? Had Ranald obtained from the girl the compliance he had never had from Isobel? She shivered. 'I can't repay you the money,' she said.

'You're already repaying it,' Thomas assured her. 'Tenfold.' He paused. 'I'm more concerned about the wench. She's a mite young —'

'*Young*?' She didn't know whether to laugh or weep. 'Not too young for whoring. And was my husband the first? Do we even know if the bairn is his? Or if there *is* a bairn?' But she knew that Jeannie MacDonell had told the truth. Ranald was incapable of living a week without seeking a woman, and the bovine, gullible Jeannie would have been an easy prey to his swashbuckling advances. No, he wouldn't have brought her to the cottage. It would have happened in the undulating, grass-choked valley where the MacDonells grazed their cattle, above Dundreggan. It was lonely there, and safe. Jeannie would have been flattered by the practised wooing of the son-in-law of Robert of Dundreggan, surrendering easily to his strong hands —

'He's an animal.' She spoke aloud, unthinking.

'Aye,' Thomas conceded. 'And not just your husband. Most men are, given the occasion.'

'You too?' she asked. 'Given the occasion?' She could feel the anger within her rising savagely. What did marriage mean to Ranald MacDonald? How many times had he come to her bed from the arms of some fleshy farm wench? And did he share with his women the joke of his virtuous wife?

She fell to her knees by the side of the litter. 'Isn't there reason for me, too? If he can be shameless, can't I?' Her lips were seeking his, and he reached for her. She came hungrily, her hands cupping his face and her mouth eagerly to his as, momentarily bewildered, he fumbled clumsily with the lacings of her bodice. 'If you want —' she said, desperately.

'With a splinted leg?' he groaned. ''Sblood — Isobel —' Then he lifted her away from him. 'No, dammit — I'd not take advantage of a woman who just wants to spite an uncivil husband —'

She wrenched herself to her feet, her eyes scornful. 'Because you're an officer and a gentleman —?'

'Aye, perhaps.' He pulled a wry face. 'It would have no plaguy significance. I know naught about women, but when I take one, it'll be because she wants me, not for retaliation.' He smiled apologetically. 'I'm not spurning you — God forbid — but in an hour's time you'll thank me.'

For a long time she gazed at him, expressionless. Then she nodded slowly. 'Not in an hour's time,' she whispered. 'Now. Thank you.'

Part II - The Chase

Chapter 14

It had been a cold, damp night, and the dawn promised little better, with a dank mist from the nearby Forth clinging obstinately to the boggy meadows, defying the first weak fingers of the rising sun. Clothing was clammy to the skin, and the men's gaiters were soaked, their muskets glazed with wetness. Cramped and huddled, their few hours of sleep marred by constant alarms from the nervous picquets, they climbed to their feet, coughing, spitting, eyes swollen, and moving surlily to the sergeants' shouts to form line.

It was not until now that they could distinguish the details of the position they had stumbled into during the dark of the early hours. A mile to their left — to the northward — lay the bleak expanse of the Firth of Forth, with the huddled rooftops of Cockenzie village, on the shore, vaguely visible. The ground fell away towards the river, so that Murray's regiment, holding the left of the fine, was fifty feet below the five companies of Lee's, who were further flanked by a battery of 2-pounder cannon and two squadrons of Gardiner's Dragoons, jostling their steaming horses into some semblance of order. And ahead of them, a thousand yards distant across the sodden hillside, was the motleyed, unbroken front of the rebel army.

As always, the movements of the shivering redcoats had been incomprehensible to Private Burt. Three weeks ago they had been in Inverness, from where all had expected Johnnie Cope to sally forth to finish this rebel business once and for all. Instead, they had tramped a hundred weary miles to Aberdeen only to be crammed into a flotilla of foulsmelling ships and taken to sea. Edinburgh, it was said, was their destination. The Highlanders were marching on Edinburgh, but Cope intended to be there first and, instead of a few frightened militia, the Pretender's rabble would be confronted by an army or horse and foot — and that would be the end of it.

Well, fester it, Johnnie Cope hadn't got there first. The Pretender's rabble had, and Private Burt and his fellows had been disembarked at Dunbar. It was a frustrating business, not alleviated by a series of rumours and counter-rumours, abortive alarms, and the tiresome groping for position that had left the men sullen and irritable. Still, when all was said, here were the rebels at last — and standing. If it wasn't so rot-gutting chilly, it might be an entertaining day.

An officer holding high a gold-laced hat was walking his horse along the ranks of infantry. Burt could now recognise Cope. 'I've no doubt, my lads, that ye' behaviour today will bring us honour! Hold ye' ranks, keep up a good fire, and ye'll shatter these rebel clods in minutes!' Burt joined in a half-hearted huzzah, wiped the damp from his pan with his spare neck-cloth, re-primed, then looked to his front. He suddenly realised that his teeth had ceased to ache.

How many rebels were there? Someone had said five thousand. Burt peered at them through the haze, but at this distance it was difficult to estimate numbers. The Highlanders' line undulated raggedly, with no division by regiments — if there were any — and its right outflanked the English by a hundred yards or more. He could see a few limp banners on poles, and the dull glitter of claymores and scythe-blades among the crowded and congealing reds, russets and greens of plaids and bonnets. A few yards from Burt, the cannon were being loaded and a dragoon sergeant was shouting for his men to come up to their ground and hold rein. Well, Johnnie Cope would finish the business soon enough. There were twenty-four companies of English foot, ready and waiting — and the dragoons. It was common knowledge that the Highlanders would never stand against dragoons.

Burt's feet were numb from the wetness that had soaked into his worn boots. He'd had a handful of hard ammunition loaf from his haversack an hour ago, and his belly yearned for something hot — mutton stew, say, with fat dumplings floating, and thick with peas and turnip — and, b'Christ, a roasting fire to drive the aching chill from his bones. The stew first, and then a swilling of gin and a big, eager wench to share a soft mattress. That was it. Alright, then, Johnnie Cope. The sooner these festerin' Highlanders were cut to bloody pieces, the better.

'Make ready!'

The shouldered muskets of Lee's fell forward into four hundred left hands, with each man of the front rank dropping to his right knee. Across the hillside the long rebel front had shivered, convulsed, and then erupted forward — starting first with the left almost opposite Lee's, the movement rippling snake-like along the dishevelled line. Faintly to the redcoats' ears came a low, ominous roar, and Burt swallowed, his finger fumbling for his trigger but knowing that to anticipate an order could earn him fifty lashes. The tumultuous sea of the enemy was flooding towards the waiting red ranks with incredible swiftness, slashing through the knee-high grass and swarming up the side of the hill, across the ribbon of the Cockenzie road. There was no sense of formation, no drilled lines — nothing but a boiling, clashing horde of racing clansmen, bare-legged, crazily screeching, and closing perilously the last few yards that separated them from the English.

'Present!'

Private Burt lifted his musket to his shoulder, pressing his cheek hard against the walnut butt. 'Od's blood — but this wasn't what he'd been expecting. The enemy should — by all the rules of warfare — be advancing steadily in dressed ranks, paced by ruffling drums, with an occasional halt to loosen a volley. There was something grossly unfair about a teeming deluge of blaspheming savages —

'Fire!'

The priming flared, the musket jolted, and Burt's ears sang. For a moment, he was blinded by a pall of black powder-smoke that rolled back over the line, choking in the throat, and almost simultaneously he heard the bark of the little 2-pounders on his right. The smoke flattened and dispersed, and the Highlanders, checked only for a few seconds by the single volley, surged on. Burt was re-loading — tearing open the paper cartridge with his teeth, ramming, priming, then blowing loose powder from the closed frizzen. Yards away from him, however, the artillerymen were throwing down their rammers and linstocks and running into the ranks of the artillery guard in the rear, and Burt, with his musket once more to his shoulder, swore contemptuously. Festerin' hell! Running for a rabble of ignorant clansmen who didn't even wear breeches —?

Lieutenant-Colonel Halkett, of Lee's, his military wig immaculately powdered and his boots brilliantly polished as if on review, surveyed the smoke-wreathed field nonchalantly. The howling clansmen were only seconds away. 'Aim low, my boys — and ram hard those charges —' He frowned, then drew his sword.

Burt fired again. Beyond the abandoned artillery pieces on the flank, a squadron of Gardiner's Dragoons was jingling forward, sabres advanced, the bob-tailed cobs nervous in the noise and keeping poor station. This, then, would be the end of it, Burt reckoned. The Highlanders would never stand against dragoons.

But the rot-gutting Highlanders had reached the unattended guns, i'faith — and, frustrated, were slashing at the pieces with their broadswords. 'Od's blood —! Was nobody fighting this festerin' battle except Lee's Foot? What were Lascelles's doing? And Guise's — and Murray's? And those lick-spit dragoons — they were breaking!

It was unbelievable, impossible. There was a stutter of wild musket-shots from the swarming, excited clansmen, one of which brought down a horse, kicking and snapping. The leading dragoons had reined, uncertain, jostling in disorder as their officers cursed desperately. Then several wrenched their mounts about, and in a moment there was chaos, with carbines and sabres thrown down and the troopers spurring for safety — anywhere, beyond reach of the horde of baying, frenzied clansmen avalanching towards them, over-running the guns and already spilling around the unnerved redcoats of Lascelles's.

'Stand, damn ye!' Halkett was shouting angrily. The Highlanders were everywhere, slashing, thrusting, eyes hot with hate and teeth bared like blood-lusty animals. Around Private Burt the ranks were melting away. Above the mêlée he could see Cope, ahorse, urging Murray's to hold firm — and then Halkett, his polished feet apart and his sword stabbing. Burt was no hero, fester it. He would have wished himself a hundred miles from this disastrous meadow, and he owed his officers nothing for twelve months of grinding drudgery during which none of them had even known his name — but he admired a fighter, be he a bare-fist miner, a gored bulldog or a game young milord. No, b'Christ, he was no hero, and the honour of the regiment could go to stinking damnation, but he couldn't leave Halkett to go down alone.

It wasn't happening, of course. Twenty-four companies of infantry and two regiments of dragoons couldn't possibly be routed by ragged, untrained peasants. Johnnie Cope would reform his line, the drums would thunder, and then these screeching savages would know what a battle was all about. But the line had gone and the redcoats were scattering, flying from their positions in their hundreds as panic seethed from platoon to platoon like a vicious powder-flare. Private Burt, spitting obscenities, lowered his head and ran towards Halkett. There were others with him — two officers with spontoons, a sergeant, and a half dozen private men uncertain whether it was wiser to surrender where they stood or hazard being cut down as they ran.

'Form line and make ready ye' pieces!' Halkett had never soiled his hands with a musket before, but he had no qualms now. 'Fire!' They were alone, encircled — a little red island in a storm-lashed sea of jostling, jeering clansmen — but the concerted volley had cleared a space, and the thin wall of bayonets had steadied. A redcoat dropped to his knees, vomiting blood, and the others fell back slowly, sullenly. There was little choice. Load, present, fire. Another man was down — but, b'God, if twenty-four companies had fought like this, the Highlanders would have been shot to crimson rags —

There was a ditch behind them, and they clambered across it gratefully, but the sergeant had sprawled, cursing. They were standing again, but it couldn't last. Burt, at Halkett's shoulder, knew that he'd never see Ludgate Hill again nor, fester it, have the fiery taste of gin in his mouth. It was a pity.

He saw the Highlander — a black-bearded oaf with an eagle feather in his bonnet — come bounding in fiercely with claymore raised, eager to cut down the gold-laced Colonel. Burt lunged, and his bayonet ran into the clansman's waist, hard and deep, before snapping off at the socket like a rotten stick. The Highlander screamed from a distorted face and fell, jerking. Halkett wiped a powder smudge from his cheek. 'Well hit, fellow.' He raised his eyebrows. 'Ye're hurt, b'God?'

Private Burt was caressing his jaw. 'Festerin' tooth-ache,' he grunted.

*

It had been Locheil's impatient Camerons who had begun the pell-mell assault against the English and, once in motion across the hazed grassland, nobody could have controlled them. The Stewarts of Appin and the MacGregors followed in seconds, and then the massed clansmen of the right — Clanranald's, Glengarry's and Keppoch's — lurched after them, quickly abandoning all pretence to order, with clan mingling with clan and the shouts of the officers lost in the angry roar. Ahead of them was the slender, red-coated lines of the enemy, silent and somehow forlorn in the damp mist that filled the hollows and pushed tendrils across the rutted Cockenzie road. If the English wanted to stand all day like reluctant wenches, the clansmen didn't. And the redcoats weren't going to have the pleasure of a leisurely exchange of volleys. Damn the preliminaries.

The nine broken men from Glen Moriston — Ranald MacDonald and John, Gregor MacGregor, Bald Ewen, the brothers Chisholm, Cluny Grant and Alexander MacDonell — went forward together. There were only nine now — Ranald's immediate neighbours. The others, unable to tolerate the impudence of his self-appointed leadership and his constant, tiresome bravado, had drifted away into the ranks of the Athollmen and the mixed MacGregors. Brave talk was a fine thing for a man who had earned its right, but there'd be a time for boasting when the German laddie's pipe-clayed puppets had been driven into the Forth, and the fire-breathing Ranald MacDonald had never been within musket-shot of the redcoat regiments.

Well, there was no avoiding the issue now. The English were there, ahead, and he knew that he was on trial. Even his closest cronies were becoming cool towards him, and he'd have to show them — or never open his mouth again. He ran forward, claymore bared, shouting them on.

The ground was sloping, undulating, and the tall September grass tore wetly at their legs. A thousand paces, someone had said, and then sword and axe. The red lines, nearer now, had crackled with tiny points of flame and then disappeared behind a wall of black smoke. His breath was coming in short pants, and he slackened his pace, feigning impatience with his fellows. Ahead, he noted with satisfaction, the Cameron's banner was already tossing and swaying over the redcoats' ranks, and he could see, through the drifting smoke, the hedged bayonets spilling into confusion. Had the English broken so easily? He barked loudly, menacingly. It wasn't his fault that the undisciplined, hot-headed Camerons had roared off before everybody else, was it? If he, Ranald MacDonald, had reached the English first —

He could see the English clearly now — three long ranks of soldiers, the front kneeling, in knee-length redcoats and white gaiters, and officers with drawn swords shouting to make themselves heard above the continuous drumfire of musketry. But the lines were disintegrating, reeling backward, with the ragged, crazed sea of clansmen surging into them, pouring into the gaps between the platoons, slashing, thrusting, hacking. A group of dragoons milled helplessly around some abandoned artillery pieces, but did nothing more than fire a few hasty shots before showing their tails and spurring away. Ranald MacDonald gave a howl of frustration. Were these pox-spawned English going to run like rabbits before he had a chance to sink his claymore into one of them? A riderless horse, with eyes rolling, clattered out of the smoke. Ranald scythed at it, missed, and cursed again.

Then he saw them — a small group of infantrymen beyond a ditch, loading and firing resolutely at the threatening circle of incensed Camerons. One of them was an officer, bewigged under a laced hat and with coat heavily braided with gold. The lace of his cuffs fell over his hands, grasping a musket which he presented and fired with the men on each side of him. Faintly, through the noise, Ranald MacDonald could hear the man's firm voice. 'Load and prime! Ready —!'

Could this be General Cope? Aye, he had the bearing of a commander, and a fine scarlet coat above his gleaming boots. The clansman who brought down General Cope would have his name spoken and sung throughout the Highlands for a hundred years, like that of Angus Og or Rory Mor — aye, and there'd be more than an eagle feather in his worn bonnet, i'faith, and no more sneers and winks when the Bard told of Ranald MacDonald with his red blade, and the killing of the English King's general.

He leapt the ditch, fell to his knees but scrambled again to his feet. The indomitable English officer was only yards from him, directing the fire of his handful of redcoats, several of whom had been struck down by the close-range musketry of the Scots. Ranald MacDonald bounded forward, his sword high and whirling. It would be easy.

Too late, he glimpsed the slight, short-statured infantryman at the officer's side — a puny fellow in ill-fitting regimentals and mired to his knees, his sodden tricorne over an unshaven face. Too late, Ranald MacDonald whirled, but the little man's bayonet had ripped into his middle, tearing upwards viciously, mortally. He fell backward, screaming Gaelic obscenities, and feeling the blood bubbling into his throat.

Behind him, on the far side of the ditch, Alexander MacDonell raised his musket and took careful aim, Ranald MacDonald had been a bladder of air, a conceited braggart — but, fester it, he'd been the first Glen Moriston man to reach the enemy, the first to die.

He fired, and watched the little redcoat crumple, then fall face downwards over the body of Ranald MacDonald.

Chapter 15

Thomas had been asleep for two hours, he supposed, when Isobel roused him. 'The haycocks,' she said, urgently. 'They're burning.'

He did not grasp her meaning immediately. 'Haycocks?'

She wore a long, shapeless shift to her feet, her unbound hair flowing over her shoulders and shimmering like molten copper in a ruddy, pulsating glare from beyond the open-flung casement. It had been a warm night, and the air heavy. Thomas sat up.

'Someone has put a torch to the hay,' Isobel repeated. 'If the flames reach the byre, there's the horses —'

Thomas groaned. For several days he had been fashioning a cradle which, secured at armpit and hip, would support his half-healed leg and permit him to move about the cottage and perhaps even hobble a few yards in the open, but he had not yet experimented with its use. On his feet he'd be capable of giving some account of himself, albeit feeble. On his back he was still helpless.

'Your pistols,' Isobel demanded. 'Give me your pistols!' The smell of burning hay filled the room, and they could hear the distant spit and crackle of the flames. Someone was hooting, jeeringly.

'Dammit, woman, you can't —!' But she had the guns in her hands, apprehensive but determined. 'If they're not driven off,' she retorted, 'it will be the byre next and the horses dead, then the thatch and ourselves. It's a mercy there's no cattle, or they'd be already hamstrung.' She lifted the door bar from its sockets.

'You'll not!' he roared. 'In God's name, drag me to the door —!' He plucked desperately at the bindings that secured his leg to the litter. He'd crawl, fester it, like a maimed whelp, rather than let a woman go into the night to meet murder-bent reavers —

But the door was open, and a new, dragon's breath of hot air poured into the room. He could see the burning haycocks, erupting sparks, and the horses in the byre were whinnying. Isobel had disappeared.

He choked, wanting to howl with enraged, bitter frustration. He was a damn' cripple — a useless hulk — and a woman was defending him with his own pistols. Infuriated, he groped for his sword — but what festerin' good was a sword to a bed-tied man?

There was a pistol shot, and his belly knotted — then a second. No, b'God, that had been a musket. Faintly, he could hear more shouting voices, followed by a third shot and a fourth in quick succession. He felt the need to vomit, then whirled with sword bared as a man thrust through the door.

It was Robert of Dundreggan, this time with broadsword and dirk at his waist, an antique snaphaunce pistol hanging by a thong from his belt, and a small, circular target on his shoulder. Behind him was Isobel and, following, a dozen men, fully armed. Thomas lowered his own weapon. 'You've come prepared,' he growled.

'I told ye before, Englishman,' Dundreggan said, 'that if there was gossiping talk I'd hear the justice of it — and if it had truth, ye'd pay for it. Well —' he nodded grimly, 'a few vicious loons heard gossip and decided to put flame to ye' thatch. Ye'd have burned in ye' beds if they hadn't been impatient and fired the haycocks first. We saw the flare a mile away.'

'They'd been listening to that canting hypocrite of a cleric — Grant?'

'Canting, perhaps,' Dundreggan nodded, 'but no hypocrite. He's sincere enough by his own standards. I listened, and if I believed half that he described ye'd have been stretched dead on the following day — and I'd not have lifted a finger to save my own daughter from a whipping. But I'm no loon, Englishman, and there's things no man alive can do if he has a shattered leg. Still —' He eyed Thomas gravely, 'ye fired a pistol at the Minister —'

'Goddam —'

'Aye.' Dundreggan raised a hand. 'I guessed ye didn't intend to murder him, and I'll not quarrel with ye' motives, man, but ye don't understand the laws of the Clan, and these are a jealous people who'll return an insult with a dirk thrust. But enough o' that. Ye' hay is being wetted down with water from the burn, and ye'll not have further trouble tonight or for a few nights to come, but ye'll need to be wary. Ye'll be fending for yeselves. There's been a battle, and the Prince is appealing for more men. I'm away to Edinburgh —'

'A battle?' Thomas stared. 'With Cope?' He calculated swiftly. If the Pretender was asking for more men, then he hadn't been killed or taken as a result of the battle. He was still at large then — and he had escaped Cope. Dundreggan nodded again. 'Aye, a battle, if ye can call it that, wi' Cope three weeks ago —'

'Three weeks ago!' 'Sblood — he'd lain on this damn' litter, desperate for news, but nobody had bothered to tell an Englishman with a broken leg. A battle, Dundreggan had said — if you can call it that. What did he festerin' mean?

Dundreggan was continuing. 'I'm calling out every willing man that's left in the Glen. That'll leave ye alone, wi' the Minister and a few others — Whigs, women, and a handful of the older cottars and grassmen. But I expect ye to remove yeself from Glen Moriston as soon as ye can sit a horse. Remain a day longer, and the Minister will have genuine cause for impeaching ye. If the House of Dundreggan is dishonoured, I'll hunt ye through the length of Scotland, to kill ye.'

Thomas was hardly listening. ''Sblood, if your Prince has been defeated by General Cope, it will be criminal to send more men to be slaughtered. I'm a soldier, and I know. Cope will be in hot pursuit, with your clans broken and scattering —'

'Cope in hot pursuit?' Dundreggan snorted, amused. 'Cope is in Berwick and his army has been whipped. Five hundred Englishmen were killed near Prestonpans and the same number wounded. The remainder were taken. Except for a few small garrisons, trapped and helpless, there's not a single redcoat north of the Tweed to offer us opposition. So we march into England.'

It couldn't be true. It was impossible. Where was Prestonpans? Likely there'd been a patrol skirmish, and five or six redcoats had been killed. In the re-telling, five had become fifty and then five hundred. Cope in Berwick? What would Cope be doing in Berwick when less than a month ago he was leading 2,500 infantry and dragoons through the Highlands? Sir John de Courcy had said that Cope would get a drubbing but, in the light of subsequent events, anything that de Courcy had said was highly suspect. English armies, even of the mediocre quality of Cope's, didn't get whipped, and Cope himself had fought in Spain and Bavaria. No, it couldn't be true.

'Ye're finding it hard to believe,' Dundreggan said. 'So did I, when the news first came — but it's right enough. The Prince has taken Edinburgh and proclaimed his father King James the Eighth o' Scotland, England,

France, Ireland, and territories overseas. There's French troops and guns expected to be landed any day, and since the nearest English forces of any consequence are south o' the Border, it's the Border for the Prince.'

Thomas shook his head stubbornly. 'It's not possible.' But *was* it possible? Could Cope have been overwhelmed by sheer weight of numbers? Even so, the infantry would have taken a vicious toll of the clansmen, and it would have been a victory of enormous cost. 'And the Prince's losses?' he asked.

'Ye'll not believe those, either. Less than a hundred.'

Thomas gave a sour laugh. 'You're right. I don't believe any of it. I don't believe your Prince has come within five plaguy miles of General Cope.' He paused. 'Have you ever seen a company of English infantry in line of battle? They're trained to load and fire fifteen times in three and three-quarter minutes — aye, even Cope's third-raters. And Cope had twenty-four companies. But you're telling me that your Prince suffered only a hundred casualties?' He shrugged. He'd been right. It just wasn't possible.

'For a man claiming Jacobite loyalties, ye've curious sentiments,' Dundreggan observed, his eyes narrowing. 'If ye're convinced that the almighty English can't be whipped, what's ye' purpose in Scotland? Ye'd have been better advised to stay in London — like the rest of ye' fine-talking English Jacobites, wi' no intention o' showing their colours until the fighting's been won. If it's titles they're waiting for, they'll not get them for the price o' Scots blood!'

Thomas considered. 'I've no liking for London Jacobites,' he said, truthfully, 'nor for being a prisoner in Glen Moriston. If you're so concerned, then you can take me with you. I'll not sit a horse, but in a few weeks I will, and I've two good horses to carry the litter to Edinburgh. I'll hazard your army hasn't so many Guards officers that it will refuse another.'

'Ye might be giving me a bluff, Englishman, but I'll accept ye' words as honest.' Dundreggan shook his head. 'No, there's no place for a maimed man. As for a Guards officer — I'd sooner have a braw young clansman wi' claymore and dirk, who loves what he dies for. Still, when ye can ride and fight, I'll look to see ye in the Prince's column. Then, and not before, I'll give ye my hand.' He turned to Isobel and reached forward to touch her cheek gently. 'Ye'll be in my thoughts, daughter,' he smiled, then was gone into the darkness.

Isobel's eyes were wet. 'He's a good man.' She closed the door against the night. 'He wouldn't lie to you about the battle.'

'I'll not suggest he would, but the news he had could be an exaggeration —'

'Can it be that you don't want to believe it? It's not easy to admit that your own countrymen have been badly beaten — but the Sassenachs have been beaten before.' She smiled sympathetically. 'The news should gladden you — you might have been fighting the English at Prestonpans, but your chance will come —'

Before Thomas could make any rejoinder there came a vague, unidentifiable noise from immediately beyond the closed door. Both Isobel and Thomas froze, their eyes meeting. Silence, deathlike, filled several long moments, and then, unmistakably, the noise was repeated.

'The pistols,' Thomas whispered, reaching for them. 'Throw open the door, and stand clear.' Deliberately, he cocked the pistols.

Isobel nodded and moved quietly. She lifted the door bar free with one movement, flung open the door, and stepped quickly to one side. On the threshold, blinking in the sudden candle-light, was Jeannie MacDonell. She bobbed a curtsy.

'Goddam —!' Thomas was as angry with his own moment of apprehension as bewildered with the girl's sudden appearance within minutes of Dundreggan's departure. She must have been waiting in the darkness. Jeannie MacDonell edged through the door and stood in mid-floor, eyeing Isobel shamefacedly.

'What's the wench doing here?' Thomas demanded. 'She was paid twenty guineas to stay in plaguy Inverness.'

In her seven weeks' absence, Jeannie MacDonell's waist had thickened appreciably, despite her tightly laced bodice of cheap satinesco, dyed a violet shade of carmine. Her flounced skirt was muddied at the hem, as were her pointed shoes with their pinchbeck buckles. Her hair, hitherto falling tangled to her shoulders, was now carried high on her head and held clumsily in place by a gilt comb. 'Faith — a lady o' fashion,' Thomas commented.

Encouraged, Jeannie MacDonell launched into a sheepish explanation in tumbled Gaelic. Isobel's lips tightened. 'She's spent the money,' she said. 'All of it.' She glanced at Thomas. 'She probably thinks the English gentleman has more.'

'Well, the English gentleman hasn't,' Thomas muttered. 'And if he had, he wouldn't throw good guineas after bad. She's a scheming little doxy, isn't she?' He frowned. 'Damme — twenty guineas in seven weeks? She must have been keeping half the population of Inverness in pies and ale.' Jeannie MacDonell was waiting, half smiling, her eyes downcast. 'There's naught else I can do for her,' Thomas added.

Jeannie's head rose quickly. She stared at Thomas, then at Isobel, and burst into petulant, weeping Gaelic, stamping her foot several times. Isobel surveyed her dispassionately.

'Now she's penniless, she's discovered a tender conscience towards the bairn to be born. Somehow the money had all gone before she could make arrangements.' She paused, then sighed. 'There are no foundling houses, as you have in England.'

Thomas grunted ruefully. 'So we're back where we were in the plaguy beginning — but poorer.' He was finding it difficult to be charitable, and those twenty guineas would have been damn' useful at a later date. 'There seems naught else for her but to face her people.' Dammit, what else was there?

Isobel was silent, then, 'No, I'd not have a mongrel bitch undergo that. You're right, she's a scheming little doxie, but it's Ranald MacDonald's bairn, and she's a right to expect some obligation.' Jeannie's tears had ceased to flow.

'You mean you'll keep her here?'

'There's no choice, is there?' Isobel's voice broke. She was near to tears herself. 'She can't go to her own people, or to Inverness. Even if you had more money to give, she'd squander it in the same way. And she can't go a'begging on the road. Winter is coming, and I'll not be responsible for a dead-born infant — even if she didn't starve before.' She drew a deep breath. 'She'll stay — but not in idleness like Inverness. She'll do her share of the house chores. She's three months to go, and Highland women expect to work in the fields until their pains begin. She'll stay, but not for pampering.' Her eyes rested on him, and for a fleeting second there was a hint of mischief in them. 'She's not convinced that the English gentleman hasn't still got pockets full of guineas, so you can prepare for some tearful coaxing.'

Thomas snorted, but there was already a simper on Jeannie MacDonell's lips.

Chapter 16

She had never had a guinea in her hand before, seldom even seen one, and to have twenty of the gleaming, yellow coins was to have a new and splendid world opening its doors to her. No longer need she be content with oat-cakes and turnip soup. No longer a musty, straw-filled palliasse under the draughty roof, crawling from her sleep in the bitter cold of the half-dawn to tend the kine and, shivering, driving them to their grazing on the wind-swept brae. In Inverness there'd be shop-made puddings and white bread, beef, tripe, herrings and river oysters. She could have a feather mattress and a coal fire, and she could lie abed as late as she wished. And she'd have a gown of red satin, and a petticoat, and shoes with buckles, and a fine bonnet —

The birth of the bairn was months away. There was plenty of time. She had gone to the MacDonald cottage on impulse, in desperation and expecting little. Isobel MacDonald was a proud one, the daughter of Robert of Dundreggan, smooth-skinned and beautiful, with her bright hair brushed to perfection instead of neglected and matted like that of most clan women. It was certain she washed every day, because there was no smell of sweat about her, and her linen was as white as new. Aye, Isobel was a proud one — too proud for a man like Ranald MacDonald.

There was a man — as lusty as a young bull. He had stretched his plaid in the hot grass below the Black Cairn, and she had not wanted to resist. She had lain with her eyes closed against the sun, her thin shift raised to her waist and his lips wet on hers. He had not been the first. There'd been fingering boys when her breasts had just begun to swell her bodice and, when she was eleven, a travelling packman had given her six pewter buttons in exchange for a hurried affair behind the hen-bothy. She had the buttons still, hidden under the roof. There'd been other men, other brief and clumsy transactions in byre and oatfield, but none like Ranald MacDonald.

And Ranald MacDonald was Isobel's husband, which made his attentions even more satisfying. She — simple, fifteen-years Jeannie MacDonell — had stolen a husband from the white arms of the well-bred

Isobel, with all her soaps and toilet waters and white-starched muslins. It had been a delicious intrigue, until the day had come when there no longer remained any doubt that there was an inexorable price to be paid for the hours of guilty ecstasy below the Black Cairn. And, almost simultaneously, Ranald had gone to the war.

There'd been nobody to confide in, and the weeks had been passing. Only she had been aware of the subtle swelling of her body that spelled dishonour for her family, and humiliation and a public whipping for herself. Her apprehension had been followed by resentment. It was Ranald MacDonald's brat, wasn't it? He'd had the pleasure of her and then abandoned her for some wild, warring adventure. It was easy for a man. Well, he had a wife — and the haughty Isobel might be anxious to avoid the implications of her husband's misconduct.

She'd not expected to find the Englishman at the cottage. He was a tall man with smooth-shaven cheeks, confident eyes, and that unmistakable air that distinguishes a gentleman from a commoner. No youth, to be sure, and with a bandaged leg strapped to a litter, but she'd not deny that he would make a presentable figure at any woman's side. It was strange that he should be in the cottage — with Ranald MacDonald absent — and he parted with twenty guineas quickly enough, to be rid of her. Twenty guineas! Well, for that price, Isobel MacDonald could have all the rich English lovers she chose.

Jeannie could still not recall how the money had melted away so quickly. Eightpence a day was a good wage for a labouring man, and a grassman receiving his food might expect only seventy-five or eighty shillings in a year. Where, then, had twenty guineas gone in seven weeks? It seemed that as soon as she changed one of the gold coins, the balance ran through her fingers like sand. True, she had a poor head for reckoning, and it was likely the town people had cheated her. She'd had her shop-made puddings and her beef — and other things, like Westphalian ham, codling tarts, roasted poultry, oranges, peaches, Canary wine and raspberry sack. There'd been two dresses, a petticoat edged with English lace, and shoes — the first she'd had to her feet. The lodgings she found on Ness-bank she had changed for better-off Church Street, where there was a woman to clean the hearth and tidy the bed. Each week she had intended to find a midwife, but there always seemed a reason for delaying the matter until, almost suddenly, the money had gone.

It had been a rude shock. Inverness was a fine place for a body with money, but having no sympathy for a penniless wench with a pregnant belly. It was mid-October, with the days becoming decidedly chill and winter rain and snow approaching — no season to be without a roof. Under different circumstances she would not have hesitated to offer herself as a kept doxie, but no man wanted a woman who was six months with child.

There remained only one solution — Isobel MacDonald's English gentleman, if he were still in Glen Moriston. She had no doubt that there were more guineas where the first twenty came from, and she, Jeannie, still held the threat of the brat. The more she considered the possibility, the more promising it became. She had no desire to be seen in Glen Moriston; her brother, Alexander, had departed the glen with Ranald MacDonald, but there remained the Reverend John Grant and others she'd rather avoid. Still, she'd have to tramp the ten miles from Inverness and need not reach the Glen until after dark. She knew every inch of it. She chuckled. Isobel MacDonald would have her illicit frolic disturbed, and the Englishman — like a rampant dog with a douche of cold water threatening — would pay.

She'd walked the ten miles easily enough — most of the way with her unfamiliar shoes in her hand — and she had crouched in the darkness, frightened, as the MacDonalds' haycocks had burned. She didn't know what it meant. There had been shots and shouting, and in the glare of the flames she had seen Robert of Dundreggan — and cowered lower, horror-struck. Then Dundreggan and his men had gone, leaving the cottage in silence but with a lamp still burning. The moment for Jeannie MacDonell had arrived.

Her entrance hadn't been quite as she'd anticipated. There was no suggestion that Isobel MacDonald and her Englishman had been locked in fervent embrace. True, Isobel had been in her night-shift, but showed no evidence of a dishevelling bed-tumble, and the Englishman was still tied to his litter with pistols in his hands.

Jeannie's initial disappointment had been followed by another. The Englishman had shaken his head, seemingly indifferent towards her predicament. There had been no glitter of gold. She had a smattering of

English, and it was plain that, tonight at least, there would be no twenty guineas. She had been ordered to the loft where, surprisingly, Isobel had joined her and the sleeping Jamie. Well, Jeannie calculated, there was always tomorrow. She hadn't fired her last shot yet, by any reckoning.

But the morrow brought further disconcertment. Jeannie hadn't been roused from her sleep at dawn for seven weeks, but now, Isobel said, there was the hearth to be cleared, kindling to find, and the fire to be re-laid and lit. Two big horses in the byre must be fed and watered, then loosened in the meadow — and all this before eating. Jeannie wrinkled her nose at porridge and bacon. In Inverness she'd have beef collops and hot girdle cakes with butter, but she'd not had a morsel for twelve hours, and ate her fill in silence.

The relationship between Isobel and her Englishman was enigmatic. There must surely be more in it than met the eye, and she'd need time to interpret its subtleties. There were no love-sick glances, no stolen hand-clasps, and she had sufficient English to know that their conversation was never more than commonplace. It was odd, but it didn't matter. The money was more important.

Well, the Englishman had the money. Surreptitiously she examined him. He might be classified as handsome and, like Isobel, he didn't smell of stale sweat, so it was likely he preferred women of the same ilk — clean and dainty and fragrant with lavender. She sniffed scornfully. On the other hand, if he had the money —

It had not occurred to her that she might be expected to remain in Glen Moriston indefinitely. She wanted to return to the pleasures of Inverness as quickly as possible, and it was only the spite of Isobel MacDonald that was delaying the Englishman putting his hand into his well-lined pocket again. Isobel wanted the satisfaction of prolonging Jeannie's uncertainty, of playing task-mistress over her husband's wench for a few days. Well, it was a game two could play. Jeannie could be demure and compliant. It was the Englishman she had to impress, not Isobel.

Her day's chores were not so burdensome as those she'd been accustomed to among her own people. She washed a few pans and polished the fire-irons, prepared vegetables, sought herbs and drew water. There were no cattle to drive down from the head-dyke, no weary hoeing of the ridges of oats and bere, no heavy creels of soil to carry to the upper slopes to replace that continually washed down by the rains.

The MacDonell women, she new, would be scouring the damp highlands for every remnant of grass, to be stored for winter fodder and to supplement the cattle's scant natural pasture. If the season was severe, many animals would die, and the weak and starving survivors would require to be carried from the byres in the spring.

When her indoor tasks were done, Jeannie brought the horses in from the meadow. They were fine, big-boned beasts, a far cry from the shaggy Highland shelties that pulled the ploughs, hauled timber and carried pack-goods, and were almost the only form of transportation north of Stirling. These tall, bay horses had never experienced a Highland winter, and the Englishman would need to find oats and hay if they were to keep their condition.

She stood for several moments, rubbing their velvet noses and then, in the dusk, went to the burn. If the Englishman was impressed by well-washed women, then Jeannie would wash — a rare proceeding. The water was icy, but she stripped to her skin and, with a filched fragment of soap, knuckled herself vigorously until she ached. Then, wringing the water from her hair, she resumed her clothes and, shivering, returned to the cottage.

When she entered, Thomas was standing triumphantly on his feet, in mid-floor. It had taken him almost an hour, with the help of a remonstrating Isobel, to strap the light cradle to his right leg, edge gingerly from the litter, and finally raise himself. He needed the support of a chair in overcoming a few seconds of vertigo, but he was erect, and determined to stay so. It was plain that his leg had knitted, and should grow stronger daily. He tested it gently — very gently. Aye, he'd be hobbling with a stick for a while, and he'd not manage a horse yet, but he was finished with lying on that festerin' fitter —

'Goddam!' he said blithely, and laughed. 'Goddam!'

Jeannie MacDonell waited for the Englishman to take notice of her, but he was far too absorbed to give her more than a brief, unseeing glance. 'A London bone-setter couldn't have done better,' he boasted, grinning. He swayed dangerously, and Isobel, with an anxious gasp, ran to give him support, but he waved her away. 'You're forbidden, woman! I'll stand or fall on my own two legs, dammit —!' He was jaunty with delight, and the ignored Jeannie pouted resentfully. Didn't anyone realise that she'd washed herself from head to foot in the freezing burn — and that she was as scrubbed-clean as Isobel?

She looked at Isobel, then paused. Isobel's eyes were on the Englishman, her expression a mixture of concern, tenderness and affection. She was slightly flushed, with her hands tightly clenched and her lips apart, unaware of anyone but Thomas. So that was it, Jeannie mused. That was it. Things were getting a little clearer. The proud Isobel was devoured by desire for the tall Englishman. She was hot for him — and he hadn't responded. Jeannie could have laughed.

It was a rich jest. Isobel MacDonald, daughter of Dundreggan, had been spurned by her husband in favour of a fifteen-year farm wench, and now she couldn't even rouse the appetite of an imported paramour. Jeannie did not know how the Englishman had reached Glen Moriston, but he'd shown no impatience to taste the delights of Isobel's chaste body. Well, it was likely that the Englishman was no different to other men — even if he did wash — no different to Ranald MacDonald. A strong, vigorous wench, with no niceties, would be more to his favour. Someone, say, like Jeannie MacDonell.

Thomas's thoughts, however, were far away from either Isobel MacDonald or Jeannie MacDonell. The resumption of his original assignment had now become a distinct possibility, and he must plan for it. He didn't believe all that Dundreggan had said, but there might be grains of truth in it, and it would be better to presume the worst. He could not contemplate, for the present, a ride of one hundred and fifty miles to Edinburgh and, anyway, the Pretender was reputedly marching on England.

Would he go for Carlisle, or into Northumberland for Newcastle? Thomas considered briefly the possibility of a cross-country ride to meet the Pretender's line of march, and then, as quickly, rejected it. He might be able to stand on his feet, but he hadn't walked yet and, as for Edinburgh, he'd certainly not ride a horse across some of the most gruelling terrain in Europe. Not yet.

What, fester it, was London doing? And de Courcy, and MacDonald of Edinburgh — and Patrick Campbell? The Pretender was balancing the hazards of a winter campaign against the advantages of a rapid southward swoop, calculated to recruit support from the English Jacobites, impress the French and throw consternation into Westminster.

But Westminster had had since late July to organise something better than Cope's force to oppose the rising. It was now October. There'd surely be battalions hurrying back from Flanders — and they'd be seasoned troops, with battle-trained artillery. They'd likely be led by the Captain-General himself, Duke William of Cumberland, who had been Colonel of Thomas's own 2nd Foot Guards only five years earlier. Cumberland was no Marlborough, but he was efficient, imperturbable, and uncommonly popular with the rank and file. He was a soldier's general, with a deal of plain good sense behind his podgy face. If Billy Cumberland couldn't come up to scratch, then there was nobody else likely to.

The healing of Thomas's leg threatened to multiply his problems rather than diminish them. Bed-ridden, there had been no advantage to be gained in speculating any course of action. Now, quite suddenly, he had to make some decision. With the two women abed in the loft, he lay staring into the darkness. He was, presumably, still a renegade in the eyes of the English, and barely tolerated by the Scots — with whom, except for Isobel, he had no desire to remain. And, aye, there was Isobel.

What was he to do about her? He was a damn' poor Lothario. Other men seemed to have the ability to sweep women off their feet, and did so without regard for inconvenient details such as a husband in the background. He, Thomas, had neither the experience nor the courage to make the first move in any affair of the heart. Twice he had repudiated Isobel, deterred by a mixture of mawkish decorum and callow fear; it was unlikely she'd offer him a third opportunity to insult her.

He was almost asleep. Tomorrow he'd walk a few paces — cautiously. He'd not put his weight onto his unsupported right leg for a week. Better a few wasted days than a relapse. In ten days he might try mounting a tethered horse. It was a pity the greys hadn't been exercised. They might be a little skittish —

In the loft, Isobel could feel the warmth of the stone chimney, a few inches from her. Sleep seemed impossible. Within reach Jamie breathed rhythmically, and nearer to the ladder was Jeannie MacDonell, invisible in the blackness.

Isobel's feelings towards the girl were an odd combination of repugnance and pity — and an unidentifiable fear. Jeannie might be easily seduced, but she was a contriving jade with less concern for her coming child, or even for the malignity of her family, than the possibility of easy money, and when she perceived that further guineas were not quickly forthcoming she might, in her desperation, resort to more spiteful means of exhortation.

And tonight Thomas had stood upright, free of his bindings, and she had seen the exultation in his face. The vision of his departure had suddenly ceased to be vague; it was a tangible thing, inexorably nearer. He'd not walk more than a few paces, and he'd not ride yet, but he was independent, now, of the score of trivial tasks she had done for him daily — that she wanted to do, because there was no other man she wanted to serve. Each day he would grow stronger and less aware of the need for her. And then, one day, she would see him no more.

What did a woman do — already married to a man who only disgusted her — when she met another to whom she'd willingly give herself at the merest beckon of a finger? Her desire for Thomas was shameless, but far deeper than just animal carnality. She had, for brief moments, entertained a glowing dream of being Mistress Margery in fact, of long years of being his wife, of bearing his sons — but it was only a dream, a ridiculous fantasy. He was an Englishman, and she was the wife of Ranald MacDonald. A husband's infidelity didn't make his wife any less married.

It didn't matter, now, whether a Stuart James or a Hanoverian George sat on a throne in distant, mythical London. She couldn't understand why she'd ever thought it did. What mattered was that, in a short time, Thomas would be gone. He might be killed on some meaningless battlefield, or he might return to his England, where he'd quickly forget a copper-haired Glengarry girl who, at a word from him, would have been tempted to abandon her husband, her glen, and Scotland, to follow him anywhere.

Her eyes were closing — then she wrenched herself into wakefulness. A few feet away from her, she was certain, Jeannie MacDonell had climbed to her feet from her mattress. Isobel could see nothing in the darkness, but she felt the boards beneath her tremble lightly, heard a soft footstep, and then the creak of the ladder. She lay unmoving, puzzled. Where was Jeannie going so stealthily? Below the ladder was only Thomas, abed —

There was a long, inexplicable silence. Isobel raised herself. Had she been mistaken?

Then, from below, she heard the cautious murmur of a voice. There was another pause, followed by a surprised ejaculation. It was Thomas.

''Od's blood! What —?' Jeannie's wheedling response was drowned by a torrent of rabid oaths. 'Goddam —! I don't understand festerin' Gaelic, but whores are the same in any plaguy language! You're damn' mistaken if you suppose I'd relish a fifteen-years slut, and if you don't take your bawdy carcass off my 'Od-rotting bed, I'll kick it off — pregnant or no!'

In the loft, Isobel turned back to her pillow, laughing soundlessly.

Chapter 17

November came in with worsening weather, initiated by a clammy blanket of mist — the 'haar' — drifting eastward from the Moray Firth, drenching the thatch and the rough stones, packed with earth and clay, of the cottars' hovels, and glazing the heather with wetness. If the coming season proved hard, both thatch and the straw from the beds might be fed to the cattle, and the bairns must sleep cold. No wheeled vehicle — rare at any time — would negotiate the roads before spring, and all loads must be conveyed in creels on the backs of ponies or women.

November was the month of speculation. The peat had been stacked, and oatmeal stowed in the driest corner — to be stringently rationed. Even in the most fertile areas the crop yield would not support a man and his family above six weeks, or at the most eight, and none would have meat oftener than once a week, on Sundays. Some fish might be caught, and there were nettles to be pulled and boiled, and there'd be hungry refugees from the Buchan heights where, during the famine of only four years earlier, thirteen out of sixteen families in one township had died from starvation.

The swirling haar was followed by sleet, slashing into the tangled broom and churning the roads to morasses. In their flimsy shelters the cottars crouched, protected from the elements only by a roof of turf laid with straw or heather, dripping water onto the open fire which, in turn, choked the interior with smoke. But there were embankments to be raised along the weak places of the river, slaughtered surplus livestock to be salted down before the meat putrified, candles to be made, wool clippings spun and, daily, the remaining cattle to be tended. It might well be a hard winter, the old ones said. How would the braw laddies fare that had marched with Prince Charlie into England?

The braw laddies, now numbering more than 5,000, were faring only indifferently. They had taken Carlisle easily enough, and had tramped unopposed across the fells — the marches that in preceding centuries had bitterly defended the Border against the Scots. At Penrith they crossed into Westmorland, with not a redcoat seen, and then on to Kendal. If they encountered no resistance, nor did they meet any cheers or waving scarves, and not a single Englishman had joined the column. Well, it was Border country, with an inborn distrust of the Scots and, once clear of it, the recruits would come in by their hundreds. These were early days.

They had marched on, in intermittent rain, past the tower of Sizergh Castle, to Lancaster, to be met by stony faces and still no volunteers. In Preston, southward still, three had come forward — an Englishman and two Welshmen. It was disconcerting. Since leaving Edinburgh less than four weeks before, a thousand rebels had deserted the Pretender. Winter was coming to the Highlands, and the crofts and farmsteads had been drained of men. How would the women and the old folk fare, with the livestock to maintain, the food to eke out until spring, and the constant hazard of lawless reavers? England was a bonnie country, right enough, and the Prince a fine-talking laddie, but neither compensated for starving bairns and plundered homes in the far distant glens.

Manchester, of course, would be the turning point. Manchester was the biggest town on their route, and would likely raise fifteen hundred — or even two thousand — stout fellows for the Stuart cause. The bells of old St. Mary's were ordered to ring out a welcome to the bedraggled banners of the clans and the small cavalcade of field guns and waggons. To be sure, there were volunteers in Manchester — two hundred shabby kerns, unarmed and penniless, who might have joined any venture that promised them subsistence. It was not enough.

It was not enough. The forces of the Crown were beginning to close in. One army, under the old Marshal, George Wade, was descending slowly from the vicinity of Newcastle while, more ominously, a second under the Duke of Cumberland, and outnumbering the rebels by two to one, was as near as Stafford. Yet a third was rumoured to be mustering near London, and the hopes of the Pretender's cause, for days sinking, had now become forlorn. The English Jacobites, curse them, had not risen in their thousands. England, it seemed, was not yearning for the return of the Stuarts, nor — mortifying though it might be — did it desire to be freed from the tyranny of King George.

The news from Scotland was of mixed quality. Edinburgh had been retaken by the English, and Inverness held, but at Perth rebel reinforcements now numbered almost four thousand, including 750 Scots and Irish regular troops in the French service. To the disillusioned chiefs in Manchester there was only one unpalatable solution. They must retreat on Scotland before the jaws of the English trap closed around them. The Highlands, at least, wanted a Stuart.

As a final act of defiance, the clansmen tramped on through Macclesfield to Derby, with Cumberland's picquets now only thirty miles away. It was the nearest that Charles Edward was ever to get to his family's lost throne at Westminster. Two days later the straggling column of ragged clansmen turned northward. It was raining from a sullen sky, and the townspeople jeered.

It was the same road over which they had confidently advanced only a few days earlier, but now there were differences. The rain was freezing under their feet, and many of the men's footwear was in a deplorable state. Many were frustrated and angry, swearing that no Englishman had stood against them, yet here they were running for Scotland like birched schoolboys. 'Wha's ye' braw red-coots the noo?' they shouted at their scoffers, who replied with flung clods and oaths. Cumberland's redcoats, indeed, were snapping at their heels, and old Wade might still cut them off from the Border. Bands of local militia-men dogged the column, albeit at a respectful distance, and stragglers were being attacked.

Discipline, never of a high order, was deteriorating rapidly. Soaked, cold and tired, the column reached and departed Manchester, narrowly avoiding open conflict with the roused townspeople. Shots were fired, and houses, shops and stables looted. With their heads lowered against the stinging, icy weather, the clansmen tramped on. There was something wrong when proud Clan Chattan, Cameron and MacDonald had to turn their backs on milksop Sassenachs. Preston, on the rain-stippled Ribble, was behind them, and they were among the sodden Lancashire hills with the road like a crumpled brown ribbon winding to the leaden northern sky.

The mud of Lancashire was repeated by the tangled fells of Westmorland, and the ammunition and provender waggons were repeatedly foundering. Far in advance of the main body a party of Highland horse had been halted in its tracks by milksop Sassenach militia and sent scuttling back while, behind, Cumberland's men, exhausted by continuous forced marching, were still straining to close the gap. The rain still fell, and the fat English sheep that had earlier grazed the moors had been driven beyond reach.

The Highland rearguard, struggling with the stubborn waggons, were still ten miles short of the Eamont river — the Cumberland bounds — when the first English dragoons had been sighted on the road to the southward. They had closed the gap at last, and were no less weary and wet than the Highlanders. Four clan regiments fought a confused night skirmish with three dragoon regiments around the terrified village of Clifton, with the dismounted redcoats giving as good as they received before retiring in good order. The Highlanders, not anxious to be embroiled in rearguard actions which achieved nothing except casualties they could afford less than the English, fell back on Penrith, streaming across the Eamont as the main column moved off towards Carlisle.

Five miles back, Bland's, Kerr's and Cobham's Dragoons stood at the heads of their steaming horses. It had been a long chase, and they had just lost. Nothing, now, could prevent the Pretender from regaining the Border and joining with his reinforcements — but Billy Cumberland would have the last word before losing touch with Charlie Stuart.

And Billy Cumberland did. Before departing Carlisle, the Pretender garrisoned the town with four hundred men — including a hundred of the English riff-raff that had joined in Manchester. Carlisle Castle, claimed the Prince, would remain a Stuart bastion on English soil, and Cumberland was incapable of reducing it. His decision was a death sentence for the ill-chosen four hundred. Ten days later the 18-pounders of Brevet-Colonel William Belford, Cumberland's artillery commander, tore the castle defences to pieces, and the garrison surrendered to captivity and subsequent execution.

Chapter 18

The Great Glen, which cleft through the mountains from Inverness to Fort William, was deep with snow, and a bitter north-east wind had persisted for days. The roads that General Wade had built ten years ago, following the strung lochs from end to end, allowed tolerable travel if they could be reached, but Glen Urquhart, Moriston and Garry were choked, and the pinched packman with his laden ponies set his boots to steam by the fire, gulped at a bowl of hot broth, and swore there must be easier ways of earning honest pence than this fool's labour.

Prices in Inverness, he said, were the highest since the famine, but he'd not cheated the old Laird — being, as he said, an honest man. He'd brought oatmeal, salt, dried beef, bacon, hard fish, cheese, butter, and a sugar loaf. Eggs were unobtainable. At great difficulty, however, he had conveyed a few extras — brawn and smoked ham, some claret from Dundee, a bolt of fine Aberdeen linen, black powder, needles, thread, buttons and combs. They were luxuries in these times, of course, and — he shrugged apologetically — would cost accordingly.

To Thomas, free now of all bindings and walking well with the aid of a stick, the man's most valuable commodity was news, of which he had been starved for weeks. He was sufficiently recovered now, he calculated, to sit a horse. He had taken his pistols down to the burn for practice, and his marksmanship was as sure as ever — as good as Sir John de Courcy's — and he had exercised his sword wrist until it ached with fatigue, cut whins and broom for kindling, and carried water. The Yorkshires had lost some of their English fat, but they were hale and impatient, and their saddlery had been checked a dozen times. His boots were greased, his sword honed and shot wallet filled. He was ready to leave.

Thomas, however, had been given no knowledge of the progress of the rising since Robert of Dundreggan's departure for Edinburgh. Even when the weather had not discouraged movement within the Glen, the local people had pointedly avoided the MacDonald cottage. Thomas had seen a distant string of black cattle being driven in from the sheilings towards the Inverwick housings, with several drovers on shaggy ponies, and occasionally he'd seen women, bowed under creels, seeking the last of the thin grass before winter's grip finally tightened, but none had approached. There were gulls driven inland from the Moray Firth, crows and pigeons — and he'd seen the tracks of fox and red deer in the snow — but nothing else. The Glen was white, vast and silent. A cricket chirped behind the hearth, which young Jamie sought but could never find, and the days and the nights passed.

Jeannie MacDonell, seven months pregnant and, like her companions, confined by the inclement weather to the immediate vicinity of the cottage, was morose and uncommunicative, seemingly resigned to the uncomfortable truth that there were no more guineas forthcoming from the odd Englishman. She had made no overtures since the rejection of her first and, logically, had seen no further use for soap and water. Despite her increasing slovenliness, she was healthy enough, and her advancing condition gave her little concern. Twice she had listened to the panting of her own mother behind a tattered blanket hung from the beams, while her father had sat by the fire, waiting for the business to be finished so that he could eat. There was naught wonderful about another bairn, another mouth to provide for.

Only Isobel was grateful for the snowfall. She could not recall one so heavy in Glen Moriston, but it would surely delay Thomas's leaving, and discourage the punitive measures of the Reverend John Grant. They had heard nothing more of the Minister — but he would not have forgotten.

The packman had news in plenty. News was a stock-in-trade scarce less welcome among the scattered crofts than the mixed wares he carried on his shelties. Aye, the Prince and his clansmen had driven deep into England, taking Carlisle and Manchester, and reaching as far as Derby without challenge, before retiring again on the Border. Likely he could have taken London had he so chose, with the redcoats running before him like sheep. True, the English towns had been relinquished, with four hundred men lost at Carlisle, but the Prince had marched into Glasgow with pipes playing on Christmas Day —

'Christmas Day!' Thomas stared. 'What day is it now?'

'It's January. The 10th or 11th —'

Christmas Day, b'God, had gone — and he hadn't known it! In London there would have been masques, and the guilds' banquets, dancing and music, the houses decorated with flowers and lamps burning throughout the night. The tables of the gentry would have groaned under their burdens of beef and capons, great pies of pigeons, eels and veal, and the streets would have rocked to the pealing of church bells —

But the packman was continuing. There was much talk of impending French landings, and the Duke of Cumberland, who had commanded the redcoat forces in the north of England, had been recalled, being replaced by one Hawley. Meanwhile the Prince's army, camped about Stirling, had almost doubled its size since recrossing the Border, with Farquharsons, Frazers and Mackintoshes, and the French regulars —

'Is there no news of the men killed or taken by the English?' It was Isobel, her voice quiet.

'Och, aye, there've been laddies frae the army fleetin' back t'they fermtouns, for seeing the folk, and there's nae mony killit.' The man seemed unwilling to pursue the subject, but glanced suddenly at Jeannie MacDonell. 'I ken ye're the MacDonell lass, tha's been swearit lost. I see'd ye' brither, Alexander, not six days sin'.' His eyes took in jeannie's swollen belly, then he reached for his boots.

There was something about the man's demeanour that compelled Thomas to follow him out to his ponies, hock-deep in the snow, and it was plain that the other had hoped he might do so. Checking his loads, he spoke quickly to Thomas, 'I did'na care to say before, Englishman, but Ranald MacDonald is killit.'

Thomas sucked in his breath sharply. 'Killed? At Carlisle?'

'No, at Prestonpans, nigh four months sin'.' He stood upright, then pushed a folded scrap of paper into Thomas's hand. 'And there's this, frae a mon namit Campbell.' Finished, he gave a shout, and the roped ponies lurched forward. The packman did not look back.

The paper was creased and damp, its inked words smudged, with no address and no signature. 'If you are still in Glengarry country I hazard that you will soon be thinking of departure. There is time still for you to complete that which was begun, and I have it from McD. that the need still remains, tho' he does not know your whereabouts, for which you can be thankful. I have other business and cannot move. C will meet H and there may be another Prestonpans. You must therefore *join C* as soon as you are able.'

There was no questioning that the letter was from Patrick Campbell, the Crown agent, and the meaning was clear enough. 'McD' referred to MacDonald of Edinburgh. 'C' was Charles Edward, the Pretender, and 'H' meant Hawley, the English army's new commander. Almost anyone could have interpreted it — even the packman, if he could read. But likely the packman was safe, if Campbell had employed him.

So he, Thomas, was required to resume his attempt to assassinate the Pretender, and this time, presumably, before the anticipated collision with Hawley — before the arrival of another opportunity for the Prince to be taken. Thomas was becoming increasingly convinced that Sir John de Courcy's professed concern for the lives of thousands of clansmen was mere fabrication. Only the Pretender mattered. He could live triumphant, but he must die if defeated. There must be no captive Prince, no Stuart in the Tower awaiting trial, no executed martyr to join the other of a century earlier.

Thomas turned back to the cottage, thoughtful. And, b'God, there was the other matter. Ranald MacDonald was dead, and Isobel wasn't another man's wife any longer.

When he re-entered, Isobel's eyes met him immediately. 'You're going,' she said, flatly. From the hearth, Jeannie watched them both.

He nodded. 'Aye.' He must go, he decided, and this was not the moment to tell her she was a widow. It wasn't even a moment for considering that she could, one day, be his wife. It was unthinkable. He was committed to murdering Charles Stuart, an act that would earn him the vilification of all Scots — and many Englishmen — and for the rest of her life Isobel would curse the weeks she had spent in his company.

'When will you leave?' Isobel asked.

'Today.' He refrained from looking at her. Better today than tomorrow, or tonight he'd lay staring into the darkness, arguing with himself, and by dawn he might have weakened. It had to be today. He buckled his spurs to his boots, laid out his cloak, pistols and sword, then went to the byre to inspect the horses. There was little to choose between them, and he saddled one at random. There were no oats, but a bag of oatmeal on his crupper would suffice until he could find better. He turned to lead the horse from the byre, to find himself confronted by Isobel. He halted, a hand smoothing the animal's withers.

'Please,' she said. 'Take me with you.'

He was silent, stunned. Then, 'Take you —?'

She dropped her eyes. 'I know I'm shameless, and I don't care. You don't have to join the Prince. There are enough Scots to do his fighting, and it isn't your cause. Many of the clans themselves are not prepared to bleed for him, so why should you? If there is no safety for you in England — your Cambridgeshire — then let me take you to the far North, to the Summer Isles. There are Glengarry there — fisherfolk and distant kinsmen — simple people with no knowledge of kings and wars. They have nothing but their fishing, and a few sheep above the sea loch, but they live in peace, and they're content.' She lifted her head. 'And if you would have me — and Jamie — I swear I will be as faithful as any wife to you. I swear you'll forget the sin of it, and no man will take me from you. The name of Ranald MacDonald will never pass my lips from this moment. Jamie thinks much of you —' she was flushing, '— and if you wanted more sons —'

'Goddam —!' He almost choked, then raised his face to hers at last. He had no words to speak. She stood, her eyes wide, golden and pleading. She was his for the taking, if only he dared to reach out —

'I know,' she swallowed, 'there are fine ladies in London, and I don't compare —' Compare? Thomas raged. No, i'faith, she didn't compare. She'd be like a graceful swan among tawdry, scratching turkeys — a young queen among tinselled drabs. If she were his wife, he'd never allow her hair to be twisted into a mountain of curls and dulled with powder, nor her smooth cheeks marred by rouge and patches. He wanted her, desperately, as she was now — fresh, unspoiled, and very beautiful. He would want her, alone, in that long, shapeless shift that hid her completely, so that he could loosen the tapes at her shoulders and lower the gown gently over her breasts, her slim belly. It would fall to her feet, and she would stand watching him, her lips apart and red.

'Madam —' He shook his head miserably. 'Isobel — I'm honoured. 'Fore God, I'm honoured, but I don't deserve it. I'm not what you think I am — or what I've pretended to be. I'm a damn' fraud — an impostor. I'm not a Jacobite. When I came to Edinburgh —' He stopped.

'You had no intention of joining the Prince?' Isobel was momentarily perplexed, but she recovered quickly. 'It doesn't matter, don't you see? I had no right to assume that, because you were in Scotland, you had come to fight the Scots' battles. It doesn't matter.' She paused, then dropped her gaze. 'I've grown to love you. I knew it weeks ago, but I was afraid of what I knew. Then I began to think that you, too —' Her voice trailed.

'Aye,' he nodded. B'God, he'd had enough of false colours. If she knew, there'd be a finish to any feelings she had, or thought she had, for him. And if she did know, there was little she could do to stop him now. She'd be hurt, like anyone was hurt when a gangrenous limb was taken off by a surgeon's knife, but she'd recover. As for himself, his task was dirty enough without adding the exploitation of an innocent woman — any woman, but especially Isobel MacDonald.

'I'll tell you,' he said grimly, 'why I came to Scotland. I'll tell you why you rode with me from Edinburgh, why the MacGregors ambushed us, and who Patrick Campbell is. When I've told you —'

'No!' She had stiffened suddenly. 'I don't want to know. If it's something that —' She shook her head. 'I don't want to know. All I want is that you take Jamie and me to the North, to the Glengarry of the Summer Isles. We'll both be fugitives — I from a husband, and you from something that I don't want to know of. We can both forget. Nobody will ask where we came from, or why. No redcoats, no family-proud clansmen —'

Thomas stood in silence. Was it really possible that, in these whimsical Summer Isles of hers, he'd be beyond the long reach of Sir John de Courcy? Would Cumberland's dragoons never probe as far as the shores of the Minch? Or was there a Highland community in which nobody would sell an English renegade to the nearest garrison? Perhaps everything was possible, but there still remained the matter of the Pretender, the French — and the clansmen who were being manipulated by both. He, Thomas, was a soldier. His orders had been confirmed by Brigadier-General Lord John Avershaw — and had come from a still higher authority. At St. James's there were very few between Lord Avershaw and the King.

Aye, he could be happy enough among these fisher kinsmen of Isobel's. He remembered something of farming from his boyhood — although, i'faith, he'd ploughed the rich Margery acres behind a team of great shires, and never a thin, stone-clogged soil with a crofter's hand plough — the back-breaking caschrom. Even when his leg was strong, he knew, he would always walk with a limp and, although willing to try, it was unlikely that he could be a successful fisherman. With every dawn he would raise his eyes to the crest of the hills, wondering if, today, a file of dragoons would be descending through the heather, with their sabres and a rope, searching for a man who had betrayed.

'You'll not understand now,' he said slowly, 'and you'll suffer offence, but in two or three weeks you'll hear a story that will sweep across Scotland like a foul wind — a story that will raise a ferment in every chancellery in Europe. The name of Margery will be a stink in men's throats, English and Scots, for a hundred years. You'll detest the memory of every day, every minute, that you've known me — and you'll never confess it to your son. But you'll remember one thing — that I didn't steal the love of a woman who believed the lies of a Judas.'

It was not to be expected that she would understand. She watched, unspeaking, as he led the bay into the open, her face now drained of any emotion. She was incapable of associating him with a crime so enormous as the assassination of a royal prince. She'd speculate on his desertion from his regiment, perhaps the theft of the few guineas he'd had, and wonder why these things should justify his spurning of her. They didn't, and there must be a deeper reason — a disdain for the soliciting of an uncultivated Glengarry woman starved of a husband's attentions.

There was no further exchange of words. He buckled on his sword, tied his cloak tight to the neck, and put the well-oiled pistols into his saddle holsters. The horse was lively, its breath feathering in the cold air as it champed and fidgeted with impatience, but Thomas mounted, his stomach sickening. A few miles of hard going in the snow would take the edge from the animal's mettle. 'Sblood, the sooner he was gone, the better. He lifted his hat, ashamed to turn his head, then kicked the horse into motion.

The sky was the colour of clay, darkening to iron-grey to the westward, where the far mountains were only shadowy hummocks through a thin flurry of snowflakes. The glen stretched ahead, undulating white, vast, and forebodingly silent. Nothing moved.

He must make for Stirling first. Stirling was the bridle of the Highlands, and the Pretender and his advisors would know that they could never march safe in Scotland until the castle had been reduced, and without it the forts of the Chain would be isolated. With an army, now, of perhaps ten thousand, and anxious to re-establish himself in the

Lowlands before Hawley's arrival, the Prince would want the threat of Stirling removed from his rear.

The snowfall was thickening, and his hands were cold. He wished he had gloves. Beneath him, the horse was churning through the snow, its neck outstretched, stumbling occasionally into a drift shoulder-high, snorting. His route, he knew, was the reverse of that he had travelled with Isobel and Patrick Campbell months earlier, but the few landmarks he recalled as he lay on the litter were gone. Somewhere ahead, however, was Wade's road — surely not completely obscured — and the long stretch of Loch Ness. He could hardly miss both.

He had time, at least, to think. He'd not see Isobel MacDonald again, and that problem was resolved. How she would fare now, alone, he did not know — and, dammit, he mustn't allow the thought of her to distract him from his purpose. There must be no mistake this time. As soon as he reached the rebel army he'd ride directly for the Pretender's quarters. Since the foray across the Border there'd be more than a few speculating English adventurers among the Scots and, if he put a bold face to it, he'd pass unquestioned. At thirty paces or less the Pretender was a dead man. Four times out of five Thomas could hit a wine-cork on a wall at that range, and with two pistols he'd stake his life on it. He'd probably have to.

Having lost all measure of distance, he was riding the fringe of a forest of spruce, and the horse was struggling to mount rising ground. Thomas blew on his frozen fingers. He didn't recall trees as dense as these between Glen Moriston and the loch. There were the Guisachan and Balmacaan forests to the northward, but he couldn't have turned full circle. Southward lay the Glendoe and, further, the great Mamore, but both were considerably further than two or three hours of slow-paced riding. Still, fester it, if he continued southward he must eventually encounter one of the lochs of the Great Glen. It couldn't possibly be otherwise.

But it was otherwise. The gloom was deepening and the swirling snow increasing, until it was difficult to see more than a few yards ahead. His hands were numbed, his cloak and neck-cloth soaked, and his breeches were wet and cold against his thighs. The horse was still going gamely, but the animal's strength would be hard taxed by the hours of dragging snow. Was there no end to these climbing trees? He must be a thousand feet above the glen and, the further he climbed, the more he must descend to find the road. His eyes were stinging, and he cursed.

The penetrating cold and the snow driving into his face must have dulled his anticipation, for he was not prepared when the horse fell. The beast had stumbled a dozen times, but had recovered, blowing the snow from its nostrils as Thomas hauled up the plunging head with a bark of encouragement. This time it did not recover. Too late, Thomas threw his weight on the reins, but the bay was sprawling with hooves threshing viciously. Alarmed for his newly-healed leg, Thomas flung himself from the saddle, hands outflung. A moment later he was engulfed in a slough of choking snow.

He clawed himself free, dreading the flare of pain which would betray another fracture, but he was unhurt. Thankfully he pulled himself upright, looking for the horse, but for several moments he could see nothing through the white flurry. He shivered, and then swore. A yard from him the ground fell away abruptly to the floor of a wide gully, the brim bristling with snow-clogged broom and young spruce which had rendered it almost invisible. Thirty feet below, only just discernible, lay the half-buried horse, its legs splayed grotesquely and scrabbling helplessly to rise.

Thomas had seen too many ruined horses on the hunting field to have any illusions about the bay's condition. He lowered himself cautiously into the gully, took a pistol from his saddle, and put a ball through the beast's head. The horse sank, and in a few minutes its bulk would be hidden under the falling snow. Thomas unlaced his holsters, powder flask and shot wallet, then paused to consider.

This was a pretty pass, i'faith, and no mistake. He couldn't remain here, and the possibility of continuing afoot was beyond consideration. There was only one sensible alternative — of retracing his steps to the MacDonald cottage where there remained the second horse — but in the past few hours he could hardly have travelled less than seven or eight miles, and it was a formidable journey for an unmounted man. Still, the sooner he began, the better.

At first, progress was not as arduous as he had feared. His horse had trodden a channel through the snow that he could follow with reasonable ease, but this was becoming progressively obscured. The light, too, never very good, was failing further as evening approached. He would soon, he knew, be in complete darkness — and as completely lost. There was a temptation to find a sheltered cranny and wait for night to pass, but he knew this could prove fatal. He was no better clothed than he had been in September, and the cold was bitter. Better to keep moving, lost or no, than to lie under a bush until he was too frozen and stiff to stir.

He pushed on. He was using his suspect right leg circumspectly, which meant that his left was soon aching with fatigue. Under his cloak he thrust his hands into his arm-pits, but his boots were already sodden. It was cold. Damn' cold. And there was going to be several more hours of it. It was festerin' queer, wasn't it? Every effort he made to reach the Pretender seemed destined to be foiled. Well, he couldn't blame any human agency this time, unless it was himself.

B'God, it was cold. His earlier tracks had long disappeared, but he was descending steeply along the fringe of the forest of spruce, the trees' foliage drooping under an accumulation of snow, like draped ghosts in the darkness among which the wind cut like a knife. He clenched his teeth to prevent their chatter. 'S'blood, he had to stop thinking about the cold. He must distract himself — like a man biting on a bullet when a limb was hacked off by a surgeon. B'God —

Isobel MacDonald? No, not Isobel. Musketry, that was it. Musketry. He wiped away the frozen crust on his lips. The Crown musket had a forty-two inch barrel of three-quarter inch calibre, weighed eleven pounds and two ounces, and fired a ball weighing one and one-third ounces. A cartridge contained four and a half drams of black powder, two dozen to every cartouche pouch, to be inspected daily — B'God, it was cold. What was he doing on this damn' bleak mountainside? Who was responsible? De Courcy? Or Avershaw? Or the French? No. It was a festerin' family named Stuart, each succeeding representative of which seemed prepared to shed the blood of thousands to establish himself king of a country that didn't want him. It was fortunate for the English that the Stuarts' persistent bids for kingship had been ill-contrived, ill-timed, and usually ill-supported — but that hadn't saved thousands of good men from dying, on the Boyne, at Sheriffmuir — and a thousand more must die, Scots and English, before the latest Stuart visionary was put in his place. Would there be another, say in thirty years time, to drive brave young clansmen and foolish old chieftains to their deaths? De Courcy's remedy was the right one, b'God, even if his reasons were not. Goddam, but it was cold.

'Od perish the Stuarts. Musketry, that was it. The musket is carried on the left shoulder, the left hand on the butt end with the thumb four inches lower than the hollow. The arm is bent and carried close to the side, the lock turned upwards, so that the lower part of the butt is level with the middle of the body —

He was sprawled flat in the snow and wondering how he had got there. He didn't remember falling, nor how long he had lain. And it had ceased snowing. He had no particular desire to rise, and he was not sure he was capable of doing so. Every stitch he wore was soaked, and he could feel his holsters, slung about his neck, pressing uncomfortably against his chest. It would be easy enough to remain here. In a short time he would drift into unconsciousness, and that would be the end of it — the end of de Courcy's murder plan and, if nothing else, the name of Margery would stay clean.

Damn' odd, he mused, the value that people put on a military tradition. His father had been a dragoon sergeant under Marlborough, and great-grandfather Ralph had captained Cromwell's 13th Troop of Suffolk Horse. A Margery had fought at Flodden, and another had left his bones at Acre. It was damn' odd, but he supposed it meant something. Over the hearth of the Margery farmhouse there were two swords — his father's sabre and an old Spanish blade that his great-grandfather had acquired at the battle of Cheriton Wood. He had thought that his own might join them one day. Well, it wouldn't.

It was very quiet. Even the wind had dropped, and the trees too heavily laden with snow to rustle —

No, fester it — there was something. There was a faint noise that his numbed senses groped to recognise. It was water — splashing water. That was odd, too. Wouldn't all water be frozen? All water, that was, except a fiercely running torrent. A waterfall.

He raised his face. There was a waterfall in the burn — the Moriston river — only yards from the MacDonald cottage. He had listened to its incessant whisper for weeks. Goddam —

He had to get himself to his feet, and that was difficult with all feeling in his legs gone. It was easier to crawl, but still desperately laborious. Several times his arms buckled, tumbling him, cursing, but he was

157

making progress, foot by foot. Was it worth this agonising effort? How could he know that the rustling murmur of water was that of the Moriston? There were probably a dozen cascading rivulets in the glen, all of which would sound the same to a numbed, half-stupefied man. It would be easier, much easier, to lie here. He could think about musketry again. The Hanoverian musket, for instance, had a bore of eight-tenths of an inch —

But the noise of splashing water was nearer, and he had to be sure. Was it a contemptible trick of his stinging eyes, or was there — in the blackness ahead — a tiny glimmer of light? He wiped the wetness from his face with the palm of his hand. 'Od's blood — it was a light, a feeble lamp-glow that threw a dull reflection onto the snow. A light meant people, shelter, warmth. Warmth? Was it possible that he could know warmth again? Warmth was a glowing, crackling fire reaching for the chimney, the burn of brandy on the tongue, and rough, friendly blankets pulled to the chin. Warmth was the essence of life, the fuel of living. Coldness was death.

He could raise himself only to his elbows and no further. He groaned. Fifty yards away, perhaps only thirty, there was somebody — perhaps Isobel, perhaps some isolated cottar — and warmth, but he was defeated. He lacked even the strength to shout.

There was one thing left. He rolled onto his back, staring at the black void of the sky, then fumbled at a pistol holster. One of his pistols had been discharged, but the other was still loaded. He couldn't tell which. His fingers, devoid of any feeling, were almost useless in the tussle with the stiff, wet buckle, and he was near to weeping with frustration when, at last, his hand closed around the hard pistol-butt. If he had chosen the wrong gun, he'd not manage to free the other, that was festerin' certain. Or if the priming was damp —

Somehow his fingers seemed to be swollen to three times their normal thickness, yet weaker than an infant's but, grasping the gun with both hands, he found the trigger and squeezed, praying. The lock snapped, there was a flash that blinded him immediately, and the pistol roared and jumped. He let it fall to his chest and closed his eyes. That, Goddam, was that. If the people behind that distant light had heard, they'd either bar their door or they'd come looking.

How did anyone measure time with his eyes closed, lying on a frozen hillside, and near senseless? Well, if an infantryman could fire fifteen times every three and three-quarter minutes, that was one volley in fifteen seconds, wasn't it? Fifteen seconds, then. Load and prime your muskets. Wait. Blow off loose corns. Wait. Make ready. Wait. Present. Wait. Fire! That was fifteen seconds. And again. Load and prime your muskets —

'Od rot it. The third man of the front rank had dropped his musket in the snow. That'll earn the clumsy oaf six days in the black hole on bread and water. Take his name, Sergeant.

The Second Regiment of Foot Guards. Redcoats lined with blue, and brass buttons. Waistcoats lined yellow. Blue breeches and hose, hat with yellow worsted lace. The men's coats were getting damn' shabby. They should have been pre-shrunk, but they weren't. And his company was to parade at the Mansion House tomorrow —

Enough of that. Open your eyes, damn you, and look for that light again. Is it still there? Aye — there were two lights, with the second larger than the first. A door was open, then — and someone had heard. 'Od's blood — get to your feet, man. It's no credit to a damn' Guards officer to be laying on his back in the snow.

When Isobel reached him, he was on his knees, fighting determinedly but unsuccessfully to lift himself upright, caked with snow and his face a whitened mask. She would never have found him but for his movement in the darkness. She did not speak, but half dragged, half carried him towards the cottage, her own shift soaked with the wetness from him. Jeannie MacDonell's apprehensive eyes peered from the loft, and Isobel ordered her back to her bed, then laid Thomas full length before the fire.

She stripped him, one by one, of his sodden garments and, with a towel, scrubbed his chilled torso until the skin flushed. It was not the first time she had seen a half-frozen man brought down from the mountainside, and minutes were more important than modesty. She kneaded his hands and feet until her own hands ached and then, as he began to stir, put more logs on the fire followed by a skillet of beef broth. Only then did she unfasten her own drenched night-shift and ease it, clinging to her, over her head. Free of it, she was aware that Thomas had opened his eyes and was regarding her silently.

'Goddam,' he croaked. 'That's the most beautiful thing I've seen.'

The colour flooded into her face and she half turned from him, her hands rising to cover her breasts, but he shook his head. 'No.' He reached up, and she knelt to meet him. 'You came back,' she whispered. He drew her down beside him, and she lay tense for a few seconds, her eyes wide and frightened as a faun's as his appraising hands invited her yielding. There was a shameless yearning in her belly, and she wanted Thomas quickly, quickly. He lowered himself to her, and she arched, splaying, then gasped as, within her, the inthrust tongue of his loins burst like a monstrous flower, agonising, ecstatic. Her arms were tightly about him, and she pressed her lips savagely to his neck. 'The broth will burn,' she moaned.

Chapter 19

The next day neither referred to the events of the previous night. It was as if nothing had happened — nothing, that is, except that their relationship was immeasurably changed. The constraint and awkwardness that had always been a part of their exchanges had gone, to be replaced by a sense of mutual fulfilment, of intimacy shared — of each belonging to the other, finally and wholly. Jeannie MacDonell must have known, but they did not care. This, Thomas decided, is how it must feel to be newly wed. From the moment she had awakened in his embrace she had been radiantly lovely, contentedly demure, as he had never seen her before. The copper-gold hair he had caressed in the firelight was a lustrous aureole, brushed until it shone like burnished metal in the sun, and her eyes, when they met his, were confidently possessive, shouting, I love you, I love you, I love you, before they left him.

The muscles of his legs and arms were stiff and aching, but he seemed little else worse for his experience on the mountainside, and from outside the cottage came the sound of constantly dripping water. The snow was thawing rapidly, and already the brae was leprously mottled with great patches of bared, brown heather. If he had delayed his departure just one day he would not have foundered. He would have found Wade's road easily enough, and been clear to Stirling. But then, if he hadn't foundered, he wouldn't have returned to Isobel.

Jeannie MacDonell, advanced now in pregnancy, no longer went to the burn for water and, when Isobel lifted the yoked pails, Thomas followed her. At the river's bank she turned to him, smiling. 'I'd hoped you would steal a moment with me.' She stood on her toes to kiss him on the lips, then added, 'My love.'

'There's something I must tell you,' he said, gravely.

She surveyed him mischievously, her head to one side. 'That you've taken advantage of a simple Glengarry woman? Fie, why so melancholy, sir?' She wrinkled her nose prettily. 'I will give you a secret, Master Margery. I was beginning to despair that you'd never attempt it.'

Thomas drew a deep breath. 'No. There's something else. The packman — when he came — brought news of your husband, Ranald MacDonald.' She stiffened, her smile fading, and he went on, slowly. 'He was killed, near Prestonpans, almost four months ago.'

'Four months —?' She closed her eyes, her face suddenly drained of colour, and for a moment she swayed. 'Four months,' she repeated, 'and every night, before I slept, I've thought of the day that he'd return.' She gazed at the sombre, black waters of the burn, floating with fragments of melting ice. Thomas remained silent. He had known nothing of Ranald MacDonald beyond a few words spoken by the man's father in Edinburgh, months earlier — 'a quick-tempered rogue' — and his own resentment of him had been inspired solely by a desire for his wife.

'I don't know,' Isobel shook her head miserably, 'how I should feel. I hated him, but I'd not wish him dead. Is it shameful that I have no tears for Jamie's father? Why don't I weep — like other women weep when their menfolk have died?' She raised her eyes to him, appealing. 'I've seen them, when the lament was played at the burying, but they loved their men, didn't they? And if there's no love, a woman can honour a man, and not shrink from his bed. When a woman has never loved, or honoured, her man, and every day has dreaded his home-coming, is she shameless for not weeping at his death?' There was a gleam of watery sunshine through the tracery of leafless birches nearby and, far overhead, a dozen rooks were gyrating, screaking. Isobel's eyes were still on him. 'You must have known,' she resumed haltingly. 'Last night, you must have known, but you didn't know the Law.'

'The Law?'

'To possess the wife of another man is cuckoldry, but to possess one who is unmarried is to make her a wife. It's the Law. In the eyes of God and the Clan you have made me your wife.' She smiled wanly. 'But it's a price I shan't ask of you. You couldn't have known.'

They stood silently, gazing at each other. 'But if you insisted?' Thomas asked.

'If I insisted,' she said wistfully. 'I could go before the Chief and his Bladier. They would listen, then contend that we were in wedlock under the Law, and the Bard would remember it for the House of Dundreggan.' She paused. 'Then for hundreds of years the bards of the Glengarry would tell of Isobel MacDonald, who loved the tall Englishman from across the Border, and how they travelled to the far land of Coigach, beyond the great mountains, and were never seen again.'

Thomas drew a deep breath. 'And in Coigach there was born a new race of great warriors and comely maidens, straight of limb, and with hair more golden than the sun that sets behind the land of Skye. Would your bards sing that?'

This time her tears came, uncontrollable, as she came to him, her lips seeking his cheek. 'My love — yes. Yes.' She raised her wet face. 'If I please you.'

'Please me?' He choked. 'My oath —!' He halted, staring to the eastward. Then he eased Isobel from him gently. 'We have visitors,' he said.

On the shallow, churned track that led from the Black Cairn two men were approaching. One, black-garbed, sat astride a muddied pony, his lean legs almost trailing the ground. The other was a Highlander, his bared knees as mired as the pony's, with a claymore at his back and a long-barrelled flintlock in his hand. He was red-bearded, and his unruly hair fell to the plaid on his shoulders. Thomas experienced a sudden shock of consternation. The black-garbed one he recognised — the Reverend John Grant. But the Highlander? Could the packman have been mistaken or lying about Ranald MacDonald?

'It's Alexander MacDonell,' Isobel breathed, then added, 'Jeannie!'

Grant had reined, pointing, but not at Thomas and Isobel. At the door of the cottage stood Jeannie, and Alexander MacDonell gave an angry shout. Thomas walked forward. 'Goddam,' he muttered.

MacDonell whirled. 'Ah — is it the Englishman, then? And ye thought yesel' safe wi' the Whig pot-lickers holdin' Inverness, eh? Ye didna suppose a MacDonell wid dare the redcoats tae cut the throat of a whoremonger?' He glared at Jeannie, cringing at the door. 'Aye, I ken ye've a gey proud belly, lass — and when the time comes, the brat'll be left on the braeside. There'll be nae English blood to foul the MacDonell line.' He turned back to Thomas. 'But first we'll gi' the Englishman his due — a death rattle i' the throat.'

Thomas frowned. 'Whoremonger? There might be reasons for wanting to kill me, but whoring's not among them, i' faith —'

'He's a liar!' It was John Grant with finger pointing. 'He's an adulterer — and this house is cursed of God. Vengeance is Mine, saith the Lord — and now has Vengeance come with sword in hand!'

MacDonald's musket rose until Thomas could see its blackened muzzle, but now Isobel interrupted. 'If adultery is your reason for killing, then you'll need to kill twice. And who are you — a broken man — to judge the daughter of Dundreggan? There'll be a price to pay in MacDonell blood. Not a stone of your house will stand on another, not a rick left unburned, not a beast alive. The MacDonell women will live and die in widowhood —'

MacDonell laughed savagely. 'There's nae quarrel wi' ye, Mistress, and there's nae court-leet in a' Scotland that'd gi' the wyte for killin' an Englishman that made game wi' his sister — an' left her wi' a fashious bastard!'

'Sister?' Thomas and Isobel spoke simultaneously, then Thomas snorted. 'You mean Jeannie? Someone's lied to you, man. The damn' packman, I'll hazard.' He nodded at Jeannie, who had lowered herself, white-faced, to the door-stone. 'The girl's had shelter here and naught more. She'll tell you herself.'

MacDonell's musket had not wavered. 'Ye've a keel tongue, Englishman, but it'll nae save ye.' Without removing his eyes from Thomas he spoke rapidly, angrily, in Gaelic to Jeannie. The girl began to cry, and MacDonell swore at her impatiently. Jeannie's eyes flickered from Isobel to Thomas, and then to Grant. 'Sàsenahgh,' she whispered, then burst into self-righteous tears.

Isobel gave an indignant cry, and Thomas wheeled, astonished. Grant's jaw had dropped, but he recovered quickly. 'Did I not say so? Whoso diggeth a pit shall fall therein! And he that rolleth a stone, it will return upon him!'

'She's lying in her teeth!' Thomas spat. He stared at Grant. 'And that sanctimonious charlatan knows it —'

'Jeannie's lying,' Isobel affirmed. 'She's lying because she fears the Minister and his whipping, and she's ill-paid the kindness she's had under this roof. She was with child when she came, and the man you're seeking is dead. He was my husband, Ranald MacDonald.'

'Och, it's nae trouble to give name to a man that's deed — and ye' ain man, scarce cauld on the stanes,' MacDonell sneered, but there was a hint of uncertainty in his eyes. He knew of Ranald MacDonald's indiscretions; the man had boasted of them often enough. Still, an Englishman was an Englishman. He shook his head. 'Ye'll nae fule me, Mistress. This gun killed the man who made ye a widow, and it'll kill the man that dirtied a MacDonell woman.' His finger tightened on the trigger.

'No!' Isobel placed herself before MacDonell's levelled weapon. 'I've told you — you'll need to kill two, and that on the word of a fifteen-years wench?' She tossed her head contemptuously towards Jeannie, watching with wide-eyed awe. 'Dundreggan will ask more proof before the MacDonell clachan is safe from burning. There'll be murder for murder.'

'The girl has said the Sassenach!' Grant impeached spitefully. 'Is there another who could know better?'

MacDonell shot an uneasy glance at the Minister. The ranting old fool was right, but he didn't have to face a blood feud with Robert of Dundreggan — and it could come to that. And could his young whore of a sister be lying? True enough, if she swore that the Englishman had forced her yielding, she might engender more sympathy — even avoid the customary flogging. She was a canny wench.

But he couldn't give ground to the Englishman. There could be some unflattering interpretations, and the whole glen would know — not least through the medium of the Reverend John Grant. No, there was another way, and just as easy.

'D'ye have a sword, Englishman?'

'Aye.' Thomas nodded. His heart jumped.

MacDonell grinned. 'Then fetch it. I'll gi' ye a chance to save yesel'. There's nae murder in personal combat.' He tossed his musket to the ground and reached over his shoulder to pluck free his claymore.

Isobel made as if to protest again, but Thomas silenced her with a touch on her shoulder. 'That,' he murmured, 'is all I ask — and damn' more than I expected.' Grant's face had tautened, his eyes expectant. Thomas stepped past the crouched Jeannie into the cottage. His pistols were within reach, but he ignored them and took up his sword. He must think quickly. MacDonell's claymore was a heavy, vicious weapon, a double-edged blade two inches wide and a yard long, and a single blow from it could cleave a man's skull to the chin. At another time Thomas would have crossed steel with MacDonell with the confidence of a man who knows the superiority of tutored swordsmanship over the clumsy slashes of any clansman. Now, however, it was a little different. His newly-healed right leg was an ungainly burden, and he'd need to fight from his left, which meant retreat. He must allow MacDonell the initiative and wait for his mistake. And MacDonell might not make a mistake.

Thomas balanced his own sword thoughtfully in his hand. When he emerged from the cottage, MacDonell was making empty passes at the air, grunting. He had wrapped one end of his plaid firmly about his left arm and drawn the other between his legs. Isobel stood, motionless as stone, and Jeannie's tear-streaked face was resolutely lowered. Grant's eyes were half closed. Thomas glanced at the sky, tested the heather with a toe, and then nodded. His blade rose.

Sir John de Courcy might have been amused. Himself an accomplished swordsman, although stiffening during recent years, the old man had given Thomas his earliest lessons in the art of cut and thrust before consigning him to a Milanese fencing master of obscure character but an undeniable talent in the use of cold steel. Emelio Caracci had clucked his tongue sadly at Thomas's initial, unimaginative sword play, but several years of determined application in the Italian's sanded courtyard had earned him the envious respect of the London military. A sword was thirty-six inches long, Caracci was fond of saying, but it required only two to kill a man. Why be extravagant? *Tocarre*!

MacDonell threw back his head and laughed, then began to sing tauntingly. 'Heh, Johnnie Cope, hae ye had ye' fill? And are ye' redcoots ranning still?' Both laugh and song were a feint, designed to momentarily distract Thomas's attention, for the next second the Scot sprang forward, his claymore whirling. The ruse was too clumsy to deceive Thomas, but the violence of his opponent's assault sent him stumbling backwards. The two blades met with a clatter, and Thomas's fingers tingled with the impact, only the hilt saving his hand. He parried and withdrew, and MacDonell scowled. 'Dinna gang awa, Englishman. I've nae finished wi' ye.'

MacDonell's interpretation of combat was based solely on agility and strength. There was no finesse. He who struck first and hardest was invariably the victor; few men could withstand one devastating blow from a broadsword or a Lochaber axe. The principle had been well proven in clan skirmishes for hundreds of years, and more recently against ranks of dull-brained redcoats. It should have been good enough, MacDonell considered, for this gyte Englishman with his slender toy of a sword, but it hadn't been. Well, let the Englishman avoid this —

He flung himself forward again. His claymore scythed savagely, a steel whiplash, and no fey gowk of a Sassenach would parry it. But there was no shuddering jar to tell of shattered bone, no gratifying spatter of blood over his sword arm. The Englishman had swayed, just inches, and then his own blade flickered. MacDonell hissed, affronted, with his cheek laid open from mouth to ear.

'Ye mirkie de'il!' He was incensed. The Englishman was making a fool of him, and he'd carry the mark for everyone to laugh at. There was the salt taste of blood in his mouth and his cheek burned like fire. He'd make an end to it, by God —

The Englishman had circled, and MacDonell was facing into the sun. Aye, he was a gey canny dandiprat, this Englishman, sure enough. MacDonell's claymore rose high, and with every ounce of his strength he lunged. The Englishman's blade met his, almost delicately, licked over the basket-guard like a snake's tongue, then buried itself in his elbow. MacDonell bellowed, his sword falling from fingers as nerveless as dried sticks. He lurched backwards, but the other's weapon was at his throat, and he crouched, waiting for the thrust that would tear out his windpipe.

'Ye damn' buckeen!' MacDonell panted. 'Will ye finish it and done wi'? There'll be nae blood-guilt, and the Minister's ye' witness.'

'The Minister?' Thomas chuckled. 'I wouldn't trust that black shaman to count the pennies in a poor box.' He lowered his sword. 'No, man, there's no sense in killing — but there's one matter unfinished. You'll ask that wench the question you asked before, and you'll ask her where and when. Then, if you can count up to nine, you might decide she's a lying little bitch who near cost you your life.'

MacDonell stared at him, glanced swiftly at Grant, then turned again to Jeannie. He made a wild figure, with the blood from his slashed face matting his beard, and his voice was an ominous growl. Jeannie, wide-eyed and ashen, shrank back. She mouthed silently for several seconds, choked, and lapsed into whining Gaelic. MacDonell snarled, shouted an oath at the sky, and the girl cringed again.

'Ranald MacDonald,' MacDonell gritted. 'That struttin' brag-mouth?' He spat, then wiped the blood from his lips with the back of his hand. 'Ye're right, Englishman — though it clags the craw t' say it. Aye, she's a lying bawd, but she'll pay, tow'd to a hirdel —'

'Fester it, do you suppose that flogging a fifteen-years wench is going to set the matter right?' Thomas shook his head. 'If there's anything you owe me, man, it's this — that you'll take the girl in charity, and let her bear her child without hurt. If she hadn't been in fear of the consequences, nothing of this would have happened. And you're man enough to silence jeering tongues, I'll hazard. Dammit, she's your kin — '

'MacDonell — ye' gun!' There was a screech from Grant, pointing. 'Ye' ain gun's at ye' feet! Put a ball through his head, and there'll be nae talk o' blood-guilt. The Lord shall direct thy hand!'

MacDonell turned slowly. 'I've listened to ye' gyte blether, Minister, and it's earned me naught but a bluidy face an' a spit sword-arm. The Laird didna direct m' hand then, did He? I'll fight ony man, but I'll nae murder — for yesel' or the Laird.' He paused. 'Och, aye, we'll tak' the wench, and she'll sit on yon sheltie. Ye' legs are lang enow to walk.' He returned to Thomas. 'Ye ha' my word, Englishman. She'll come to nae hurt — nor the bairn — and I've nae quarrel wi' ye feyther.' He nodded at Grant. 'But ye'll ware yon kirkman. He gants hate for ye, and nae mistake.'

'There'll be a reckoning,' Grant seethed, but he tumbled from his saddle quickly enough as MacDonell stooped for his claymore, and watched sullenly as Jeannie, avoiding the gaze of Thomas and Isobel, took his place. MacDonell shrugged aside Isobel's offer to bind his wounds. They were naught, he said, that couldn't be mended by binding raw onion against them, and likely a dram or two of old whisky to slocken the throat. 'If it means anythin' to ye, Mistress, ye' man died well at Prestonpan'. It were better he did. Alive, he might ha' filled the glen wi' killing — your folk and mine — and all for an hour wi' a wench i' the heather.'

Thomas and Isobel watched the ill-assorted trio wend slowly away towards the Black Cairn and Inverwick — MacDonell leading the pony with Grant trailing, ankle deep in the half-melted snow. Isobel's hand sought that of Thomas. 'There was a moment when I thought I'd be widow again after one day wife.' She smiled up at him. 'And what, then, would the bards sing of the Summer Isles, in the fair land of Coigach?'

What, indeed? Thomas pondered. There was still the Pretender.

Chapter 20

He had left the cottage before dawn, but not before he had lain for almost an hour in the cold darkness, torn by indecision. It must be now, or not at all. His resolve had been stretched almost to breaking point, and tomorrow would be too late. Tomorrow he would ask her again about the Summer Isles, and the land of Coigach, and it would be too late.

For four days he had possessed a wife, and in a single moment he could choose to possess her for four years, or forty. It would be so easy. Coigach, or Skye, or by sea to Antrim. Would de Courcy pursue for ever? Or at all.

But he had left the cottage before the first light of dawn, while she still slept. She had stirred and murmured softly as he eased himself from the warmth of her, but she had not wakened. His weapons, cloak and saddlery were in the byre, deposited during the previous day deliberately to leave himself no trivial pretext for evading departure. His clothes were near to hand. He carried his boots, lifted the beam from the door as quietly as possible, then stepped softly into the damp night. For a long minute he stood motionless, listening, but he could hear nothing from within.

The glen had been drenched with moonlight, and silent. There was time, still, for him to change his mind. She was deep in sleep, and he could climb beside her again with, if necessary, a mumbled excuse that she'd have forgotten by morning. It would be easy.

Even when he led the horse from the byre, a hand over its nostrils, the reality of his leaving was oddly lacking. The snow had almost gone from the low ground, and the few remaining fragments clinging to clumps of whin were silvered by the moon. Well, it was now — or not at all. Which was it to be, man? The chilled fingers that tightened the bay's girths were not his, nor the foot he lifted to a stirrup. He was a coward, without the courage to tell her that Coigach was only a dream, that the weeks in Glen Moriston had been only a brief interlude of no meaning or value. So he had crept away in the night, choking back the shame of it. She would waken as the sun pushed its golden fingers through the casement, and she would feel for him, but his place would be empty and cold. Jamie, tumbling from the loft, would stand thumb in mouth, his eyes wide and questioning, and then she would find the empty byre.

On the high brae he reined, and looked back. He could see the cottage far below, isolated and tiny in the vast, hushed glen. It was a lonely place for a woman and a child.

When she did awaken, he'd be miles away, beyond the Great Glen, and this time there'd be no returning. Weeks might pass before the news of the Pretender's killing reached her. Then she would remember, and never again would she speak of the Summer Isles in the land of Coigach.

He drew his cloak tighter and kicked his horse on.

Chapter 21

It was a confused, ill-disciplined battle, fought in dusk and torrential rain, with both sides claiming victory, an empty claim on Hawley's part, since most of the English regiments had retreated from the field in disorder, leaving behind their baggage, and many of their tents, several standards and colours, and more than three hundred prisoners. The Pretender's staff, however, had little to be complacent about. When the English dragoons — Hamilton's, Cobham's and Ligonier's — had been flung back from the Highlanders' line, many of the Clanranald and Glengarry men had scattered jubilantly to plunder the bodies of the dead and wounded, while others wandered at will about the field, disorganised and achieving little. The teeming rain, too, had quickly rendered the clansmen's firearms useless. This was not a factor of too great importance, since few Highlanders were accustomed to using their muskets after the first volley, but threw them aside and resorted to claymore and axe. Still, three English regiments — Ligonier's, Price's and Barrel's — better served by their ready-made cartridges, had stood their ground stubbornly, their ordered musketry scything down the Highlanders in swathes. Scores of disheartened Scots fled the field, convinced that the battle was lost and, even when the redcoats had abandoned Falkirk and fallen back on the road to Linlithgow and Edinburgh, too few clansmen could be dragged from their pillaging activities for pursuit to be considered.

When Thomas reached Falkirk, the battle was four days past. The English had returned to Edinburgh to lick their wounds and prepare for the next move, while the rebels had trickled back to the sprawling camp at Bannockburn or to the sterile siege of Stirling Castle. Falkirk had recovered from the disquiet of a battle only a few hundred yards away, and the townpeople had already taken advantage of the spoils overlooked or scorned by the departing Highlanders. There were small boys bartering redcoats, belt and musket balls, and officers' chests lay smashed and rifled, with unwanted items strewn and trampled in the mud. The rising ground southward of the town was thickly scattered with the white, naked bodies of the dead, both English and Scots, abandoned now except by a few gypsies searching for the occasional finger-ring or locket overlooked by the clansmen and townspeople. They would lie there until the stink of putrefaction spurred the parish elders to order a pit to be dug for the corpses to be flung into and forgotten.

A number of dragoons' horses had been slaughtered for no other reason, it seemed, than spite against their erstwhile owners, while army victuals had found their way into every kitchen — salt beef, cheese, bread, and the flour intended for powdering the redcoats' heads, but which made a welcome supplement to the Scots' unvarying oatmeal drammach. There were family groups of sightseers from the surrounding villages, the women averting their eyes from the naked bodies on the hill as their menfolk talked knowingly of enfilade volleys, closing files and turning flanks. Nobody paid any attention to Thomas.

He rode over the hill to the bogland on the far side, but there was little to indicate the battle dispositions, and the many accounts to be had in Falkirk were as widely different as they were improbable. At a quiet place by the Glen Burn he dismounted and considered. Several things, at least, were apparent. Hawley had been given a drubbing, but he had retired, seemingly in reasonable order, on Edinburgh. That the rebels had failed to press home their advantage but had chosen to disperse on less important activities suggested either an ominous over-confidence or a disintegrating discipline. Either promised disaster. De Courcy had been right about the rebels so far, and he was likely to prove right to the end. The British Army might lose battles but it seldom lost a war. There was an odd inevitability about eventual victory that France, Spain, Holland and Bavaria had recognised with surprise and burned fingers — and the Pretender must be a fool if he thought himself any nearer Westminster than he had ever been. The English could afford to lose several battles, however humiliating. The Pretender dare not lose one.

He walked his horse back to the road, then westward along the line of the ditch and turf rampart of the old Roman wall. To his alarm he found himself riding the fringe of a chaotic jumble of tents and make-shift shelters, cooking fires and scattered piles of refuse. There were Highlanders everywhere, of every age and description — ragged, barefoot boys, gaunt and uncouth clansmen, sullen-faced greybeards and, here and there, a strutting dandy in velvet, lace and tartan kilt of crimson and green. There were no picquets or vedettes, no indication that an English army was hardly more than twenty-five miles away, and none gave Thomas more than a second glance as he passed within yards of the nearest group.

It still seemed incredible that a horde of such ignorant cut-throats could have twice put drilled regulars to flight. The air was thick with the smoke of mutton grilling over dozens of fires, of rotting meat garbage and shallow-dug midden pits. There were horse lines ahead, and he reined. Horses meant cavalry — of some kind — which suggested a higher quality than that of the unkempt clansmen behind him, and he needed news of the Pretender's whereabouts.

A few seconds later he realised that cavalry was a flattering title for the score of wasted animals which could not have made knackers' fare in a tinklers' horse market — and their owners, who seemed more numerous than their mounts. Sprawled or crouched, their weapons laid aside, several wore the grimy scarlet and knee-boots of Gardiner's Dragoons, but most were young men, conventionally attired, though weather-stained, with the air of honest breeding. Were it not for their cockades and occasional tartan sashes they might have passed in any English county for the sons of yeomen farmers and town merchants. As Thomas swung from his saddle a dozen pairs of eyes flickered enviously over his big Yorkshire. One, a willowy youth in a dusty, plum-coloured coat and grey English gaiters, rose to his feet with a sigh.

'You're neither the Duke o' Perth, nor Lord George Murray, so with a horse like that you must be newly arrived.'

'Aye,' Thomas agreed cautiously. 'But what's the horse to do with it?'

The other shook his head ruefully. 'Horseflesh is damnably scarce, friend. Priority's given to the Life Guards and Fitz-James's Horse — the pretty gentlemen from France. That's where the best of ours have gone, and where the rest of these shambling nags will go within a week or two.' He delivered an exaggerated bow. 'The Perthshire Horse, at your service, sir, and likely soon to be the Perthshire plaguy Foot.' Then he shook his fist angrily at the adjacent camp of the Highlanders. 'And a few days ago those ignorant savages butchered twenty or more good English cobs — for being English!'

Thomas was hungry, almost penniless, and the smell of the scorched mutton made his stomach writhe. 'I was thinking,' he said, 'of finding the Prince —'

The Scot laughed. 'Aye, you all do. You all think you have to offer your trusty blade to His Royal Highness in person — on your bended knee, eh? And the Prince will choke back his tears, put his royal hand on your shoulder and pledge you the eternal gratitude of the House o' Stuart!' He laughed again. 'You'll learn different, friend. But first, you've a famished look, and if your teeth can battle with yonder veteran tup, you're welcome. I'm Fergus MacDaniel, of Montrose.' He paused expectantly.

Thomas hesitated. 'Johnson,' he said. 'Thomas Johnson.' MacDaniel put his head to one side. 'Aye, well — all the Englishmen are Johnson, Smith or Roberts. It's plaguy odd, but it's your business, friend — and if the redcoats take you, you'll still hang whatever your name is.'

The Prince, Thomas learned, might be at Bannockburn, or Stirling, or anywhere else, but the despondent Perthshire Horse didn't know. Wherever he was, he'd be wining and dancing among the gentry, and there were more immediate problems for a troop of cavalry that mustered two men for each of its animals. And the Perthshires weren't alone in anticipating the indignity of being progressively unhorsed. Baggot's Hussars and Lord Pitsligo's were similarly damned in order that the bucks of the Prince's bodyguard be allowed to present a brave show. 'If you're wise,' MacDaniel advised, 'you'll not make yourselves conspicuous in the vicinity of the Prince's gentlemen — not, that is, if you want to stay mounted.'

It was imperative, Thomas agreed mentally, that he stayed mounted. To be horseless would not only considerably reduce his chances of killing the Pretender but almost certainly eliminate all possible hope of his own survival. The depleted Perthshire Horse could be most accommodating. In its company he must, sooner or later, come within reach of his quarry and, the deed done, none of these sorry hacks would gallop half a mile in pursuit. Moreover, if the Prince's bodyguard were remounted from the same source, there was little to fear from them either.

MacDaniel was eager to talk, recounting his departure from Montrose during October last, escorting the arms and supplies landed from two

French ships that had slipped through the Navy's net. He had furnished his own horse, a nineteenth birthday gift from his burgher father and now being ridden into the ground by a French popinjay of Fitz-James's — all of whom considered themselves officers and potential viscounts. Thomas listened with only one ear. His new companions showed little curiosity in his arrival among them, and it was probable that inexperience and over-confidence had dulled their suspicions of anyone not wearing a redcoat. There seemed nobody in authority, no duties, rations, fodder, no troop orders. Men came and went as they chose, drank ale or watered brandy, slept or sprawled — and swore about Fitz-James's. God help them, he mused, when Billy Cumberland's veterans — the men of Dettingen and Fontenoy — reached Scotland.

That night Thomas slept in the horse lines with his horse tethered to his spur leather — a precaution that MacDaniel suggested was hardly necessary. If Fitz-James's wanted the horse they didn't need to steal it. Thomas retorted that he, in turn, had no intention of being deprived of his horse by any method. The next day followed the same pattern of the first. There was an issue of the remaining ammunition bread from Hawley's waggons, but the Perthshire troopers had to forage for all additional supplies, including fodder — and fodder was desperately short in Falkirk. Local winter stocks had almost gone, and the Stirlingshire farmers, more concerned for their own cattle than for the plight of the rebels' horses, had a habit of spiriting away all feed reserves when the Scots foraging parties were abroad.

The youthful MacDaniel had attached himself to Thomas — and the Yorkshire bay — with an enthusiasm that was almost pathetic. Watching Thomas draw the charges from his pistols before cleaning them, he suddenly asked, 'Have you written a will, Master Johnson?'

'A will?' Thomas chuckled. 'That's another way of saying that, if I'm killed, you'd like the horse, eh?' He nodded. 'Aye, lad. There's nobody else to claim it.'

MacDaniel returned a rueful shrug. 'It's not that —' He looked wistfully at the bay. 'Well, when you've joined an army with your own horse and saddlery, expecting to be a damn' cavalier, and then find you're reduced to shanks's mare —' He paused, brightening. 'But if the bay's going to be mine — only if you're killed, o' course — I'll see it cared for, fed, watered, curried. I'll help forage.' He paused again, then suddenly pointed. 'Aye, and there's the man you were wanting to see, Master Johnson — the Prince, wi' Lord George and the Irishman, O'Sullivan.'

Thomas sprang to his feet, then cursed. His guns were drawn, his horse unsaddled and tethered, and only thirty yards away on the Bannockburn road was the man he had sought for six frustrating months — to kill. The Prince, slim-figured and ruddy-faced, was astride a handsome grey gelding, and sat well. He wore a Highland costume, with a white cockade in his velvet bonnet and a broad blue sash edged with gold. There was a sword at his waist with a basket hilt of silver. The thirty yards had narrowed to twenty, and Thomas could have put a ball through the young man's head with consummate ease.

Accompanying the Prince were several gentlemen and, behind them, a double file of mounted guards in blue coats lined with red. Hundreds of clansmen were on their feet, shouting and waving bonnets, and the Prince bowed in the saddle, his hand lifted. Aye, Thomas mused, just one pistol, and this damn' comedy would be laid in ruins. Fergus MacDaniel had moved hurriedly to stand futilely obscuring the Yorkshire, but the cavalcade had passed without pausing.

Thomas tossed down his empty pistols wearily, and then stared. A few yards behind the last of the trotting escort rode another horseman, a lean, sallow-faced man in a long, serge horse-cloak and a battered, black hat. It was Patrick Campbell, his eyes ranging lazily over the clansmen's tangled camp, the piles of refuse, the Perthshire's tethered horses. Thomas did not move. Campbell's eyes swept past him, halted, then jolted back, widening in surprise for a single second. Thomas gave him the merest nod before the other's gaze swept emptily beyond his head.

MacDaniel was occupied with the bay and, allowing a minute to pass, Thomas strolled with as casual an air as possible towards the Bannockburn road, kicking at the stones. On both sides was rising, open moorland, studded with clumps of gorse, and the Prince's company had already vanished beyond a bend. The road was empty.

He might have expected nothing else. Campbell, a Crown agent and probably even now engaged in spying, would not wish to be compromised in the middle of the rebel camp. Still, Thomas would have welcomed an exchange, however brief, with someone who was a link with MacDonald of Edinburgh, Sir John de Courcy, and everything that was reminiscent of a civilised, peaceful England. Campbell, for whatever motives, was an accomplice.

He was about to retrace his steps when Campbell's voice spoke from a shock of hawthorn a few feet away.

'I thought ye'd not resist the temptation, Master Margery. Ye'll never make a conspirator. No — don't turn ye round. Ye' leg's mended?'

'Aye, well enough,' Thomas replied to the deserted road.

'Then listen. Billy Cumberland will reach Edinburgh in the next day or two, and he'll be marching westward wi' horse, foot, and a regular artillery train. If I know Cumberland, he'll waste no time, and he means to make the clans pay for Prestonpans and Falkirk wi' bloody interest. Ye can see as well as I can the condition o' the rebels, and their time's running out fast. Lord George Murray knows it, and so do some of the chiefs. Today it was decided that the rebels would retreat northward into the Highlands, to refurbish and recruit.'

'Cumberland won't give them the chance, b'God,' Thomas said. 'Not now. He'll follow. As you said, Cumberland wastes no time.'

'Right. As well as the artillery, he's been reinforced with two battalions of infantry and three squadrons of dragoons. And there's another thing. The Navy has ships on both coasts — to stop the French getting in and to stop rebels getting out. Scotland's a net, and the Pretender is marching into it. Cumberland's going to pull the draw-string, fast and tight, but before he does, ye've got to be inside, because when the clans are finally cornered, the Pretender will abandon them, like his father and grandfather before him. Aye, mark my words. The Stuart hasn't been born who'll shed his blood for others. He'll be hunted down and, 'less he has wings, he'll be taken whether Cumberland wants it or not — and I'll wager Cumberland doesn't.'

'Nor King George.'

Campbell chuckled. 'Nor, for that matter, Patrick Campbell. There's more Scots than ye'd suppose, Master Margery — including a few of the titled gentlemen at Bannockburn — who'd be relieved to see the Stuarts finished and done wi'.'

There was a moment's silence between them, and then Thomas said, 'I'll do it as soon as I'm able — before Cumberland interferes.' He paused. 'And when it's done, what then?'

'Afterwards?' Campbell hesitated. 'It's a question o' circumstances. If ye get clear, I recommend ye strike westward, for Argyll — Glen Orchy say. Ye can lie low there as safely as anywhere in Scotland — which might mean nothing once the English are loose, but having a place in ye' mind is better than aimless wandering. Besides —' Thomas could sense his grin, '— Glen Orchy's not too far from Glen Moriston, if ye ever thought o' returning.' Before Thomas could reply, a lumpish leather purse fell damply into the mud at his feet. 'Ye'll need some victualling money. I'll charge it to MacDonald o' Edinburgh. He makes a rare profit among the clansmen wi' his English broadcloths. He's even dressed the Pretender's Lifeguards.' There was a slither of hooves and a final laugh, and Thomas turned, but Campbell was already spurring his horse away towards Bannockburn.

Part III - The Kill

Chapter 22

Everything was wrong. Everything.

The position was badly chosen, flat and exposed. The battle orders were those for yesterday, not today. The weather was unfavourable, with a strong wind and intermittent rain blowing directly into the clansmen's faces. The men were exhausted with marching, hungry, cold and wet. The Prince's advisers could not agree; they had been at logger-heads for hours, while the clansmen waited, shivering. Nobody had tested the ground over which, presumably, the clans were to advance. Nearly a thousand of the total of eight thousand Scots had failed to reach the field in time.

Everything, Thomas speculated, was festerin' wrong. If Cumberland himself had disposed the Pretender's forces, he could not have balanced matters more weightily in his own favour.

He could see over the muddled rebel line to where, five hundred yards beyond, stood the English — long, geometrical ribbons of scarlet and white under a leaden sky, motionless and silent except for a continuous, ominous rolling of regimental drums. There was a glittering ripple as the bayonets of the six battalions of the front leapt to their muskets with a crash that the Highlanders heard across the moor and then, once again, that unnatural silence that carried more foreboding than all the jeering shouts and chants, the skirling pipes, of the restless clansmen.

It wasn't just today. Things had begun to go wrong from the moment the clans had retreated from Falkirk. It was a march of which every stage seemed more confused than the previous one. Nobody seemed to know where they were going, or why. Men had deserted at every mile, artillery pieces and carts were abandoned, and the commissariat had foundered. There was no food or clothing, no money, remounts or fodder. The column, splintered into dozens of indisciplined groups, lurched through rain and snow towards the Highlands, herding into two divisions beyond Crieff. Thomas, with Fergus MacDaniel behind him, had followed the scarecrow cavalry on a circuitous, mud-spattered route towards Inverness, with every day the knowledge that, behind them,

Cumberland's redcoats were remorselessly following. At Inverness the surviving mounts of the Perthshire Horse had been requisitioned for the Pretender's Life Guards.

Thomas, at least, still had his bay, a fact he had reason to bless as he stared now across the wet expanse of Culloden Moor. He had never mustered with the Perthshires and, when the speculating eyes of French and Scottish gentlemen fell on the big Yorkshire, they also noted that Thomas had a hand on a pistol butt. He had been within feet of Lord George Murray on a score of occasions, and knew a dozen chieftains by sight, but of the Pretender he had seen nothing. Charles Edward, in his dainty Highland costume, was lisping his way through a series of soirées, dances and receptions, seemingly insensible to the worsening military situation and to the fortunes of thousands of half-starved clansmen struggling through the mountain passes with Cumberland in merciless pursuit. But Thomas could see the Pretender now.

The small throng of dismounted Perthshire Horse stood shivering on the uneven, rising ground behind the left of the rebel line. With other unhorsed cavalrymen — Baggot's Hussars — and two companies of Lowlanders, they formed almost the entire reserve strength of the army. Two hundred yards down the hill were the Irish and French contingents, part of the second line, and the same distance further spread the massed, jostling clansmen. To Thomas's right, however, along the ridge, flew the Stuart standard, around it gathered a dozen gentlemen, including the Pretender on his well-groomed grey. Thomas felt yet again for the locks of his pistols.

'Why don't we charge?' somebody asked plaintively, and it was a good question. The Highlanders sole battlefield tactic was a concerted, headlong rush against an enemy position, trusting to carry all before them by sheer weight and savagery. It had been successful at Prestonpans and Falkirk, and it was the only tactic which might conceivably be successful on Culloden Moor. That being so, there was no profit to be gained by waiting, growing colder and wetter, while Cumberland's artillerymen meticulously sighted their guns. The clansmen had never before received the attention of professional gunners, and they were likely to find it a chastening experience.

Thomas could visualise the scene in the redcoat lines across the moor. In anticipation of the day's fighting, the men would have had a better breakfast than usual — perhaps meat or cheese with their bread — and likely a tot of brandy. Cumberland knew the value of a full, warm belly. Like their enemy, they'd be wet and tired — they'd marched just as far — but the weather would be on their backs. At this moment the cornets of foot would be inspecting the men's ammunition and ramrods, while among the dragoons the farriers were making a last inspection of the horses. Between each of the first line battalions there'd be the encouraging presence of a pair of three-pounder pieces already, for certain, loaded, ready and waiting.

Sooner or later, Thomas calculated, one of two things must happen. Either the English would open fire, or the Highlanders would be ordered to charge. Whichever it was, all attention would be drawn to the battle-line, and that would be the moment for him to walk his horse towards the Prince. Who would notice a lone, walking horseman of the reserves when two armies were locked in murderous combat only hundreds of yards away? Fitz-James's and the Life Guards were a musket-shot's distance from the Pretender and his aides, and Thomas had few fears of their marksmanship or the quality of their horses. It seemed simple enough, and he had rehearsed it mentally a hundred times. One shot through the head, with the second pistol held ready. Then away, crouched low and spurring south-westward for the head of the big lochs. He'd be a mile away before any chase was started, and with any ordinary luck would have shaken it off by dusk —

Down the hill the soaked and famished clansmen were impatient for something to begin. This was a gey cauld place, with the rain turlin', to wait for some bauchlin' fool to gi' the word. Then it happened. One of the Highlanders manning the rebels' guns, frustrated, thrust his linstock at a touch-hole. There was a roar, and the first shot of the battle had been fired. The clansmen howled, throwing their sodden bonnets into the air. Something had happened at last.

The reply came almost immediately, brutally. There were puffballs of black smoke punctuating the English line, flattening in the rainy wind and rolling out across the moor. Thomas knew what they were and sucked in his breath, tensed. Seconds later the barrage of hurtling shot smashed into the clans. The Scots' shouting had suddenly lost its jubilance, and the Lowland reserves were crouching.

Below, the rebel line heaved, sighed, and then, with almost incredible swiftness, the English guns vomited again, the red points of flame only vaguely visible through the smoke crawling leprously towards the Scots. The rebel line heaved again, and the pipes had shrieked to a stunned silence. Now, Thomas thought. Now it's time. He could smell the powder smoke, and there were ashes in his mouth.

He dismounted. Better to lead the horse for a hundred paces, then mount again before he reached the Pretender. It would be even less conspicuous. He shouldered the bay around, casually, and MacDaniel, holding his hat on his head as though it might be blown away by the guns, glanced at him questioningly. The distant thunder of the cannonade was now almost continuous, with the English artillerymen firing and reloading with dedicated, rapid precision. In the dense ranks of the clansmen there was blood-spattered carnage, the Highlanders blaspheming, jostling. Crimson was mingling with the rain that slashed into the trampled, greasy heather, with men sprawled and crumpled, or crawling among the legs of their crazed fellows. Along the ridge, the horses of Fitz-James's were fidgeting, frightened, eyes rolling, and the Lowlanders, only yards away, were edging backwards, stumbling into each other.

There was a screech, and Thomas turned. The air was filled with flying clods and several Lowlanders were on the ground, contorting. MacDaniel was half bowed, tugging his hat over his ears, and there were men running. Thomas pulled at the horse, but the animal wrenched backwards, tearing the reins from his hand. MacDaniel, his face twisted with fear, shouted. 'B'Christ! The horse!'

The bay had fallen back helplessly on its haunches with ears flattened and teeth bared. Then it rolled sideways, coughing. A hind leg hung only by rags of flesh. MacDaniel fell to his knees, sobbing. 'The horse, b'Christ! The horse!' Thomas was near to retching. Avoiding the animal's snapping jaws, he plucked the nearest pistol from its holster, cocked it, and put a ball between the bay's eyes. Fester it, he was becoming a damn' proficient horse-killer. He swore, loudly and bitterly. MacDaniel, more concerned with the death of the horse than with the three sodden corpses only feet away, raised his fists to the teeming sky and shrilled profanities at the distant lines of redcoats. Thomas began reloading the pistol under his cloak.

That, fester it, was that. All hope of killing the Pretender *and* escaping with his own life had died with the horse. He had to have a horse. There was a stupid, childish doggerel running through his mind — '*For want of a horse a battle was lost; for want of a battle a kingdom was lost …*' This situation was just as ludicrous. He was standing two hundred yards from the Pretender with loaded pistols in his hands. De Courcy, if it were possible, would have offered him his entire string of Godolphin blood stock, Lord Avershaw his peerless Hessian mare — a gift from King George. Goddam, at a snap of his fingers he might have commanded any damn' horse in the royal stables, just to ride two hundred yards of soggy, Scottish moor.

Several of the English guns had raised their sights. There were spouts of muddy debris behind the French-uniformed Royal Scots, climbing towards the Pretender's standard where the Prince and his gentlemen sat their horses, and the smoke from both British and the few rebel pieces had already reached over the clans' line. MacDaniel pointed at the distant rebel cavalry, already almost obscured. 'Look at 'em. Sitting there like lords o' creation, on *our* horses.' He clutched again at his hat as a ball struck the earth in front of the cowering Lowlanders and spun high in the air. 'They're cavalry, aren't they? Not cherries on a plaguy cake? Aren't they supposed to charge enemy guns?' At another time the idea of the pitifully few, ill-mounted rebel horsemen charging anything would have caused Thomas to chuckle. Still, MacDaniel had said something. He, Thomas, wanted a horse — and Fitz-James's and the Life Guards had horses. If there were going to be any loose mounts they'd be among the rebel cavalry, not here behind the Lowland reserves.

For the moment, however, he found it impossible to drag his eyes from the smoke-wreathed massacre of the clan battle-line below him. He could see the Athollmen of the far right — their bedraggled banners still raised — the wild Camerons, Appin, Fraser and Macintosh, disordered now and torn by gaps festooned with dead and maimed. Nearer, and more distinctly, he could see Glengarry, Keppoch and Clanranald, the men still holding their ragged line, but many on their knees in the mud with targets and even plaids raised before their faces. Somewhere among them, Thomas realised, was Robert of Dundreggan, and likely Alexander MacDonell — and perhaps even the freckle-faced Alloa boy with his rusted claymore. What crass stupidity of the Pretender was keeping these defenceless clansmen standing before this murderous bombardment? 'Sblood — a half-wit could see that they must go forward or backward, anything but remain motionless while the English gunners tore them to bloody rags with insolent ease. And the watching ranks of redcoat infantry hadn't yet fired a shot.

Thomas's personal frustration was almost subordinate to a mounting anger at a situation that allowed a handful of titled, self-seeking gentry to drive thousands of simple-minded men to useless slaughter. There'd be bitter weeping among the crofts and clachans of the Scottish glens for today's black crime on rain-soaked Culloden Moor. B'God — and did the Bonnie Prince, on his fine grey horse, intend to fight and die among his loyal clansmen? The Stuart hasn't been born, Campbell had said, who'll shed his blood for others. Well, Thomas gritted, we'll festerin' see.

He flung his buckled holsters over his shoulder and pushed his way free of the thronged Scots. MacDaniel, misinterpreting his intentions, shouted, 'Johnson — it's not finished yet, man —!' but his remaining words were lost. Between Thomas and the Stuart standard, hung from a spruce pole, was a flat expanse of slippery moor, with the sky behind it so sullen that it was difficult to distinguish the hill crest. There were scattered men climbing away from the line, stooping, running, and then, careering pell-mell down the slope from the direction of the Pretender, a man on a horse. Thomas halted, tempted for a moment to hazard a shot, but the man was beyond reasonable range of a pistol — and, Godammit, there was murder enough here without him contributing to it. He turned his head as the rider plunged determinedly towards the shattered clan positions, then choked on an oath as a hurtling ball smashed the horseman's head from his shoulders. The horse, terrified, thundered on, with the blood-drenched, headless corpse sagging grotesquely from its saddle. A pistol shot, Thomas mused, might have been cleaner after all.

He had almost reached the lank-hanging, red and white standard, but now he could no longer see the Pretender. The hoof-trodden heather had been churned by several cannon-shot, and there were a number of men, both on foot and ahorse, including two officers in the blue coats faced with red of the French service. Beyond, through the smoke-haze, four ladies with skirts raised above their ankles, and accompanied by their harassed consorts, were scurrying for a closed coach halted in a sunken road that he had not known existed. Hereabouts, too, was a fresh scattering of dead, several pinned beneath mutilated horses that still kicked feebly. But there was no Pretender, no grey gelding. A youthful gentleman in a feathered bonnet and with his velvet coat spattered with mud was shouting at the increasing trickle of clansmen hurrying with lowered heads from the battle-line, but none heeded the lone, angry voice.

'Od's blood — where was the damn' Pretender? He'd left his standard, for certain. It was surely impossible that he had taken to his heels so early in the day? Aye, it was impossible. It was more likely that Campbell's prediction of the Pretender's behaviour was prejudiced and that the man had ridden down to share the straits of his clansmen. It was a gesture he owed them. From where he stood, Thomas could see the entire panorama of the battlefield, and he scanned the tumult below to catch a glimpse of the Prince, easily recognised by his distinctive horse and, it was probable, a mounted escort.

The rain, he was aware, had almost ceased and, as a flare of sunlight broke through the heavy cloud, the English gunners loaded grapeshot.

Cumberland's artillery commander had chosen his moment well. Bewildered and shaken by several minutes of crushing solid shot, the clansmen were now exposed to a murderous drenching of screeching pistol balls that slashed into their ranks, tearing down men in their dozens. All remnants of discipline had now gone. Many flung themselves on their faces, others reeled back to thrust a way through the equally demoralised second line, where a few, angered beyond control, ran blindly forward into the smoke to seek a reckoning with the guns, and to be brought down at leisure by the waiting redcoats.

Through the continuous, sullen roar of noise, Thomas did not hear the orders shouted, but he saw the whole Highland centre suddenly burst outwards, followed seconds later by the clans of the right. He stood, rooted, aghast at the savage spectacle of massed thousands of clansmen flooding across the empty, sodden expanse of moor that separated them for the English. Pipes were screaming crazily, and a great, sighing howl, of hate, frustration and relief rose from a tossing sea of plaids and bonnets, tangling claymores, scythe-blades and muskets, with bared, scrabbling legs churning and splashing through the soggy heather. Nothing, it seemed, would stand against the ungovernable fury, the sheer weight, of this massive charge. But as the wind plucked at the pall of powder-smoke Thomas could also see, far distant, the long lines of English infantry, firm and unmoving. He saw the front ranks fall to one knee and, battalion by battalion, the silver ripple of six thousand muskets coming to the shoulder.

*

When the three MacDonald regiments of the Highlanders' left — Glengarry, Keppoch and Clanranald — went forward across the moor, Robert of Dundreggan went with them. He had bared his sword and flung his plaid over his left shoulder, and ran with the young men until, his breath failing, he slowed to a dogged tramp. There was a scattering of others with him, older men, and those of less enthusiasm. Dundreggan waved them on, compelling himself to trot, his feet splashing through the waterlogged heather. Ahead, between the gaps in the mêlée of clansmen, he could see the long redcoat lines — Pulteney's and the Royals, although he could not have named them — and the waiting muskets, the sergeants with their shouldered spontoons, and several mounted officers.

He had survived the shrieking grapeshot, survived the first thunderous, point-blank musketry volley that scythed down the clansmen in swathes and halted the headlong MacDonald charge as though it had run into an iron wall. Dundreggan trotted on, avoiding the slumped and contorted dead, and the wounded who crawled and jerked in the ankle-deep water, and thrust through the clansmen reeling back from the van. Thirty yards away were the redcoats, loading, presenting and firing methodically into the massed confusion of thwarted Highlanders. A few of the Scots were firing back, but most had flung away their muskets and now surged backward and forward in the flame-pitted smoke, slashing futilely at the ranks of levelled bayonets, shouting, some even tearing up stones to throw at the enemy beyond their reach. The dead lay in piles.

But it was not an English bullet that brought down the white-haired Dundreggan. Of the twelve artillery pieces with which the rebels had begun the battle, all but one had been quickly silenced or abandoned. It was the remaining gun, on the extreme left flank of the rebel line, that fired its last, erratic shot at the enemy hardly visible through the smoke. The spinning ball flung Dundreggan into the mud, his back broken and his old snaphaunce musket unfired.

*

Alexander MacDonell, with his kilt pulled between his legs and frenzied with anger, had been in the forefront of the Glengarry when Pulteney's had fired the first, devastating volley that whirled away the MacDonald van like windblown chaff, and he found himself almost alone in the fog-like smoke. Prestonpans hadn't been like this. At Prestonpans the redcoat ranks had splintered and disintegrated under the weight of the charging clansmen, but here they were standing firm in drilled lines, the front kneeling, and the few desperate Scots who had come within claymore's reach of them had died on a hedge of bayonets. Morton was gone, and Bald Ewen, and young Cluny. They'd run forward with him, shouting, into the death-smoke, and they lay now among the hundreds in the wet heather, pitiful humps of sodden tartan, their shouting silenced.

Like scores of his fellows, MacDonell had thrown aside his musket for the last, heedless rush intended to flood over the cattle-like English, but which now was incredibly halted, baffled and helpless. He could see an English officer laughing, the confident redcoats with mouths blackened, tearing at their cartridges with their teeth, and yard by yard the clansmen around him were falling back, forced back by the hammer-blows of musket fire against which their claymores were useless. There were fresh shouts to MacDonell's left, and he whirled, panting, to find the remaining Glengarry streaming away in disorder with the swords of dragoons slashing at their heads. The anger within him choked his throat. He wanted desperately to fling himself on the grinning English, to slash and thrust, to tear with gouging hands, but he turned away, stumbling with a curse over the dead that strewed his path and with no backward glance. It was enough. Men were flesh and blood. He could hear cheering behind him, but they were English cheers, taunting, and the mighty MacDonald were broken. He flung his sword into the mud.

*

When the MacDonalds broke, young Fergus MacDaniel knew that the day was lost, and for the first time since he had left Montrose six months earlier he was genuinely frightened. He had never cared for the ragged, unkempt clansmen, but he regarded their fighting qualities with awe, and the possibility of them ever retreating in disorder from the same men they had thrashed at Prestonpans, and at least forced into withdrawal at Falkirk, had never remotely occurred to him.

There was very little awesome about the clansmen now. They were running, and scores had already reeled past the Perthshires' position with the Lowland reservists following suit. Below, the Irish infantrymen in the blue French uniforms were firing doggedly in an attempt to cover the flying MacDonalds, and on the distant right fighting was still raging as the Athollmen, Cameron and Appin hurled themselves against the English. The dragoons, however, were coming closer, fanning out as they rode, slashing with their sabres, among the Highlanders. MacDaniel, with fear gripping at his belly, began to run diagonally across the rear of what had been the second line, now largely dispersed. A party of horsemen was spurring across his path, and he recognised the Prince, hatless and tense-faced, and the Adjutant-General, O'Sullivan. It was finished, then. Finished.

He felt cheated. He'd done nothing of note at Falkirk, and little enough of anything except tramp endless miles through mud and cold. There had been no thunderous cavalry charges with swords high and the Prince's banner flying in the wind, no fine, jingling parades with the ladies blowing kisses, no captured English officers bowing as they presented their surrendered swords.

He glanced over his shoulder, then broke again into a shambling trot. Christ — he didn't want to die. He was only nineteen, and he wanted to be home in Montrose, to hear the evening bell of the Old Church, to watch the deft brown fingers of the women heckling the strikes of flax in his father's work-house. He wanted to see Glas Maol again, and drink forbidden whisky with the sailors from Riga and Rotterdam. He wanted to lie with a woman, and watch cockfights, and provoke the old men of the watch —

He heard the horse blowing behind him, and the splatter of hooves on the marshy ground, but little else. The big English dragoon from Nottingham leaned forward in his saddle and brought his sabre down with stunning force on MacDaniel's unprotected head. The boy's legs carried him on several yards before he pitched to the ground, out-spread, his skull shattered.

Chapter 23

Thomas, too, had caught sight of the Pretender, just at the moment when the Prince was turning his horse away from the fighting and, accompanied by two dozen gentlemen of Fitz-James's, spurring southward towards the track that led to Belvraid, a mile away. There was some jeering and raised fists, and the troopers of the escort were drawing their swords to clear a path through the hundreds of fugitives from the battle, stumbling in the same direction. Thomas dragged his pistols free and ran. It was just possible, he considered, that he might reach the road further on its route before the Pretender did. He recalled the sunken road. It had high banks, steep and slippery. He'd be able to see the Prince approaching while the escort wouldn't see him — and they'd never climb free of the road before he had been lost in the turmoil of flying clansmen. It was just possible. B'God, it had to be possible. A half mile away the rebel army was being ruthlessly slaughtered — and the killing wouldn't end on Culloden Moor. If the Pretender rode free he might, yet again, rally fighting men around him, and the whole senseless, murderous business would begin again. There could be another Culloden Moor, in Argyll, say, or Ross or Ayr — this year, or next, or in ten years time.

He threw a last glance over his shoulder. Cumberland had unleashed his dragoons. That meant that the clansmen were broken and the bloody pursuit was about to begin. There wasn't much time.

It was further to the road than he had thought, and the boggy turf so torn by hundreds of feet that progress was slow, but he could see the road now — a long, curving gully. It must join the better, Inverness road westward, but the Pretender would avoid Inverness, for certain. He'd strike beyond the lochs into the Aird country, and further, to the Fraser glens — a natural labrynth in which he could hide from searching redcoats for weeks. Alternatively, if some enterprising dragoon colonel moved a squadron quickly, the Pretender could still be taken before nightfall. There was a £30,000 reward for his capture, but there'd be some perplexed wig-scratching in Whitehall if another Monmouth were dragged to London.

Thomas dropped to his knees, twelve feet above the road, thronged with retreating rebels. Some, weaponless, ran in undisguised despair from the gunfire behind them, others marched stolidly, sulky-faced, with snarling oaths for the jostles of the more anxious. Filthy with mud, many near to collapse from weariness and weeks of privation, they streamed southward — clansmen, townsmen, ruined gentlemen, boys and white-haired elders, with here and there the ragged scarlet of an English deserter stumbling blindly from the certain penalty that followed treason.

There was a commotion on the road beyond his sight, but seconds later, above the heads of the press of fugitives, he saw a mounted officer of Fitz-James's in his French coat, sashed at the waist. Behind him followed ten or twelve troopers. Thomas rose on his knees and cocked both pistols. If he could be undisturbed for a few more seconds the whole business would be finished. He looked quickly in both directions and then, with an angry oath, whirled.

The wide, greasy moor behind him swarmed with running men intermingled with pursuing groups of dragoons, sabres hacking. The battleground was hidden by rising ground, but he could still hear distant musketry and, almost a mile distant, could smell the powder smoke from the English lines. Only forty yards away a man was stumbling through the clinging mud on failing legs, his strained face grey and frightened. Behind him a single redcoat cantered easily, unhurriedly savouring the moment, his sword raised. He leaned forward in his saddle, grinning, and his blade fell viciously. The running man sprawled with legs still jerking, his head blood-drenched.

Wrenching his horse around, the dragoon searched for another victim. His eyes fell on Thomas, still kneeling, and he hooted, kicking his horse on. Thomas rose to his feet slowly.

The man on the ground was MacDaniel — Thomas was certain. He stood waiting, motionless, with his hands at his sides until the approaching dragoon was almost upon him, then raised a pistol. The sudden horror in the redcoat's face was almost comical. He dragged on his reins desperately, throwing his horse into a rearing halt, its hooves slithering. Thomas's bullet struck him in the chest, just below his knotted neck-cloth. There was incredulity in his widened eyes, his open mouth, as he fell sideways with clawing hands outflung.

That, Thomas decided, was murder, and he could hang for it. He snorted. Goddam, enough had happened already to hang him six times over. There was something more important — the dragoon's horse, standing over its late rider. A well-fed cob, it carried the embroidered housings of Cobham's 10th Dragoons and a carbine in a brass-tipped bucket holster. No acquisition could have been more welcome at this moment. A redcoat sergeant was shouting, pointing, and a half dozen others of Cobham's had turned from their pursuit and were wheeling towards him. Thomas thrust his pistols into the waist of his breeches and swung into the saddle. His father, Adam Margery, had once been a dragoon, and had laughingly told him that the English horse never galloped. A redcoat trotted, and occasionally cantered — but ask him to gallop and he'd fall off. Well, likely disciplines hadn't changed since Trooper Adam Margery rode for Marlborough. This damn' dragoon horse was going to gallop.

He lashed with his heels. There was a rattle of pistol shots, but whether intended for him it was impossible to tell. On the road below the troopers of Fitz-James's had disappeared, but they could not have travelled far. His horse was responding well, and the dragoons, not yet in great number, might well decide that a single horseman was not worth a prolonged chase. He could see a clutter of cottages and farm buildings ahead — Balvraid — and he spurred towards them.

Balvraid, at the junction with the Inverness road, was a teeming ant-hill. Hundreds of rebels, fled from the lines during Cumberland's bombardment, had reached thus far before drawing breath and, not yet convinced that the comrades they had deserted on the field were defeated, lacking leadership and incapable of decision, milled aimlessly about the road and the few cottages. Many had stood in the front line — Farquharsons, Gordons, MacLachlans and MacLeans — and had turned away when the clans had surged forward to take their claymores to the English. Now some had regained their belligerence, stamping and swearing that they had been betrayed. Harassed officers, waving the swords they had declined to use earlier, shouted contradictory orders and were ignored. The mud was littered with trampled white cockades torn from bonnets.

There were Lowlanders, too — Edinburgh apprentices and labourers, Dundee weavers and Glasgow vagrants, ill-armed and apprehensive, wishing themselves a thousand miles from Culloden Moor, but preferring the safety of numbers to the uncertainties of the forests and mountains southward. Who knew if the clans had been beaten? None of them, they vowed, would have run if the others hadn't.

Of the Pretender there was no sign. A few claimed to have seen him, but predictions of his intentions were confused. He would have crossed the Nairn river at Faillie, one suggested. No, a second claimed — he'd make a stand at Inverness, to be sure, because he had the army's money, of which Thomas failed to see the relevance. A third affirmed authoritatively that the Prince would retire through Ruthven and Glen Mor, where he would be joined by reinforcements — of a nature unspecified. Any further debate was terminated by distant shouts of 'Dragoons!' and Thomas turned his horse away from the chaos of the Inverness road towards the Nairn.

What now, B'God? The Pretender and a sizeable escort couldn't simply dissolve into nothing, but there was a wide choice of directions he might have taken, and every irretrievable mile could be taking him further from his quarry. There was one certainty at.least. The Prince must be riding in a generally southward direction until he faced the choice of passing to the northward or southward of Loch Ness — a twenty-five mile barrier. There were Frasers on both sides but, if he were the Pretender, Thomas calculated, he'd make for Castle Dounie, the lair of old Lord Lovat on the Beauly Firth and the gateway to the vast wilderness of the far North, where a small army could vanish from the ken of man. That was it. He had to decide one way or the other. He pulled his horse around in the direction of the Ness river and the setting sun.

*

It was a bleak, lonely journey. He rode across the desolate Aird, guided only by instinct, until he reached the sands of Beauly Firth to look down on a foreshore peopled by grey seals and lamenting gulls. Across the wind-rippled water, northward, lay the isthmus of Black Isle, and Cromarty. There was a tang of bog-myrtle in the air, and he had glimpsed red and roe-deer, an eagle like a floating black cross against the sky, pine marten and fox, but he saw no man until he descended to the cultivated fields and little white-washed houses beyond Kirkhill. He could smell peat smoke again.

He was not the first with the news. There had been others, swifter, before him — native Frasers, men of the Chisholm, and Mackenzies homing to their far, western forests. The crofters and cottars of Kirkhill and Beauly watched with worried eyes the road from the East, waiting for the distant glitter of steel and the tapping drum that would tell of approaching retribution for the young men who had shouted for a Stuart. The crops were showing well, the meadows lush with new grass. It was a pity.

No, they had seen or heard nothing of the Prince, nor had any wish to. Thomas rode on, across the neck of Millbuie, until Cromarty Firth lay at his feet. He'd been wrong. The Pretender — 'Od rot him — hadn't come to Fraser country.

He turned at last to retrace his steps. He was weary, damn' weary, and the clothes he had worn since de Courcy had despatched him from Halstead Hall, ten months ago, were near to rags. His boots were broken at the toes, and his hair, uncut for many weeks, hung over his back in a long queue. He must present a raffish appearance, but he possessed no mirror to gauge. Above all, he was damn' weary.

A mile from the Beauly river he sensed something wrong, and he checked his pistols and the dragoon carbine. It wasn't the smell of peat in his nostrils, but of charred timbers and thatch. The rooks were circling restlessly above the trees, and the fields were empty of workers. At Beauly he saw the reason. The little cottages were roofless, the white walls scorched, doors broken, and domestic chattels scattered the road, smashed and trampled. He saw a dead cattle-dog, its jaw shattered. The venerable pile of Castle Dounie was a blackened shell, with wooden outbuildings in ashes, young fruit trees axed. In the adjoining fields an attempt had been made to fire the crops, but the corn was too green for much damage to be done. All cattle had been driven off, save for a fine old stud bull, which had been shot. The ruins were deserted.

Following the firth, the clachan of Kirkhill was hidden from him by trees, but he could see smoke rising above them. He knew what was happening in Kirkhill, and he was helpless to intervene. Within minutes he sighted the flames on the skyline, the cascading sparks and whirling soot, near the crash of axes and the crackle of burning. Only a hundred yards away a dozen whooping redcoats were chasing a flock of terrified sheep towards the road, and he could see more soldiers on the hill, waggons and horses. He drew back into a copse of firs, and waited.

He waited for an hour, deep in thought. His activities since the battle on Culloden Moor had been abortive. He'd not found the Pretender, who might by now be anywhere in the length and breadth of Scotland, on any of the islands off the west coast, or even aboard a ship running for France. Goddam, he'd failed, and he was weary — weary of weeks of vagrancy, of dirt and wet, of chill nights in the heather, and the constant looking over his shoulder through every mile of the muddy, rutted road. It was Patrick Campbell who had said that a definite objective was better than aimless wandering.

Was there any further point in seeking the Pretender until he had established his whereabouts? And who would know? He gazed up the hill. The early flames had died, but the thatch of the houses still glowed red, incandescent, and the air above them shimmered with heat. The redcoats were preparing to march, with cattle and sheep herded and the waggons loaded with spoil. He heard the spirited ruffle of a drum.

Well, old Lord Lovat had nothing to blame but his own treason for the burning and looting of the Beauly lands. It was a cost he must have contemplated before sending three hundred clansmen and two sons to support the Pretender. The pity was that hundreds more, unconcerned with distant battles, must share the penalty. But it had always been so, and Cumberland was no different to any other army commander expected by London to obliterate the embers of rebellion with a mailed fist.

And the Frasers would not be the only clan to be punished for its chief's ambition. The simple people in scores of glens throughout the Highlands would be waiting in terror for the tramping feet of redcoats. Glen Moriston was only a day's march from Inverness.

He led his horse back through the copse before remounting, then rode in a wide circle, almost to the edge of the firth, turning southward. There was a climbing track here which pointed at the heart of the Glengarry country, and Wade's road and Loch Ness could be scarce more than ten miles distant. His horse had long needed the attention of a farrier, its shoes worn to wafer thinness, but they'd last ten miles. On either side, now, the terrain was thickly wooded, the dense firs, like chasm walls, obscuring all vision save ahead and behind. He urged his mount on with a kick.

Open moorland spread before him at last, and he descended into Glen Urquhart, relieved that, as yet, he'd seen no smoke, no burned-out crofts, no mutilated cattle to mark the passing of vengeful redcoats. An hour later he stood high above the dull glitter of Loch Ness, flanked by Wade's military road running northward to Inverness and southward to Fort Augustus. The day was clear, the sky scarcely clouded, although the April wind from the Moray Firth penetrated his thin clothes. Below him were the few roofs and the mill of Invermoriston scattered about the mouth of the smaller glen and the black Moriston river. He stared at them and then cursed. He could see smoke.

And — Goddam — he could see scarlet coats, tramping westward into the shadows of Glen Moriston. But they weren't English redcoats. They wore dark tartan kilts and plaid bonnets — and he'd wager there were sprigs of myrtle in those bonnets — 'Od fester them. He didn't need to guess. They were the Argyll Militia — the Campbells — loyal to the Crown and eager for the blood of their old enemies, Clan Donald. They'd needed no second bidding to add to the slaughter of their own countrymen on Culloden Moor, and it was a cruel wit that had sent them to wreak punishment on the defeated Glengarry. There were old scores to settle that had nothing to do with King George, smouldering feuds handed down from father to son — and a heaven-sent opportunity to add another dozen verses to the Bard's triumphant war-song. There'd be no quarter.

Thomas wrenched his tired horse about, flogging it across the high saddle of land that separated the Great Glen from the twisting Moriston. Isobel and the child were twelve miles away, and he'd reach them easily enough before the tramping militiamen did, but there was a hideous doubt in his mind. No punitive force entering the Glangarry lands would number less than two, perhaps three companies. There could still be MacDonalds who would show fight in defence of their families and homes. There were farmsteads and clachans at Dundreggan, Inverwick, Torgyle, Balnagarn, and Cluanie on the loch, and they'd take time to burn and pillage before Isobel's isolated cottage was reached, but Thomas had seen only the tail of the Campbell column. The van could be hours ahead.

His horse was flagging, but Thomas would ride until it dropped rather than pause. Below and ahead were soft green meadows girdled by a dry-stone wall, a clutter of farm buildings and a long, grey house roofed with elm shingles and built around a paved yard. There was washing drying on a line, and birds were singing, but Thomas's belly was twisting. He reined nearer to the house, a hand feeling for his carbine. The building was silent, its windows flung wide, and the yard was littered with smashed furniture and ripped bedding, shattered glass and pottery. A heavy oaken door, gouged by axes, hung crazily on its hinges, and slashed sacks of corn and upturned milk-churns were strewn everywhere. The mouth of a well was clogged with debris.

There was worse. Two corpses, stripped of clothes, hung by their necks from an upper window — a man and a youth. The naked body of a woman lay in a puddle of blood on the stones.

With nausea in his throat, Thomas veered away. The Campbells — 'Od rot them — had already passed this way. How far had they reached? His horse was coughing and would not sustain this pace much longer — but, fester it, he had to reach Isobel before the Campbell jackals —

Attempting to cling as closely as possible to the river, he might never have seen the cottage, obscured by trees and low in a hollow, if he had not heard the scream. It was a mean little structure, scarcely better than a drover's bothy, part rough stone, part turves. For a moment he persuaded himself that the scream had been the cry of a bird, and would have pushed his horse on, but it came again, and he reined.

For a few more seconds he could see nothing more than just the cottage, the trees and high weeds. Then he did. A man in a red coat and a kilt appeared at the open door, a musket with bayonet fixed held aloft. He was laughing. On his bayonet was transfixed an infant.

Thomas dropped to the ground, freeing his carbine with his eyes on the Highlander. Goddam — there was more than one. He had detected a vague flurry of scarlet in the shadow of the cottage wall. And then the scream came yet again, desperately. It wasn't the infant, that was certain. He fell to one knee. It was a long shot for a short-barrelled carbine, but he needed to reduce the odds. He fired, then saw the Highlander jerk and spin backwards. Thomas ran forward, a pistol in each hand.

A woman lay in the bracken, writhing, her skirts torn from her. One Highlander held her down by her shoulders as she twisted her bloodied face from side to side. A second man was flung across her, a knee thrust savagely into her groin and a fist flailing. There was another woman, white-haired and shapeless, crouched with her old, brown face pressed to the wall, weeping. Thomas hardly noticed her. Neither of the Highlanders had heeded the report of his carbine, obviously attributing it to the man he had just shot. They were stragglers, Thomas guessed, raping and killing among the few hovels overlooked or disdained by their main column. It was fortunate for him they only numbered three.

He had reached within six paces of them when one scrambled to his feet, staring. It was almost unfair at such range, but Thomas made amends by placing his shot precisely between the man's eyes. The other Highlander, aghast, glanced down at his fallen companion and then mutely up at Thomas, but there was blood on his fists, and Thomas experienced no stab of regret as he squeezed the trigger of his remaining pistol. Then he drew a much-needed breath. The woman in the bracken was Jeannie MacDonell.

She lay panting, her eyes closed and her tongue probing her broken lips. The old woman by the wall began screeching maliciously, clawing at her hair, and then Jeannie burst into jerking sobs. Thomas was impatient to be gone, but he went to the front of the cottage and dragged the body of the first Highlander from the door. He wrapped the dead infant in its murderer's plaid and placed the tiny, weeks-old body on a dirty mattress in one corner of the earthen floor. It was Ranald MacDonald's child. He returned to Jeannie MacDonell, still in the bracken, vomiting, her legs drawn up and her hands pressed to her bruised pelvis. He lifted her and carried her into the cottage, then put her down beside the infant. The old woman seemed unhurt, and he left her mouthing venomous Gaelic. He had time for nothing else.

He sighted smoke again, far to his right, but it was too distant northward for Isobel's cottage — perhaps even in the next glen. There were likely more than one raiding party in MacDonald country on this clear April afternoon, a score of little bothies burning. There'd be other Jeannie MacDonells battered and raped in front of their helpless families, children bayonetted and old men hanged from their own rafters.

The horse was failing rapidly, but Thomas was on familiar ground now. He could see the olive and russet sweep of the wide braeside he remembered, the line of six tall spruce standing like sentinels against the sky, and in a few more seconds he'd hear the splashing of the waterfall. Then he saw the cottage, and his belly twisted. There was no smoke save for a thin trickle from the chimney, no scarlet coats, and he sobbed. Dear God, he gritted, let her be safe.

He wrenched his mount to a halt and flung himself from the saddle. Nothing had changed since his departure. Nothing. It was as if he had never left. With three paces he had reached the door. It was closed but unbarred, and he pushed it open.

A man whirled with a pistol in his hands — a tall man in a laced red coat and tartan trews and a feathered bonnet. Thomas stared.

'B'God,' he croaked. 'It's Patrick Campbell!'

'B'God,' Campbell said. 'It's Thomas Margery.'

There was a stifled gasp from the hearth. It was Isobel, her eyes wide with amazement and disbelief. Thomas's throat had knotted. 'Thank God —' he choked. 'Thank God you're safe.' She said nothing, but she ran to him, and he knew she was about to cry. He took her in his arms, his lips in the silk of her hair. He was trembling, and no words would come. Words were meaningless. She raised her face, her lips reaching for his, and there was wetness on his cheek. 'Thank God,' he repeated at last.

Campbell had lowered his pistol and was watching amusedly. Thomas, with Isobel still pressed to him, glanced at the Scot. 'Why are you here?' He eyed the other's scarlet coat. 'You're a redcoat?'

Campbell nodded. 'Aye — and I always have been. Major Patrick Campbell, at ye' service.' He gave a little bow.

Thomas pushed Isobel gently aside. 'There's Argyle Militia in the glen — your own murdering brood. They've sacked Invermoriston and Dundreggan, and the MacDonell bothy. They'll be here next —'

Campbell nodded again, patiently. 'Aye. Two companies — as ye say, my own murdering brood. That's why I'm here. I'd given orders that none should approach this house, but we've lost some deserters on the march and I had to be sure.' He grinned apologetically. 'Ye can't trust Campbells to be men of honour in the MacDonald lands.'

Thomas gave a snort of disgust. 'And you're condoning this murder? You're responsible —?'

'Not responsible, nor condoning, Major Margery. It was inevitable, and ye know it. I'd never prevent it, but at least I might save something.' He glanced at Isobel. 'And there's another thing. It won't be the last raid. There'll be more, and worse. Next time I shan't be here.'

Thomas's thoughts were chaotic. 'I'll take Isobel away,' he said, 'and Jamie. There are places where the military won't reach. There must be.' He felt Isobel's fingers tighten on his arm and knew her eyes to be on his face. He looked down at her. 'If you'll come?'

Her voice was a whisper. 'You are my husband, by the Law.'

'It could be a strange country, strange people, strange customs —?'

Her cinnamon eyes held his, and they had both forgotten Campbell. 'Anywhere,' she nodded slowly. 'The Summer Isles, or China — or even your English Cambridgeshire.' She paused, reflecting, then nodded again. 'It would be right for your son to be born in England — and October is a short time away.'

Thomas's jaw dropped, and Campbell coughed discreetly. 'England, then, is it? And the sooner ye start, the better. In a few days this plaguy country will be swarming wi' soldiers, and everyone will be suspect.' He pushed a hand into a pocket. 'I've a few blank warrants o' immunity, ready signed, that'll get ye both safe to the Border —'

'England?' Thomas breathed. 'You know damn' well I can't go into England. There's a rope waiting for me if de Courcy's people get their hands on me, B'God —'

Campbell suddenly laughed. 'Ah — that? It's all finished wi', Major. All the Jacobite fence-sitters in London have suddenly become loyal King's men. Besides, Sir John de Courcy is dead —'

'Dead? De Courcy dead?'

'Aye, a week after Falkirk, it seems. In his sleep, after a twenty-five mile foxhunt an' four bottles o' port.' He paused.

'Ye can have my word. England's open to ye. Not the Guards, i'faith. Ye'll never flutter the hearts o' the ladies-in-waiting again.' He shrugged. 'But farming in Cambridgeshire, say —'

Thomas was silent for several pensive moments. Farming in Cambridgeshire? It was damn' odd, but he'd never thought seriously of it before — never in his years at St. James's. Growing wheat and barley was a far cry from the scarlet and gold of the 2nd Foot Guards, and de Courcy had once mentioned campaigns in Florida and Mexico — and Canada and India — but likely they were only the brandy-fuddled dreams of an old man, and had died with him. Wolfe, Howe, Clive and Margery — all part of a grander scheme, he'd said.

'There's an unfinished matter,' he said. 'The Pretender.' Campbell thrust out a lower lip. 'Aye, I know what ye're thinking, but he's broken. More important, so are the clans — which is a damn' better thing for Scotland than she's realised yet. It was a bloody experiment, but the Pretender's proved one thing, that the courage of a few thousand Highlanders isn't enough to compel a king on a country that doesn't want him. The Stuarts are as dead as the Tudors and Plantagenets, ye'll see. And I'll wager the French won't burn their fingers wi' Scotland again.'

Cambridgeshire, then. Sawston village and the little church of St. Mary-the-Virgin. They'd be there in May, with the hawthorn blossom and lilac, and he'd show Jamie the best place for sticklebacks, at the bottom of Five-acre Meadow. And Isobel —

He took her hand. 'Not the Summer Isles,' he said. 'Not the land of Coigach beyond the great mountains. Will you bear my son in Cambridgeshire — by the Granta river, on the London coach road?'

Her lips told him.

Printed in Great Britain
by Amazon